DEATH IN THE LONG WALK

A TWISTY AMATEUR SLEUTH MURDER MYSTERY

THE BREAKFAST CLUB DETECTIVES
BOOK 1

HILARY PUGH

Housemouse Press

PROLOGUE

His heart pounding in his chest, judgement clouded, and head dizzy with fear, he staggered breathlessly through the trees. Terrified and disorientated by what had appeared in front of him, he could only hope that his sense of direction was leading him the right way. Once clear of the trees and away from the thing he'd seen, or thought he'd seen, he might feel safer. Out in the open, the menacing branches no longer clouding his judgement, he could find his way more easily. If he knew where he was, he could make his escape from the something or someone who was waiting for him.

Things appeared to be moving towards him. The branch of a tree, or something more frightening? A creature with antlers, or a body swinging on a rope, its face leering at him as it gasped for a final breath. He groped for his phone, eventually grasping it in a shaking hand, pulling it out along with everything else in his pocket. Something fell to the ground at his feet. He didn't care about that. All he needed was the light his phone could give him, and he had a firm grasp of that now. There would be enough of a glow to see his way through the trees to safety. He reassured himself that it was never completely dark here. The Great Park was surrounded by towns with their streetlamps and lit-up office blocks. Even in the park itself there were *fleeting headlights from passing cars, although the shadows they cast distorted everything around him.*

He pushed on, certain now that he was heading in the right direction, sensing he would soon be out in the open, but for now barely able to see his way ahead. And then, to his relief, he glimpsed the pale, moonlit surface of the Long Walk. Once there, he would be near the town and safety. As he was about to emerge into the open, he tripped on a tree root and dropped the phone. The light went out and he was in darkness again. He stumbled forward, falling onto his knees in the wet grass. He felt around for the phone but found only nettles and stones. He forced himself to stand on shaking legs, only to fall again and lose his sense of direction. He could see nothing now except the dim light of the town on the horizon. Then even that was obscured as he felt something fall on him, something warm and soft covering his face and forcing him to lie prone on the wet earth. He couldn't breathe, but his fear ebbed away as he stretched out his hand and felt the comfort of the hard surface. He had reached the Long Walk. He closed his eyes and let himself sink into oblivion.

1

W as he too old to be a detective?

Jonathan Cardew, Jonny to his friends and family, woke up on the first morning of his retirement and wondered what to do with the rest of his life. He knew what he'd like to do. It was what he had wanted for most of his life, from when he was thirteen and had been deeply into Sherlock Holmes. He had an ambition to solve murders. And now, at last, he was free of the work he'd done conscientiously for the last forty years but never enjoyed very much.

Jonny had been struck down by covid within hours of the first lockdown starting. He and Belinda had caught it at the same time, but while Belinda had recovered in days, it had taken Jonny many months. How grossly unfair was that? He'd always been fit and healthy. He ate his five a day, most of the time. He took exercise, well, he led an energetic life, which was the same thing, wasn't it? He lived a hardworking and blameless existence, rarely the worse for drink, not overweight, or maybe a pound or two – nothing to be concerned about – and not suffering from undue stress. And then he caught covid. He had to admit that he'd been luckier than many. He'd avoided intensive care and the brutal intervention that implied. But his recovery had been slow. Long covid, they called it now. At the time no one really knew very much about the disease. He'd simply suffered from debilitating exhaustion, an irritating cough that dragged on and on, and an inability to taste or smell anything he ate. Not that he felt like eating, which at least meant he dropped the extra pounds he'd been carrying. His doctor, consulted from time to time over a video link, could do very little for him. The only reason anyone could think of for why Jonny had been affected so badly was that he had suffered from asthma as a child. There had been some worries, unfounded as it turned out, that the disease could leave scars and he might experience it again.

And then he'd recovered. And retired. And there must be murderers out there who needed catching, but possibly not by him. He was too old, wasn't he?

Until he retired, Jonny was the CEO of Cardew Packing Solutions (CPS), founded by Cardew senior, Jonny's father, and occupying a site on the Slough Trading Estate. The company, as its name suggested, provided cardboard boxes, bubble wrap, vacuum packs – pretty much any way anyone had ever thought of to pack things – ready to transport them to wherever they needed to go in a way that would allow them to arrive at their destination unharmed by the rigours of their journey. With so many people locked up at home and shopping online, CPS flourished during the pandemic. It was considered an essential business and not only kept going for the duration but actually increased both its workforce and its profits. After the many months it had taken to feel energetic enough, Jonny returned to work to find his son Marcus doing an admirable job and decided, unlike his father before him, to step back and allow him to formally take over.

Now Jonny could do something else with his own life. Take a gap year, perhaps. He reached for his iPad and googled *gap years for seniors*. Then a newsflash flipped onto the screen. It was from a local news page he subscribed to, one that sent him eye-wateringly boring stuff like *Cat rescued from tree in Cookham* or *Wheelie bins stolen from Goshawk Road*. He was about to delete the new message but then he read it: BODY FOUND IN THE LONG WALK. He no longer wanted to go on a gap year. But he was unable to find any more details about the body.

Jonny had always looked forward to retiring. After leaving school, he had been sent by his father to learn all there was to know about packaging in cities all over the world. He did learn all there was to know about packaging and also a lot about falling in love and partying in different languages and cultures. He returned home with a head full of new ideas, which his father refused to discuss, never mind put into place. For a few years Jonny kicked around the factory, feeling bored and wondering how his father would react to him taking up an altogether different career. A police detective, for instance. But then his father died of a heart attack, and Jonny was left with little choice. He took over the company and vowed that if he ever had a son who wanted to work in the business, he would listen to his ideas and then step back and let him take over.

Jonny and Belinda did have a son, but following in *his* father's footsteps was rarely mentioned until Marcus showed an enthusiasm for packaging that Jonny had never felt. On his sixteenth birthday, Marcus had begged his father for a holiday job and Jonny placed him under the care of one of his floor managers. It was a job Marcus returned to every holiday until he left university. Once home from his own gap year, something Jonny had encouraged Marcus to do before he became bogged down in cardboard for the rest of his life, he took up a permanent post with his father and by the time he married Jennifer, a trainee office manager from a neighbouring business park, and had become the father of Justin, he was every bit as capable of running the company as Jonny himself – better, his mother Belinda commented wryly, because Marcus actually enjoyed what he was doing– the upside being that it left Jonny free to find something he *really* wanted to do. For the next few years Jonny thought about retirement, but he was too young; it would be self-indulgent. Even with Belinda's encouragement he was unable to think of anything he wanted to do apart from being a detective and it was probably too late for that. He couldn't spend the rest of his life doing nothing, could he? But then, poleaxed by covid, he found himself doing exactly that – nothing – and he became used to the idea.

As he slowly recovered, he and Marcus put together a restructuring plan. Marcus would become the new CEO and take the company forward into a greener, more sustainable future. Jonny would remain on the board and carve out a new role for himself. The new role had yet to make itself clear to Jonny. He had an idea that it would include sponsorship and charitable work which, as Marcus pointed out, would fit in well with their new ethical image. Jonny moved into a smaller, more modern office with a view of the Slough arm of the Grand Union Canal, which ran through the trading estate. Most days he stood at the window watching passing boats and wondering what to do with the hours that stretched ahead of him. Was he really too old to train as a detective? Probably. He toyed fleetingly with the idea of writing a crime novel – murder in a packing factory? But he had no knowledge of either methods of killing people or of the procedure the police adopted in solving crimes. Instead, he bought himself a Kindle and downloaded box sets of crime stories, which he smuggled into the office in his coat pocket. Then he waited for the date of his real retirement to arrive.

The formal handing over was to take place on Jonny's sixtieth birthday, at which point he would cut his office hours and just potter in for board meetings. They planned a celebration for the employees in the afternoon and a family meal at a restaurant in Bray in the evening. Unfortunately, the birthday coincided with the state funeral of Her Majesty Queen Elizabeth ll. The CPS celebration was postponed, and the factory closed to allow the employees to watch the funeral either on television or by taking the short train ride to Windsor to line the Long Walk and watch the slow progress of Her Majesty's cortège to her final resting place. Going out for a slap-up meal would be disrespectful, and in any case Belinda, or Councillor Cardew, as she was known more widely, was invited to a reception held to mark the occasion and to pay her respects to the new king. Jonny stayed at home and ate toasted cheese sandwiches while watching *Only Connect* on television. None of which worried him. He liked toasties and there would be no one to witness his inability to do much connecting, it being one of the UK's hardest quizzes. They could go out for dinner any time.

Now on his first non-working morning, Jonny lay in bed, enjoying a pleasant sense of freedom. Then he remembered Belinda's parting words as she bustled out to attend to council matters. 'Don't forget Mrs Gage.'

Mrs Gage had cleaned the house for them for years. Until her enforced break due to the pandemic, she had been *old school*, arriving for work in a wraparound overall with her hair covered by a knotted scarf. She had been happy, although Mrs Gage never showed much sign of ever actually being happy, to use whatever cleaning products and equipment they could provide. But lockdown had changed that. Mrs Gage had now joined forces with a group of other cleaners who had named themselves *Windsor Mops* and drove around in small yellow vans with a logo – a grinning woman inside a yellow sun, brandishing an old-fashioned feather duster. Mrs Gage was now kitted out in orange trousers and a sunshine yellow t-shirt bearing the same logo under the words *Windsor Mops,* which were embroidered in a shade of orange that matched her trousers. She now brought her own industrial-style vacuum cleaner – for insurance reasons, she muttered darkly – which sounded as if it was powered by a jet engine, and a bright yellow toolbox containing an array of dusters and tins of floor polish, sink cleaner and stuff to remove limescale from around the taps. They no longer left an envelope of cash for her on the kitchen table. The moment Mrs Gage left the house, money was extracted from Belinda's bank account by an app called *Gocashless*.

But two things hadn't changed. Belinda still got up two hours early to give the house a good clean before Mrs Gage arrived. *Why?* Jonny asked. Belinda had given him a withering look. 'You can't expect her to clean around all your clutter,' she said.

His clutter? The few things he may have left lying around were nothing compared to Belinda's cardboard files, piles of leaflets, minutes of recent council meetings, and countless other things to do with her role, about which Jonny took little interest. That was not really fair. Jonny was immensely proud of his wife: a local councillor for the last ten years; spokesperson for culture and leisure; tipped to be mayor in a year or two and respected by fellow councillors of whatever political shade. Jonny managed to be encouraging without having to know very much about the workings of the council and what Belinda actually did.

The other thing that hadn't changed was Mrs Gage's opinion of men. Men, she believed, belonged at work. This had never been a problem when Jonny was working. They rarely passed the time of day until her return to work after lockdown, when Jonny was still stuck at home barely able to get out of bed. Neither did Mrs Gage approve of invalids of the male variety. 'Man flu,' she muttered as she drove the vacuum cleaner around the bedroom. She was not a quiet cleaner, and all Jonny could do was bury his head under a pillow and pretend to be asleep until she'd finished. Once he began to feel better, Jonny went out for long walks on cleaning days. Probably, he thought wryly, Mrs Gage had played a major part in his recovery.

He looked at the clock by the bed. Half an hour before Mrs Gage was due and he had no intention of being there when she arrived. He got up, showered and dressed, and then wondered about breakfast. Not here, obviously, not if he wanted to avoid a meal accompanied by the disapproving mutterings of Mrs Gage, her dusters and pots of cleaner lined up on the table in front of him. A hint that the kitchen absolutely had to be tackled first. He wasn't going to argue. He'd walk to Windsor and find a café serving all day breakfast, buy a newspaper and stroll up to the castle to watch the clearing up after the funeral.

It was a pleasant autumn day and the walk from his house to the town centre would do him good. There was a wide choice of eating places: big chains like Starbucks; department store cafés; hotels with posh dining rooms and smaller places tucked away from the more touristy areas. It was the last of these that Jonny fancied today. Somewhere small and quiet with personal service and a menu free of modern fads like smashed avocado and sourdough toast. He wandered past the shops in the old station, strolled into an alleyway and down some stone steps, at the bottom of which he found exactly what he was looking for. *Jasmine's*. He could see through the window that it was by any standard scruffy with mismatched chairs placed at tables that could have been sourced from a skip. A blackboard standing on the pavement outside announced delicacies such as beans on toast, poached egg, full English and porridge. Jonny hadn't had porridge for years. This was just what he was looking for. He opened the door and went inside. Choosing a table near the window, he picked up a laminated menu and looked around. A few people were seated at tables munching their way through well-loaded plates of the kind of food that doctors warned would induce high levels of cholesterol. A black and white cat snoozed in a sagging armchair, one of a group arranged around a fireplace containing an imitation log fire, not currently in use. A dark-haired young woman stood behind a counter next to a hissing coffee machine of the kind Jonny remembered from his teenage years. 'Hi,' she said, leaving the machine and crossing the room to where Jonny was sitting. 'What can I get you?'

He replaced the menu on the table in front of him, smiled at her and ordered porridge and coffee. While he was waiting, he opened his newspaper and spread it out in front of him. He hoped there would be more about the body and he wasn't disappointed. There was the same headline that had flashed briefly on his iPad screen.

BODY FOUND IN THE LONG WALK

It was unusual for this area, where most people died decorously in their own beds or quietly in hospitals. He read on.

The body of a man was discovered by a dog walker in the early hours of Tuesday morning. Police are unable to give more information until the identity of the victim has been established and a post-mortem carried out.

2

He was here again. That would be the third time this week and he always sat at the table by the window. He was working his way through the menu, so perhaps when he'd tried everything he'd stop coming here and go somewhere else. Jasmine hoped not. He was polite and friendly, and quite attractive even though he was old. Same age as her dad probably. She was sure she'd seen him before but couldn't remember where.

Jasmine Javadi and her dad Karim ran the café together. Dad had been there for years. Ever since he left Iran during a revolution or something. He didn't talk about it, so Jasmine didn't know much about Iranian history. Only that her dad had to leave in a hurry. He met her mum at a Persian culture evening in London. Her mum was British and not interested in Persian culture. She was studying catering and was short of cash because living in London, even then, was hideously expensive. She was at the culture evening to do the washing up for a bit of extra money. It was dead romantic, Dad said. Jasmine couldn't see how falling for her mum when she was up to her elbows in greasy water was more romantic than meeting her, say, at a party. But she supposed the young didn't get out so much in those days. Anyway, Dad and Mum got married and bought the café together. They called it *Suzy's Diner* after Jasmine's mum. Suzy died when Jasmine was fifteen. They kept the name for a few years after that, but when Jasmine finished her catering course Dad made her a co-owner of the café and renamed it after her. They dropped the word *diner* because someone pointed out that it wasn't a diner, it was a café. Diners apparently are all stainless steel and look like caravans. Dad didn't want to be done under the Trade Descriptions Act. In any case, 'Jasmine' had a lot more letters in it than 'Suzy' so he had a new sign painted and called the café *Jasmine's*.

They were doing well. The café was in a prime spot just a short walk from the castle, down an alleyway and some stone steps, tucked away from the shops in the expensive part of the town. People came because they were *not* Costa or Nero. Since finishing her course, Jasmine had become an expert at second-guessing what would bring in customers. Dad wanted to completely refurbish the place last year when people started to come back after lockdown, but Jasmine persuaded him not to. What was needed was somewhere comfortable, a reminder of what it was like before the pandemic. There were loads of places with posh furniture and shiny new fittings. What they should offer was good old-fashioned comfort. A place where people came in and said things like '*My mum used to have a chair like that*', and settle down for a slow cup of tea and one of her dad's pastries – which had to be tasted to be believed – in a chair that reminded them of the past.

Omar Kayyam was very popular as well. Jasmine got him from a cat rescue place because they had mice. Dad said the health inspection people might object, but when consulted they said they were fine with cats as long as they were kept out of the kitchen. Mice were more of a health hazard apparently, and anyway Omar really lived with Jasmine and her dad in the flat upstairs. Jasmine had never actually seen him catch a mouse – thank goodness; she wouldn't know what to do with a dead mouse. But they must have moved out the day Omar arrived because she hadn't seen one since.

Karim appeared from the kitchen with a tray of sandwiches, which Jasmine stacked in a glass cabinet on the counter. Most sandwiches were made to order for the lunchtime crowd who came in from the nearby shops and offices, but they kept a few ready wrapped for anyone in a hurry.

'We need to get Ivo in,' said her dad. 'Get him to fix that bit of loose skirting in the passage outside the kitchen. I keep tripping over it.'

'I'll give him a call,' said Jasmine, picking up her phone and tapping in the number. While she was waiting for an answer, the good-looking man from the table by the window came to pay for his breakfast, tapping his card onto the machine and leaving with a cheery wave. Then Jasmine remembered where she had seen him before. It was a few years ago, during the gap between leaving school and the start of her college course. She'd worked as a canteen assistant for three months in a factory in Slough that made cardboard boxes. The canteen was at the back of a collection of buildings and usually she went in through a staff entrance. But occasionally she was given the job of serving refreshments at board meetings and to guests who were there to discuss contracts about matters of packing. On these occasions Jasmine, bearing loaded trays or trundling a trolley, presented herself at reception, a stylishly furnished area with an expensive blue carpet and comfortable chairs. She would be scrutinised by the receptionist, a girl of around her own age dressed in a short black dress and high-heeled shoes, whose fingernails were long, unchipped and bright red, and whose hair lay in a carefully casual way around her shoulders. Once Jasmine was passed as suitably dressed – she always was, since she had been warned in advance to wear her most presentable clothes – she was allowed to take the lift to the managerial offices, more often than not to the boardroom. It was there that she caught occasional glimpses of Jonathan Cardew. On one occasion he was about to chair a meeting and Jasmine read his name on a card he had placed in front of him. It struck her that his name was also that of the company itself. Must be someone important, she assumed. *He's only the bloody chairman*, she was told, having mentioned it on her return to the canteen kitchen after her first refreshment-bearing mission. And here he was now, in her café. Who'd have guessed?

He hadn't recognised her, but Jasmine wouldn't have expected him to. People serving food in boardrooms were usually invisible, even when they were young and attractive (Jasmine refused to be falsely modest. She knew her long hair and dark eyes attracted attention). But when serving boardroom refreshments, she was also reassured by her invisibility. It would be nothing short of creepy if it had been any other way. Although there had been one or two visitors who leered at her as she poured their coffee; one even put a hand on her thigh as she leant over the table with a plate of sandwiches. But Jasmine was no shrinking violet and this particular so-called gentleman would, she hoped, have some explaining to do when he arrived home and someone, hopefully his wife, found the pockets of the jacket that he'd slung over the back of his chair stuffed with mangled, and by now putrefying, prawn mayo sandwiches.

And now Jonathan Cardew had turned up at her café for breakfast on three occasions. She didn't wonder why. Doubtless he had his reasons. What interested her was that he could be just the person to help her with her plan.

For a while now she had been going out with Stevie, the son of a local vicar. Not a serious relationship, they assured each other, but they liked the same music, enjoyed talking to each other and had similar political views. Once a week, Jasmine joined Stevie as a volunteer in the church hall at the back of his dad's church, which was currently acting as a food bank. It was here that Jasmine and Stevie thought up their plan for a breakfast club. For Stevie this was not much more than a daydream. Most of Stevie's life was one big daydream, his father often told him with a sigh. But for Jasmine it was the start of something much bigger, far more practical and very exciting. She'd learnt a lot at college, not only about running a catering business, but also about publicity and sponsorship.

Jasmine's breakfast club plan was both to provide free breakfasts to those who needed them and to sell membership to people who worked locally. They'd pay an annual subscription and get breakfast every day, plus the knowledge that they were contributing to a worthwhile project. They'd be able to offset the expense as a charitable donation. Anyone on benefits, homeless, or who was eligible for food bank vouchers, would be offered free membership. The food bank was currently strained to breaking point and the committee who ran it loved Jasmine's idea. They offered her any support they could give as long as it wasn't financial. She put together a business plan, took it to one of the banks in the town and asked for an appointment with their small business consultant. She and Stevie visited an adviser and while Stevie sat silent, awed by the occasion, Jasmine talked about business plans and fundraising. The adviser studied the plan and suggested that they would look favourably at a start-up loan as long as she and Stevie could raise a certain amount in local sponsorship. Jasmine's dad promised his support by employing an extra cook at his own expense. Stevie's dad agreed to run jumble sales and a raffle to raise money. Stevie would help with leaflet drops and washing up. All Jasmine needed now was a local business sponsor. And Jonathan Cardew struck her as the perfect person to approach.

She wouldn't ask today. She needed to put a proposal in place and be able to give him something he could take away and think about, probably discuss with his financial people. Right now, he had his head buried in the newspaper, no doubt trawling for more news of the body they'd found in the Long Walk. They still didn't know who it was, and the gossip was that he was either from out of town, one of the tourists who had come to watch the funeral procession, or it was one of the homeless, but that was less likely because although people were living on the streets around the town, there were not that many of them. Windsor was a prosperous place on the whole and people looked after each other. The half dozen or so regulars who camped on the pavements of the shopping street all knew each other and someone would have noticed if one of them had gone missing.

So that was Jasmine's evening sorted. She'd spend it putting her notes together ready to give to Mr Cardew next time he popped in for breakfast. Assuming that he did pop in again. But even if he didn't, there was nothing to stop her visiting him at work. She could catch up with some of her old workmates at the same time.

3

I vo Dean washed his hands and carefully put his tools away. 'All done,' he said, picking up the toolbox and looking around for Harold, who had wandered into the café looking for somewhere warm and comfortable to lie down. If it hadn't been for Omar, he'd probably have taken his chances with one of the chairs, but Harold had an uneasy relationship with cats and Ivo could see that his dog had settled himself into a corner quite close to where he was working.

'What would we do without you, lad?' said Karim, reaching into his wallet and handing over three twenty-pound notes.

Ivo took the money and stashed it away in the back pocket of his jeans. Not bad for three hours' work. The Javadis were always good to him. The café was in an old building and there was always something that needed doing. But Karim and Jasmine also recommended him to friends, and in the last year he had built up a nice little business. Three years ago, he'd been living on the streets, evicted by his mother's landlord only days after her funeral, every penny he had used to pay off her debts. Then the pandemic struck. For many this had been a tragedy, but for Ivo it was the start of his new life. He'd been removed from his spot outside Superdrug and allocated a caseworker, who sent him to a hotel on the edge of the trading estate in Slough. It was a very basic hotel but for Ivo, who had no experience of hotels of any kind, it was unaccustomed luxury. He had his own bathroom as well as clean towels and bedding once a week. For six months he was warm and well fed. And best of all, he was allowed to keep Harold with him.

The caseworker also found him work a few minutes' walk away at a company called CPS, who made a lot of cardboard boxes. Ivo didn't know what CPS stood for but guessed that cardboard and packing came into it. He couldn't explain the S and didn't like to ask anyone. And it didn't matter. He was earning money, so whoever they were, he was grateful. It was Ivo's job to stack the flat packs of boxes into bundles of thirty and run them through a machine that slung nylon tape around them. Then they were loaded onto trucks and driven away to... well, Ivo had no idea where. Companies that did a lot of packing, he supposed. And judging by the number he loaded every night, there were many people who did that. He'd never had a real job before. All the time-keeping and form-filling confused him until the head of human resources, a motherly type called Dawn, took him under her wing. She took care of his paperwork and opened a bank account for him.

Ivo knew it wouldn't last. Sooner or later lockdown would end, he'd have to leave the hotel and he'd be back on the streets. But the six months had given him time to think things over. However grateful he was for the job, he didn't want to spend the rest of his life packing boxes. He had always been good with his hands, so as soon as he had saved enough of his wages, he bought a set of good quality tools and set himself up as a handyman. He talked it through with Dawn, who tried to persuade him to go for one of the company's apprenticeship schemes, but realised his heart wasn't in packing. Instead, she made leaflets for him, found him a room in a hostel and added his name to the waiting list of a housing trust in Windsor.

It took six months to reach the top of the waiting list and in that time, Ivo had been able to save enough to pay the deposit on a one-bedroom flat at the top of a block close to Windsor Racecourse. Things were looking up. Until the letter arrived.

'You okay, lad?' Karim asked. 'You look a bit peaky.'

Ivo shrugged. He wasn't all right. Not at all. But what could he do?

'Grab yourself a seat in the dining room,' said Karim. 'I'll bring you a nice cooked breakfast. Put a bit of colour back into those cheeks.'

It would take more than that. But Ivo pushed his toolbox into a corner where no one could trip over it, gathered up Harold's lead and settled them both at a table in the dining room.

Not many here this morning. The breakfast rush was usually over by nine, when people had to be at work, and Ivo knew it would be quiet until lunchtime. He looked around. A couple of elderly women were gossiping over cups of coffee and biscuits, and at a table by the window Jasmine was talking to a posh-looking bloke. Ivo would normally chat to Jasmine, but this morning she had spread out the contents of a folder and posh bloke was reading them through. Better not to interrupt.

He took a newspaper from the shelf and was reading about the body in the Long Walk when Karim placed a plate of food in front of him. A full English breakfast: bacon; sausages; two fried eggs and hash browns. Usually this would have had Ivo's mouth watering, but today he didn't feel hungry. He cut up a sausage and gave it to Harold. And that's when it really hit him between the eyes. While working, he'd been able to put it out of his mind, but now he had to face it. This would be the very last time he'd feed a sausage to Harold. He pushed the plate away and sank his head onto his arms, sobbing bitterly, unaware of anyone else in the café.

A moment later he felt an arm around his shoulder. 'Oh, Ivo,' said Jasmine. 'What's happened?'

Ivo sat up and took the tissue she was holding out. He wiped his eyes and sniffed, reaching down and stroking Harold's head. 'It's Harold,' he sobbed.

'Is he ill?' Jasmine asked. She reached down and held Harold's head in her hands. She gazed into his eyes and stroked his nose. 'Does he need a vet?'

Ivo shook his head. Harold had never been ill. He was rugged and healthy. A regular visitor to a pet charity who checked him over and injected him with things that would stop him picking up diseases. 'It's the housing association,' he muttered. 'Bloody contract.'

Jasmine looked surprised. 'But I thought that was going really well. You said you liked it there.'

'I do like it there. Or I did, but now they say I can't keep Harold.'

'But why?' she asked. 'He's no trouble.'

'They said it was in the contract. No pets. I got the letter last week. Harold has to go by this evening, or they'll evict me.'

'Oh, Ivo, that's terrible. What are you going to do?'

He shrugged miserably. Nothing he could do, was there?

'Can you take him to the animal shelter?' she asked. 'Perhaps they can find someone to give him a new home.'

'There are so many dogs needing homes now, with the cost of living and everything. And if they can't find anyone, well... you know what that means.'

Jasmine nodded. 'We can't let that happen,' she said. 'And we can't have you back on the streets. It's not safe out there at the moment. There must be something we can do.'

He appreciated that. He liked that she'd said *we* not *you*. It made him feel less alone. Not that there was anything she could do.

'Excuse me.'

It was posh bloke. What did he want? *Sorry to interrupt your business meeting,* Ivo thought bitterly. Bet he'd never had to face anything like this. Life's easy if you're rich.

'I'm sorry to interrupt,' the man continued, 'but I couldn't help overhearing. Perhaps I can help.'

'And just how can you do that?' said Ivo angrily.

'Hear him out,' said Jasmine, patting his arm.

'I should introduce myself,' said posh bloke, pulling up a chair and sitting down next to them. 'I'm Jonny Cardew.'

'Oh yeah.' How was that supposed to help?

'I live on the edge of town, and we have a big garden,' he said, reaching down to stroke Harold, who licked his hand. He looked up and smiled at Ivo. 'Your dog could come and stay with me.'

Ivo stared at him. 'He's called Harold.'

'Yes, of course, and Harold would be very welcome. He seems to like me.'

'He's my dog,' said Ivo, tugging the lead a bit closer. 'And he likes everyone.'

'I've got time to spare,' the man continued. 'I could bring him to see you whenever you want.'

'And he'd still be your dog,' said Jasmine. 'He'd just be staying with Mr Cardew until something's sorted out.'

'Let's drop the Mr Cardew. Everyone calls me Jonny. And Jasmine's right. Take him to the dog rescue and if he's lucky he'll be given a new home and then he'll belong to someone else. Let him stay with me and he'll always be your dog.'

But could Ivo trust him? This Mr Cardew, Jonny. Once Harold moved into some posh house, Ivo might never be allowed to have him back. 'How do I know you'll look after him properly?'

'Ivo,' said Jasmine. 'Of course Mr Cardew will look after him properly. He owns a big factory in Slough and his wife's on the council. And he's going to be part of the breakfast club.'

Jonny nodded. 'Looks like I'll be around here quite a lot.'

'With Harold,' said Jasmine. 'So you can pop in here to see him. The only difference is that he's not going to be sleeping in your flat.'

Ivo wasn't sure that owning a factory qualified anyone to care for a dog. A wife on the council was more reassuring. The council were interested in things like animal welfare, weren't they? He was coming round to the idea. His only alternatives were to say goodbye to Harold forever or for both of them to be back on the streets again. 'Well,' he said. 'If I tell you what he eats and that...'

'I tell you what,' said Jonny. 'Let's take him for a walk now and you can tell me everything I need to know.'

Ivo nodded and started eating, his appetite returning. 'We could go to the Long Walk and see where they found that body,' he said, wondering if there would be blue and white crime scene tape and a white tent like they had on the telly.

Jonny grinned. 'Just what I was thinking,' he said.

'You're a right grisly pair,' said Jasmine. 'It's exciting, though. Do you think it could be a murder? I'd come with you if I didn't have lunches to serve.'

THE CASTLE GROUNDS were still closed after the funeral, so Ivo, Harold and Jonny walked to the Cambridge Gate and down the Long Walk from there. There was no sign of any police activity, a disappointing lack of crime scene tape and white tents. They walked further down a hill and then across a road. The walk began to climb again, and they looked up towards the George III statue, the King astride a copper horse at the top of the hill. Jonny had paused at the side of the walk, to catch his breath Ivo assumed, and stopped walking to wait for him to catch up. But Jonny had found something. Ivo walked back to where he was on his hands and knees, brushing the grass aside. 'Look,' he said. 'Something's flattened the grass. And over there you can see footprints and tyre tracks.'

'Do you think this was the place?' Ivo asked. 'There's not much to see.'

'I suppose any evidence will have been taken away by the police,' said Jonny. 'They'd need to preserve everything they find until they know the cause of death and who the guy was.'

'You'd think someone would have missed him and reported it,' said Ivo. 'It's sad if some poor bloke died and no one even noticed he was gone.'

'There's been nothing in the papers to say he's been identified,' said Jonny. 'Or on the Internet.'

'Why are you so interested?' Ivo asked.

Jonny shrugged. 'Time on my hands, I suppose. But also, I feel the same as you. I want to know he was missed.'

They stood and looked down at the spot and Ivo shivered, suddenly sad for the person who had died there. It was too deserted.

There should be bunches of flowers to mark the place. Like they do when someone died in a road accident. A few days ago, further up the walk towards the castle, there had been a carpet of flowers, thousands of them, left by mourners for the Queen. They'd all been cleared away now and Ivo didn't know what had happened to them. He looked down again at the footprints just visible on the ground in front of him. In a day or two there'd be nothing left of them either.

They were well away from the road now and Ivo let Harold off his lead. He watched as he scampered away from the Long Walk and disappeared into some trees. He was enjoying the freedom, Ivo thought, watching as he ran in and out of the bushes, nose in the air and tail wagging. Then he stopped at the foot of one of the trees and started barking. He'd seen something glinting in the branches above him. Ivo moved closer, trying to see what it was. 'Look,' he said. 'There's something hanging in the tree. It looks like a necklace.'

Jonny stared up into the branches. 'Too big for a necklace,' he said. 'It's more like a chain of office. The kind of thing mayors wear.'

Ivo grabbed a low-hanging branch and swung himself up into the tree for a closer look. 'It's a weird thing,' he called down. 'A kind of pendant on a chain. It looks like a tree with antlers.' He wedged himself between two branches and reached into the pocket of his jeans for his phone. Then he jumped down from the tree and showed Jonny the photo he'd taken.

Jonny studied it for a moment. 'Can you send it to me?' he asked, reeling off a string of numbers. 'I'll try to find out what it is.'

'Okay,' said Ivo, tapping the numbers into his phone. 'You don't think we should get it down and take it to the police, do you?'

Jonny shook his head. 'The police will have done a thorough search and anything like this would have been bagged up and kept as evidence.'

Ivo thought about that for a moment. 'So you think this was left here after the police had finished?'

'I think it was left as a memorial and you know what that means, don't you?'

Ivo scratched his head and then realised what Jonny was getting at. 'They know who the dead man was. But if they knew, why didn't they tell the police?'

'We can't be sure they didn't, can we?'

'Wouldn't everyone be talking about it if they had?' Ivo imagined it would have been the only topic of conversation in the café. Everyone had been gruesomely fascinated by the body in the Long Walk.

'I don't know,' said Jonny. 'I'll see what I can find out when I get home.'

Ivo sighed. He had a job that afternoon at a house in Dedworth. He needed to be on his way. 'I'd better get going,' he said, putting Harold back on his lead and handing it to Jonny. He bent down and put his arms round Harold's neck. 'You be a good dog,' he said tearfully. 'I'll see you soon.'

'You've got my number,' said Jonny. 'Call me any time you want to see him.'

'I'm working for a lady over in Egham for a couple of days,' said Ivo. 'I'll need to get the early bus. But I've nothing on Friday morning.'

'Then meet me at *Jasmine's,*' said Jonny. 'I'll buy you breakfast.'

Ivo nodded, then walked away, back down the Long Walk towards the town centre. He didn't look back.

4

—————

Jonny watched as Ivo walked away. Harold sat with his head on one side as if wondering when Ivo would turn and realise he'd forgotten him. Jonny tugged gently on the lead. 'Come on, old boy,' he said. 'My house is this way.'

Harold, Jonny thought, was not going to be any trouble. He seemed willing enough to trot at his side as they made their way home, pausing at a Tesco Local to pick up tins of dog food. Any trouble was likely to come from Belinda when she discovered they had now become dog owners. No, not owners. Jonny remembered the promise he made that Harold would always be Ivo's dog. Dog sitter was a better term, although he doubted that would make a lot of difference to Belinda. They were still in charge of a dog, weren't they?

Arriving home, Harold found a quiet corner of the living room where he sat and scratched while Jonny planned a special Belinda-pleasing meal. A neighbour had left a box of aubergines on the doorstep with a note saying they were fresh from his greenhouse. A bumper crop this year, apparently. And not suitable for freezing. A search of the freezer revealed a pack of top-quality minced lamb, and the larder was always well stocked with herbs. Moussaka then. One of Belinda's favourites. He popped the mince into the microwave to thaw and turned his attention to Harold, who was still scratching and, Jonny noticed for the first time, didn't smell very nice.

BY THE TIME Belinda arrived home after her council meeting, the moussaka was bubbling away in the oven, Jonny had opened a bottle of red wine and Harold was curled up asleep on an old blanket Jonny had found at the bottom of the airing cupboard. Jonny had given him a bath in the guest bathroom, having rejected their walk-in shower as impractical. He'd rubbed Harold down with three towels, now in the washing machine, and dried him with Belinda's hairdryer.

Belinda swept in and draped a camel hair coat over a chair in the hall. 'Something smells wonderful,' she said, kissing Jonny, who was standing anxiously by the kitchen door. 'What have I done to deserve this? Ah,' she said, looking down at Harold, who had left his blanket to sniff Belinda's legs. 'Didn't know you were planning on getting a dog.'

Jonny took her by the hand and led her into the kitchen, where he poured her a large glass of wine, served up the moussaka and explained Ivo's situation to her.

'Poor lad,' she said, tucking into her meal. 'This is delicious, by the way.'

'I'm planning on doing more cooking,' said Jonny, smiling. 'Now I've got my appetite back and food actually tastes of something again.'

'Excellent idea,' she said, taking a gulp of her wine. She looked at Harold, who was now sleeping peacefully, and returned to the subject of Ivo. 'I'm not surprised. Those housing trust managers can be quite up themselves. Power crazed.'

'Could you do anything?'

'For Ivo? I could try, but they'll just say he broke their contract. Not much I can do really. I'll ask around, see if anyone knows of any dog-friendly rentals. But it's not easy finding anywhere right now. Ivo was actually lucky. Single young men aren't exactly top of the waiting lists. But you did the right thing and it'll be fun having Harold around.'

'We did talk about getting a dog, didn't we?'

'I said it would get you out walking a bit more,' she agreed.

'And Harold's a nice dog.'

'He seems well behaved,' she said. 'But why does he smell like a tart's boudoir?'

'I gave him a bath,' said Jonny. 'And how do you know what a tart's boudoir smells like?'

Belinda ignored the question. 'What did you wash him with?'

'Some stuff I found in the guest bathroom. It said it was shampoo. I only used about half a bottle. And a bit of conditioner.'

Belinda sat back in her chair and roared with laughter. 'That was the shampoo Sylvia gave me for my birthday.'

The dreaded cousin Sylvia who turned up once a year on Belinda's birthday and showered them with expensive and generally useless gifts.

Belinda leant forward to give him another kiss. 'Jonny, my darling. That dog wash probably cost around forty quid.'

'So thank you, Sylvia.'

'I don't think we need to tell her,' said Belinda. 'Anyway, apart from adopting dogs, what have you been doing today? Not one of your office days, was it?'

'Take a look at this,' he said, passing her the folder Jasmine had given him. 'I think it could be the charity project I've been looking for.'

Belinda cleared a space on the table and opened the folder. 'Interesting,' she said. 'It looks like a well-thought-out plan. Do you think it could work in an area like this?'

'I think it could. It's an affluent town but the food bank is under pressure even here. I like the idea that it's going to be part charity and part profit-making, and Jasmine already has contacts wanting to sign up for the paid membership.'

Belinda grinned at him and poured the coffee. 'I'm guessing one of them is you.'

'Definitely. I've already sampled their breakfast menu.'

'And the next step?'

'I'll get our finance people to check it over and then put it to the board. But I think Jasmine's done her research and she's already got the bank on her side.'

'How soon can she get it going?'

'I've put it on the agenda for next week's board meeting. I'm pretty sure they will vote it through once it's got the okay from the accountant. After that it can all move quite quickly.'

'That's great,' said Belinda. 'It's so good to see you fired up again.'

'It's good to have the energy. I thought I was going to spend the rest of my life feeling half asleep. You hear long covid mentioned but most people don't know the half of it.'

'Perhaps you should work on that as well. There must be support groups you could talk to. Let people know that recovery is possible.'

'Maybe,' he said, looking doubtful. 'I'll see how the breakfast club goes first. I wouldn't want to tempt fate. I don't know for sure that I won't relapse sometime in the future.'

'So you'll keep up the brisk walks and healthy eating?'

'Of course. Ivo and I did the Long Walk today. Almost as far as the statue and back. We wanted to see where the body was found.'

'Was there much to see?'

'Very little.' He turned his phone on and swiped to the photo Ivo had taken. 'We found this hanging in a tree close to where all the police stuff had been.'

Belinda took the phone from him and studied the picture. 'Do you know what it is?'

'No idea. Too big for a necklace, I think. Some kind of chain of office?'

'Could be. It looks a bit spooky, though.' She handed his phone back to him. 'Might be worth checking out local folklore groups.'

'As far as I know the body hasn't been identified yet. Perhaps when they know who it is, this pendant thing will make more sense.'

'We've been asked to check out the libraries,' said Belinda, whose special interest as a councillor involved fighting to keep them open.

Jonny laughed. 'That's a bit of a long shot, isn't it? Are they expecting to check out everyone with an overdue book in case they died before they could return it?'

'You're way behind the times, my love, and the police aren't that desperate. What they think is that as the libraries are now drop-in centres for advice about legal stuff and benefits, one of the volunteers might have noticed a missing client.'

'So they think it could be someone down on their luck, homeless perhaps?'

'They'll be doing the same round doctors' surgeries, probably at the food bank as well. Someone must know who he is.'

'Do you think I should tell the police about the thing hanging in the tree, or will they think I'm just wasting their time?'

'You should tell them. If they don't take you seriously then it's their problem.'

5

Katya Roscoff looked out of her window and wondered what had happened to the promised Indian summer. A couple of warm September days was all they'd had that year and now it was October and she felt cold. There was no way she'd put the heating on yet. Even with the promised help, her fuel bills had doubled. They had for everyone, she supposed, but not everyone was trying to exist on a police pension. When she'd decided to retire, things hadn't been too bad. But she still had another eight years to go before her state pension kicked in and that was assuming they didn't hike up the pension age again. When she started work it was sixty for women. She'd been fifty-eight when she reached her thirty years of police service and retired. She'd always planned to do this. Only a couple of years to wait. But then the age was raised to sixty-five. She could see the fairness of that since men already had to wait that long. And now it was sixty-six. But she could still manage. She wouldn't be rich, but she had enough to get by. And then prices started to take off.

Stop it, she told herself. *There are others a lot worse off than you.* She'd manage. She was good with money, budgeted well, had a nose for a bargain and didn't have expensive tastes. To make sure she remained cheerful, on a shelf in her kitchen she kept a jam jar, into which she put her change. Every Monday she checked the amount and treated herself to whatever she could afford. Something special to brighten up the week. This week there was six pounds and twenty-five pence. She'd take a brisk, warming walk into town and treat herself to breakfast. She'd already chosen where she would go. A café called *Jasmine's*. She'd seen it on many of her walks but had never been inside. It was a nice, comfortable-looking place with shabby armchairs and a cat. Katya missed her own cat. He'd died last year, and she hadn't the heart to replace him. Couldn't afford it now anyway, not with the price of cat food and vet bills. She'd find a comfy chair, or perhaps a table by the window, make her breakfast last, eat slowly and read the papers from cover to cover. Then she'd wander round the shops, stop off at the market perhaps and buy some cheap veg. Then she'd come home and make soup, enough to last three days. After that she'd curl up in front of the telly until bedtime. *Not an exciting life,* she thought glumly.

KATYA PUSHED OPEN the door of *Jasmine's* and peered around. It was busier than she expected. The armchairs were all occupied and there was a man sitting at the table by the window. A smartly dressed man who didn't look as if he needed to be there for the warmth. He probably lived in a house where they had the heating on all day. But he did have the ugliest dog she'd ever seen sitting close to him. Well-off people had upmarket dogs, didn't they? Golden retrievers or German shepherds. So perhaps he wasn't well-off at all – just careful with his clothes. She tried to see what he was eating and how much of it was left. Perhaps he would leave soon, and she could grab the table. She fidgeted by the door for a few moments, but he was taking his time. *What the heck,* she thought. The table was big enough for both of them, wasn't it?

She walked over to the table, keeping a wary eye on the dog. 'Mind if I sit here?' she asked, pulling off her hat and the scarf she'd made after unravelling a hand-knitted jumper she'd bought at a charity shop only to discover it was several sizes too small, and dumping them on a spare chair.

The man looked up and smiled at her. 'Of course not,' he said, moving his newspaper out of the way.

Katya sat down.

A pretty girl with long, dark hair came over. 'What can I get you?' she asked.

Katya studied the menu. She ordered poached egg on toast and a black coffee. The prices were not bad at all. She'd have enough left for an iced bun to take home for her tea.

'Good choice,' said the man sitting opposite. 'Karim's an expert with eggs.'

'You're a regular here?' she asked.

'Jonny Cardew,' he said, holding out his hand. 'I'm here most days.'

She took his hand and shook it. 'Detective Sergeant Katya Roscoff,' she said, wanting to give a good impression. 'Retired.'

'Nice to meet you,' said Jonny.

'That your dog?' she asked, peering under the table at the black dog who had edged closer to her in the hope of scrounging a piece of toast.

'That's Harold,' said Jonny. 'I'm looking after him for a friend, Ivo. He should be here in a minute.'

Her coffee arrived and she spooned in some sugar. 'I suppose you're going to ask if I'm Russian,' she said.

'I wasn't, actually,' said Jonny. 'Although Roscoff does sound a bit like a character from War and Peace. So, are you?'

'My great-grandfather was Russian. I grew up in Leeds, but I've been down here with the Thames Valley coppers all my working life. What about you?' He seemed like a nice bloke. She might as well get to know all about him. It was lovely and warm in the café, and he might even offer to buy her a second cup of coffee.

'I've lived round here all my life,' he said.

'Are you retired as well?'

'Semi-retired. I work a couple of days a week usually, although it's flexible.'

Katya sighed. 'Sometimes wish I'd stayed on,' she said. 'But I was never going to make inspector. I'd have ended up as the office drudge. I get bored, though. And cold.'

'Do you keep up with your colleagues?'

'Oh yeah, one or two. I sometimes go to the pub of an evening. But they don't have much time these days. Too many cuts. Work spread too thin.'

'Can I ask you something?' said Jonny as her breakfast arrived.

'Go on then,' she said, cutting into her egg and letting the yolk soak into the toast, just as she liked it.

'I've just been to the police station. I thought I'd found some useful evidence to do with the body they found in the Long Walk, but they made me feel like a nuisance.'

Katya tutted. 'No call for that,' she said. 'What was it?'

Jonny showed her the picture on his phone. 'It was hanging from a tree near where the body was found.'

That was interesting, Katya thought. She'd wandered up there herself and had been told to push off. Nothing to see, they said. Foul play not suspected. Had they even identified the body or established the cause of death? Too lazy to pursue it any further in her opinion. 'They've cleared the scene,' she said. 'They'd have bagged up any evidence and taken it away.'

'That's what they told me.'

'So that thing you found, it must have been left there after they'd gone.'

'That's what we thought, but it could still be evidence, couldn't it? Someone trying to leave a message or something.'

She used a piece of toast to mop up the remaining egg. He had a point. Could her ex-colleagues have missed something? She wouldn't be surprised.

'I don't suppose there's any way you can find out more, is there?' Jonny asked. 'I know you've retired, but if we at least knew who this guy was we might be able to find out why someone was hanging things in trees.'

Not impossible, she thought. 'Why do you want to know?'

'Just interested. It would be nice to solve a mystery.'

'Fancy yourself as one of those amateur sleuths, do you?'

'Why not?'

'Mostly because that only happens in crime fiction. And we don't even know if a crime was committed. Perhaps this chap just dropped dead while out for a walk.' Although if there *was* more to it, why not let this Cardew bloke take an interest? She might just look into it herself. It would be a way to pass her time and she could do with some company. They couldn't do much without help from someone who knew their way around the CID squad, though. And who could do that? She smiled and drained her coffee cup. She knew just the person. Lugs Lomax, the detective inspector she used to work with. Pour a couple of pints into him and he'd tell her anything she wanted to know.

Before she could tell Jonny about Lugs, the door was opened by a skinny lad and the dog suddenly went crazy. Harold had crawled out from under the table and started running round in circles, tail wagging – at least the half tail he had left was wagging – and bumping into chairs, then charging towards the door where he leapt into the boy's arms and slobbered joyfully, licking his face and hands. This, Katya assumed, must be Ivo. She watched as he put Harold down on the floor and crossed the room to join them at their window table, Harold still running in circles around him.

'Sit,' said Ivo firmly, pulling out a chair as Harold obediently settled himself back under the table.

'I've not seen him that lively in days,' said Jonny. 'I guess he's pleased to see you.'

'He's missed me,' said Ivo. 'But not as much as I've missed him,' he added, fondling the dog's ears.

'He's been very well behaved,' said Jonny. 'I think he's felt a bit lost without you.'

'He's definitely missed you,' said Jasmine, putting a cup of tea down in front of Ivo. 'Mr Cardew's been in with him every day and Harold's looked all around for you.'

'Jonny, please,' said Jonny. 'We're business partners now.'

'Really?' said Ivo.

'Mr Car... Jonny's company is sponsoring the breakfast club,' said Jasmine. 'We signed the contract this morning.'

'Going to introduce us?' asked Katya, realising she was no longer the centre of attention.

'I'm sorry,' said Jonny. 'This is Ivo Dean. A handyman of extraordinary talent and owner of Harold, who you've met already. And Jasmine here owns the café with her father. Katya's a retired police officer,' he said, turning to Ivo and Jasmine. 'We've just been talking about the body in the Long Walk.'

'Did you tell her about the necklace thing we found?' Ivo asked.

'He did,' Katya replied before Jonny had time to take a breath. 'Police told him he was wasting their time. Wouldn't have been like that in my day. We're going to find out what really happened.'

'We are?' said Jonny, looking surprised.

'Yeah, why not? You've got time on your hands, and I've got contacts with the local police. We'll do some detecting together.'

'Can I join in?' asked Ivo. 'It was me that found the thing in the tree.'

'Course you can, love,' said Katya, feeling a surge of generosity. 'And Harold. He can be our bloodhound.'

'And me?' said Jasmine. 'I'm an IT whiz. I can do the online research.'

Katya sat back, feeling pleased with herself. Looked like she'd made new friends and found a way to fill up her time. The food wasn't bad either.

'Seems we're a team then,' said Jonny, looking, Katya thought, rather bemused. But he'd get used to the idea. And he'd been the one to suggest it, hadn't he?

'How about I get us all a coffee to celebrate?' said Jasmine. 'On the house,' she added as Katya looked dubious and reached for her purse.

'A double celebration,' said Jonny. 'The breakfast club and...' he paused for a moment, 'the breakfast club detectives.'

'Right,' said Katya, unwilling to waste any more time and with a slight concern that they could all change their minds. She delved into her bag and found a scruffy exercise book and a pen someone had given her to celebrate the diamond jubilee. 'We should get going. Jasmine, you can search the Internet and see if you can find out anything about this pendant. Ivo can send you the photo of it. Jonny and Ivo, go back to the Long Walk and see if it's still there. Then check out a larger area. You might find other things left in trees.'

'Er, what are you going to do?' Ivo asked.

'I'm going to take a police friend out for a beer and get him to tell me all they know about the body. We'll meet back here the day after tomorrow and compare notes. That okay for everyone?'

They all nodded. *Nice to be in charge again*, Katya thought.

6

'On the house,' said Jasmine, putting a plate of Jonny's favourite breakfast dish down in front of him.

She was getting to know him well. She knew his favourite breakfast without even having to take his order. 'What have I done to deserve this?' Jonny asked as he sat down at his usual window seat and Harold settled himself under the table, where he could keep an expectant eye on the door.

'I've a favour to ask,' said Jasmine.

She was looking at him in the way he imagined a daughter might look at her father when about to ask for something inconvenient or expensive. 'Ask away,' he said.

'It's about an opening celebration for the breakfast club. I've signed up eight paying members, nine if we include you, and another six referred by the food bank.'

Not a lot, Jonny thought. But he didn't want to dampen her enthusiasm and he was sure the membership would grow once word got around. 'Are we ready for a celebration yet?'

'I thought that before we get too many more, we could have them all here together and get someone from the local paper to come and take photos.'

It was a good idea. Once it took off, they'd be working shifts and the café wouldn't be big enough to have all the members in at the same time. Jonny was already thinking they might need to expand and had his eye on some of the neighbouring shops. If one of them became vacant, and in the current economic climate this was more than likely, he'd jump in and rent it. But it was early days and he'd not mentioned it to Jasmine yet. 'What did you have in mind?' he asked. 'Just getting the local press to take pictures of people eating breakfast doesn't sound very exciting. Perhaps we could get someone to crack a ceremonial egg.'

Jasmine laughed. 'I thought we'd have a plaque on the wall and get a local celebrity to unveil it. The guy who did our shop sign could make it. I thought something like *Jasmine's Breakfast Club* and then the date it started and the name of the celebrity who opened it.'

'Sounds good,' said Jonny. 'Do you have someone in mind?'

'I thought you might ask Mrs Cardew to do it.'

'I'm sure she'd be flattered,' said Jonny. 'Not sure she thinks of herself as a celebrity though.'

'But she's always turning up to open things and getting her picture in the paper.'

That was true. Belinda was often asked to make speeches at local events. Probably because she was arguably the most presentable and photogenic member of the council. Although, if those he'd met were anything to go by, the bar was set fairly low. He couldn't remember if she'd been named on a plaque before, but she'd be tickled by the idea. She could use the photo on her website. 'I'll ask her this evening,' he told Jasmine.

The door opened and Katya struggled in, clasping two plastic carrier bags which she pushed under the table next to Harold. 'Weekly shop,' she explained, removing a knitted hat and bending down to unlace a pair of what Jonny knew as bovver boots. 'Oxfam shop,' she said, pointing at the boots. 'Not broken in yet. Killing me feet.'

'I'll get you a coffee,' said Jasmine.

'Thanks, love. You've not forgotten the meeting, have you?'

Jasmine shook her head. 'I've got Stevie in to cover so I'm all yours. I'll just get my laptop.'

'Where's Ivo?' said Katya. 'We can't start without him. Hope that dog doesn't kick up the same fuss as last time. He'll get us chucked out.'

Jonny was thinking the same, but as Ivo came in Harold stood up, yawned and ran a couple of circuits of the café, wagging his tail. Then he slumped down again under the table. Ivo scratched the dog's head affectionately. 'Looks like he's getting used to me coming and going,' he said.

Jasmine returned with coffees for Ivo and Katya, her laptop under one arm.

'Let's get started,' said Katya. 'I hope you've all got something to report. Jasmine, you can keep the minutes.'

Jasmine opened up her laptop and looked around at them hopefully.

Jonny felt like the kid who'd not done any homework. *Might as well kick things off though,* he thought. 'Ivo and I went back to the Long Walk and had a good look around. The pendant is still there, and we checked out other trees but didn't find anything. Sorry, it's not much.'

'Anything to add, Ivo?' Katya asked.

Ivo pulled a scrap of paper from his pocket. 'Whoever put that thing in the tree meant it to stay there,' he said, showing them a complicated diagram of how it had been fastened to the tree, which included a list of screws and nails, a length of wire and the tools needed to put it all in place.

Jonny was impressed. All he'd noticed was that the thing was firmly fixed to the tree. 'We took some measurements as well,' he said. 'Paced out how far that particular tree was from the road and the monument.'

'I made notes,' said Ivo. 'Shall I read them out?'

'Maybe not just now,' said Katya. 'They might be useful later.'

'Shall I make a folder for all that kind of stuff?' Jasmine asked. 'It would be good to keep it all together on the laptop.'

'Good idea,' said Katya. 'Did you find out anything about the pendant?'

'I couldn't find anything like it,' said Jasmine. 'But the design is interesting. That branch and antler motif is linked to the Herne the Hunter legend. Do you all know about that?'

'Something to do with an oak tree in the park, wasn't he?' said Jonny.

'He's a scary ghost,' said Jasmine. 'Rides around the park wearing antlers, rattling chains and freaking out the wildlife.'

'Perhaps the dead man was frightened to death,' Ivo suggested.

'Chased by the ghost of Herne the Hunter, who then returned and left a pendant hanging in the tree? Hardly,' said Katya.

'You got a better theory?' muttered Ivo.

'Did you find out anything about the dead man?' Jonny asked, hoping this wasn't all about to become a bad-tempered joke.

Katya opened her notebook. 'He was in his fifties, balding and slightly overweight. No obvious sign of the cause of death and nothing on the body to identify him. And that's important.'

'Why?' asked Ivo.

Katya sighed. 'It's obvious, isn't it? No one goes out for a walk, particularly in the dark, without a phone or a wallet, or even some small change. What does that tell you?' she asked, with an expression that suggested she was dealing with a class of particularly stupid children.

Jonny and Ivo looked at her blankly.

'That he was robbed,' said Jasmine.

'Thank God one of you has some brains,' said Katya. 'It was clearly a murder by someone who robbed him.'

'Couldn't he have died naturally and been found by someone who stole his stuff?' Ivo asked.

'He could,' said Katya. 'But what kind of heartless person robs a dead man and doesn't even bother to report the death?'

'A desperate one?' Jonny suggested. 'Someone who is scared to go to the police?'

'We can't possibly guess until we know who the dead man was,' said Jasmine.

'That has to be our next step,' said Katya. 'We have to find that out, then perhaps we can discover a motive.'

'How on earth are we going to do that?' Jonny asked.

'Right,' said Katya. 'Jasmine can look at missing persons sites on the Internet. Ivo, go round tool shops and ask if they remember anyone buying the stuff on your list recently.'

'That might find the person who nailed up the pendant, but it won't tell us who the dead guy is,' said Ivo.

'It'll be connected somehow,' said Katya.

'What shall I do?' asked Jonny. 'Stroll around town asking if anyone's missed a chubby bald guy recently?'

'Keep Ivo company,' said Katya.

She's run out of ideas, Jonny thought.

'I'll keep on at my police buddy and make sure he tells me anything they find out.' She crammed everything back into her bag. 'Same time the day after tomorrow? Great,' she said, not waiting for a reply.

7

Jasmine tapped a teaspoon against the cup she was holding, and the room went silent. She'd gone to a lot of trouble, Jonny thought, with flowers on the tables and balloons hanging from the ceiling. She was standing next to a small plaque on the wall near the counter, which was covered with a blue silk scarf attached to a cord with a tassel. 'If I can have your attention,' she said. 'I'd like to thank all our founder breakfast club members for coming this morning. You will each find a badge on the table in front of you. I hope you will wear it with pride and help to spread the word. Remember that for every one of you who has joined the membership scheme, you are helping to support the community.'

She and Jonny had agreed on the need to be tactful. No one need know who was a paid member and who was not. All the badges were the same. There was no need to point out charity cases. Some people fell on hard times, but they were as entitled to their dignity as anyone else. He was pleased to see that, as far as he could tell, the members were chatting to each other regardless of whether they had paid or not.

'I'd like to welcome Councillor Cardew,' Jasmine continued, 'and thank her for agreeing to officially launch the club.'

She handed the cord to Belinda, and Jonny watched his wife with
pride. She'd taken a lot of trouble to look her best, but then she
always did. She wore jeans and jumpers at home but had a wardrobe
of stylish dresses, suits and coats for public appearances. She looked
stunning whatever the occasion. They'd been married for more than
thirty years, and he didn't regret a second of it. Today was no exception. She'd gone for a shade of fuchsia pink and Jonny thought it was
a pity that the paper didn't publish colour photos. He wondered
vaguely if the local TV station had taken an interest and looked
around, hoping he might see someone with a video camera. There
were a few people with smartphones and one or two, he thought,
were videoing the event. But none of them looked like TV people,
although he didn't really know what they would look like so he could
be wrong. Not to be upstaged by Belinda, he'd worn a suit and a grey
and pink striped tie. There was a time when he'd worn a suit every
day. He had a wardrobe full of them, but since his retirement he'd not
bothered very much with how he looked. But today was special and
he was glad he'd made an effort.

Belinda was about to start her speech, after which she would pull
the cord and reveal the plaque, when the door flew open, banging
back against the wall and Katya charged in waving a piece of paper.
'I've got it,' she shouted, in a way that reminded Jonny of Neville
Chamberlain's *Peace for our time* declaration in 1938 that he had been
taught about at school.

This was definitely not the time for noisy declarations of any kind
and Katya's was unlikely to be anything as momentous as Chamberlain's. He jumped up and grabbed Katya by the arm, shushing her
and leading her to a chair as far as possible from where Belinda was
standing. Katya was muttering crossly about her right to freedom of
speech. 'You can tell us in a minute,' Jonny hissed at her, signalling to
Belinda that she should continue, which Belinda did, managing not
to show any hint that she'd been rudely interrupted.

The plaque was successfully unveiled, and Karim emerged from
the kitchen with a tray of breakfasts, followed by Stevie with a similar
tray. It was what most of the people were waiting for and silence

descended as everyone tucked into a plate of celebratory bacon and eggs.

'Can I talk now?' Katya asked impatiently.

Jasmine handed her a plate of food.

'I'm not a member,' said Katya, picking up a knife and fork and setting about the food before anyone could take it away from her.

'On the house,' said Jasmine. 'You've obviously got something important to tell us.'

'It can wait until I've finished my breakfast,' Katya said, scowling at them as if she had been the one who was interrupted.

Probably best to wait until it's a bit emptier in here, thought Jonny.

After a while the café began to clear. Belinda was picked up by an official car and driven off to her next engagement, and people began to drift away.

'Right,' said Jonny. 'Tell us what's on your piece of paper.'

'Where's Ivo?' Katya said. 'I'm not going through this twice.'

He was helping to clear tables and Jasmine called him over. 'We can finish that in a minute,' she said. 'Katya's got important news.'

Having been silenced when she arrived, Katya now took her time. She cleared a space on the table and spread out her sheet of paper in front of her. 'They know who it is,' she said, looking pleased with herself. 'This is a copy of the press release. It'll be in the paper tomorrow.'

'The body?' asked Ivo.

'Of course the body,' said Katya. 'Who else would it be?'

'Only asking,' said Ivo. 'Hurry up and tell us then. Some of us have work to go to.'

Katya started reading.

'The body of a man found recently close to the Long Walk in Windsor Great Park has now been identified as that of local resident Mr Raymond Irving Pierce. Mr Pierce, a carpet salesman, was reported missing by his wife Stella on her return from visiting a cousin in Spain. The police have appealed to anyone who might have seen Mr Pierce on the day of his death to contact them.'

'Is Irving his middle name or part of his surname?' Ivo asked.

'No idea,' said Katya. 'Does it matter?'

'It's an unfortunate set of initials,' said Jasmine, laughing.

'Do they have any idea how he died?' Ivo asked.

'Not yet,' said Katya. 'There should be a post-mortem report soon and possibly an inquest.'

'What do the police know about him?' asked Ivo.

'There doesn't seem much to know,' said Katya. 'He lived near Virginia Water, went fishing a couple of times a week, belonged to a bridge club and sold carpets.'

'I suppose it depends on the post-mortem,' said Jasmine. 'If he had a heart attack or something like that, there'd be no need to ask any more questions.'

'Any thoughts, Jonny?' asked Katya. 'You've gone very quiet.'

'I know that name,' said Jonny. 'I can't remember how, but I know I've heard it before.'

'Perhaps you bought a carpet from him,' Ivo suggested.

'We don't really have carpets,' said Jonny. 'Just parquet flooring and some rugs.'

'Well, let us know if you remember,' said Katya. 'It could be important.'

'Is that it, then?' asked Ivo. 'All sorted?'

'Of course not,' said Katya. 'Pierce was obviously murdered, and we need to find out who did it and why.'

'We won't know that until after the inquest,' said Jasmine.

'Take my word for it, he was murdered.' Katya's expression was determined.

'How can you be so sure?'

Katya sighed. 'We've been over this. First, he was robbed. And then someone left that thing in the tree. Neither of those would have happened if he just died while out for a walk. It's definitely murder, and I intend to find out who did it.'

'Isn't that a job for the police now?' asked Jonny.

'That useless shower? They wouldn't recognise a murderer if he was standing in front of them waving a gun and a carving knife.'

Jonny was beginning to regret ever getting involved. It had been quite exciting when it was just speculation, but now they could be talking about someone he actually knew, he wasn't so sure. 'There's not much we can do, is there?'

'There's plenty we can do,' said Katya. 'But if you want to drop out, then go ahead.'

Was that what he wanted? He was in two minds, but then the thought of the other three making what could be important discoveries made him decide to stay with it.

'Jasmine,' Katya said. 'You need to get onto that Internet and find out all you can about our Raymond. You too, Ivo. You must have mates in the carpet fitting trade. I'll keep nagging until I know the cause of death. And Jonny can go home and think about how he knew the guy. We'll meet back here the day after tomorrow.'

That didn't seem to leave much room for discussion, so they all nodded and Katya picked up her bags and left.

8

It bothered Jonny for the rest of the day, and it wasn't until he was taking Harold for his evening walk that he remembered where he had met Raymond Pierce. He and Belinda had been at a charity event where various businesses had been nominated for awards for services promoting cultural events. Must have been four or five years ago and he couldn't remember the details, but he didn't think Raymond Pierce had won anything. There must have been something about it in the local paper, and with any luck a picture of the nominees. And if Raymond was the type to get himself nominated for an award, he would have left some kind of a digital footprint, which hopefully Jasmine would find. Or she would if she did as instructed, or should that be ordered, by Katya.

Belinda would remember the occasion. And even if she didn't, it would be in her records. Belinda was a scrupulous record-keeper. Everything from expensive dinners to a single cup of coffee that she'd been given in her official role was recorded on her register of interests. And this had been a dinner in an expensive hotel.

As he walked, Jonny began to remember more of the occasion. It was a formal dinner held in the kind of hotel that hosts conferences and weddings. It was also, he remembered with embarrassment, the venue for a speed awareness course he'd attended having driven past a speed camera at thirty-seven miles an hour. He'd spent a morning watching the kind of videos that left him feeling he never wanted to get behind the wheel of a car again. But that feeling had passed when he realised how inconvenient relying on buses would be. It had, however, turned him into a maddeningly slow driver. But that was irrelevant and in the past. He put it out of his mind and trawled his memory for details of the award event.

He attended a lot of dinners with Belinda, and he recalled that at this one they had been separated. He was used to it. Belinda was usually seated with the high and mighty; the mayor, or someone who had made a large financial donation, occasionally the local MP. Jonny would be consigned to a far table along with various others of little importance. On this occasion he had found himself sitting next to a pleasant, rather quiet woman who introduced herself as Stella Pierce. 'I don't usually go to this sort of thing,' she told Jonny. 'We don't socialise much together.' Raymond, Jonny understood, usually went to the kind of functions where wives were not invited. He didn't like to think what that implied. He'd never been anywhere that would exclude Belinda. He'd liked Stella, he remembered now the occasion was coming back to him. They'd talked about their lives. She didn't have a job but sat on a few charity committees and liked going out for lunch. He told her a bit about running a packaging factory. Both had agreed that their lives didn't make for riveting conversation and turned to behaving a little like naughty schoolchildren sitting at the back of the class. And now the poor woman was a widow. What a shock that must have been after what he assumed was a pleasant couple of weeks in Spain with her cousin. He wondered if they had children, or anyone else who could help her through a difficult time.

JONNY AND HAROLD returned from their walk and found Belinda in the kitchen making a lasagne. 'I remember the occasion,' she said when he asked her about the dinner. 'But not the people involved.'

'I liked Stella Pierce,' said Jonny. 'I wonder if I should call on her and offer my condolences, but maybe she won't remember me and she'll think I'm being intrusive.'

Belinda put the lasagne in the oven and set the timer. She stood up and gave Jonny a kiss. 'How could she forget your handsome face?' she asked. 'I think she might welcome a visit. Take her some flowers. You don't need to hang around if you think she doesn't want you there.'

How would he know that? Okay, he'd be able tell if she was openly aggressive. What if she was just politely uncomfortable? But Belinda was usually right about things like that. He'd just have to hope he was sensitive enough to know the difference.

Jonny checked the Pierces' address, a street close to the entrance to the Saville Garden car park. He decided to visit her the next day, taking Harold. He could say he was just passing on his way for a walk in the park, which would give her an excuse not to say very much.

RAYMOND HAD CLEARLY BEEN a success in the carpet trade. The house was a modern, detached building in a gated development of six executive-type residences, each with a double garage and pillared portico. Houses like that, Jonny always thought, were an example of triumph of image over substance. He'd seen a similar estate under construction once and watched the pillars being unloaded from a truck, carried easily by two workmen, designed to resemble marble but probably made of polystyrene. But he was being unfair to both the architect and the residents. Anyone who could afford to live within striking distance of the Saville Garden would have the kind of income that could stretch to a decently built house, not to mention a team of surveyors who would ensure that the house *was* decently built. Besides, he was here to comfort a grieving widow, not to insult her architecture.

The door opened before Jonny's finger reached the bell and he was face to face with the woman he recognised from a few years back. She greeted him with a warm smile, not what he'd expected from a grieving widow. 'I'm sorry if I'm intruding at a difficult time,' he said. 'And you probably don't remember me...'

'Oh, I do,' she said. 'I remember speculating on the mayor's ability to keep his chain of office out of the soup. And you're not intruding at all. To be honest, I'll be glad of a bit of company. Can you stay for some coffee?'

Jonny handed her the bunch of flowers he had bought on Belinda's advice from an upmarket flower shop opposite the castle. 'That would be very nice,' he said. 'If you don't mind the dog.' He suspected the house would have cream-coloured carpets and that Harold wasn't exactly a cream carpet kind of dog.

'He's very welcome,' she said, bending down to stroke Harold. She held the door open for them and led them into a living room overlooking a well-manicured garden at the back of the house. The carpet was pale green, but probably just as susceptible to paw prints as cream. He instructed Harold to sit and hoped that he'd not trodden in anything wet or muddy on their walk from the car park. Stella didn't look concerned as she opened a door into the kitchen and turned on an expensive-looking coffee machine.

'I'm so sorry for your loss,' said Jonny, watching as she arranged his flowers in a vase, which she placed on a coffee table.

'To be honest,' she said, 'it wasn't really a surprise. Raymond's lifestyle wasn't what you would call healthy.'

'Do you know what happened?'

'He collapsed while out walking. A heart attack, apparently. The first I knew about it was when he failed to turn up to meet me at Heathrow and I had to get a taxi home. There was no sign of him when I arrived back here but that was not so unusual. He belonged to this group who often met at night. But if you don't mind, I'd rather talk about something else.'

'Of course,' said Jonny. The house felt very quiet. Was Stella alone? Surely she should have someone with her at a time like this. Jonny had no idea if they had any children. 'Is there anything I can do to help?' he asked. 'Anyone I can call to be with you?'

'That's very kind of you, but I have everything under control, and I prefer to be alone.'

She held out her hand to stroke Harold. 'I'd like a dog,' she said. 'But I'm probably going to sell up and move as soon as everything's sorted.'

'Will you stay in the area?' Jonny asked, thinking of the luxury block of flats that was going up near the town centre. A controversial development that had kept Belinda at lengthy planning meetings, after which she came home in a foul mood muttering about the need to provide affordable homes. Not places to make the rich even richer.

'I might,' said Stella. 'But really I'd like to move abroad.'

'You have family in Spain?'

'I do, but I wouldn't want to live with them.'

'Are you on your own here?'

'Yes, we never had children. To be honest I'm relieved.'

That was a strange thing to say. Wouldn't having family be a comfort at a time like this? He couldn't imagine how he'd cope if he suddenly found himself on his own. 'Do you have a date for the funeral?' he asked.

'In a couple of weeks, as long as the coroner releases Raymond's body soon.'

'Is there any reason why he wouldn't?'

'There seems to be some confusion over the cause of death, but I'm sure it will all be sorted in a day or two and then I can move on with my life.'

Jonny wasn't sure how to reply to that.

'Have I shocked you?' she asked.

He wasn't sure how to answer that either. But yes, he did feel uncomfortable with her lack of feeling.

'It wasn't a happy marriage,' she said.

No. He'd already worked that out for himself.

'You see, Raymond...' She stopped. 'You don't want to hear about that,' she said, pouring him a second cup of coffee and leaving him intrigued to know what it was she hadn't said.

He swallowed his coffee and thought it was probably time to

leave. He stood up and pulled Harold's lead out of his pocket. 'If you're sure there's nothing I can help you with, Harold and I had better get on with our walk.' He searched his pockets for a pen and notebook. Tearing a page out of the book, he wrote down his phone number and email. 'Let me know if there's anything I can do, won't you?' he said, handing it to her.

'Thank you,' she said. 'You've been very kind.'

WALKING AWAY from the house and into the park, Jonny thought of all the questions he should have asked. First and foremost, what was Raymond doing in the Long Walk late at night? It was three miles or so across the park from where he lived; hardly a gentle evening stroll. The body was found by a dog walker early in the morning and the Long Walk was a popular place for evening walks. According to Katya's police chum, no one had seen Raymond in the park earlier in the evening, so he must have gone there after dark. But why? Was he meeting someone? A bit of cheating while his wife was away in Spain? But with his wife away, there was no point in walking all the way across the park. There were plenty of quiet spots much nearer home.

Stella's lack of emotion also worried him. Even warring couples must feel something if one of them dies suddenly. But Stella had seemed calmly relieved by the whole thing. And what was this group Pierce belonged to? A group that met at night, a group that Stella had clammed up about almost as soon as she'd mentioned it. Then he remembered the pendant hanging in the tree. A replica of a strange tree with antlers for branches, symbol of Herne the Hunter. There had to be a connection. Was this mysterious group just a bunch of men who played at ghost hunting? Was Pierce out late that night looking for evidence of Herne the Hunter, and had one of his ghost-spotting colleagues left the pendant in the tree as a mark of respect? But if so, why not just come forward and say so. Why the secrecy?

He sat on a bench by the lake and let Harold run around after squirrels while he got out his notebook and made a list of things to

mention at the next Breakfast Club Detective meeting. If they were
going to have meetings and make notes, they needed something
shorter to call themselves. But the initials BCD sounded too much
like a remedy someone had recommended recently. Belinda had gone
out and bought him some a few months ago to boost his immune
system. CBD, a substance made from cannabis plants, which he'd
always assumed must be illegal and which Belinda referred to as his
can't blame the dog pills. They'd not done him any good at all as far as
he could tell.

He started a new page and wrote *Breakfast Club Detectives* at the
top. He'd just have to put up with the long name. He wasn't going to
risk confusing it with a dubious remedy. The first item on his list was
to ask Katya if she'd discovered the actual time of death. There was
no way they could know what kind of crime it was until they knew
that. Early morning or evening could just mean an innocent walk.
Something he frequently did himself, even before Harold moved in.
A death late at night would be far more suspicious. The next was to
find out about groups of people who met in the park at night. Definitely something suspicious if combined with an unexpected death.
That could be difficult. Night-time meetings were almost by defini-
tion secretive, with members probably vowing never to tell anyone
about them. Jonny couldn't imagine how he'd even start that kind of
search. But he thought of something more manageable. He could get
to know people Raymond worked with. Perhaps he could express an
interest in new carpets for the boardroom at CPS and chat to Pierce's
colleagues. Find out if he was suspected of having an affair. Could
Pierce have been the victim of a jealous husband?

Jonny read through his list and felt quite pleased with himself.
He'd have something to contribute at their next meeting. Katya had it
all her own way at the moment, giving them simple tasks to do but
keeping the real detective work for herself. And that was right since
she was the only one with police experience. But if Jonny was going
to become an amateur sleuth, he should do it properly. His list was
just the start.

9

Jasmine kicked off her shoes and wriggled her toes guiltily in front of the gas fire. She glanced at the smart meter and decided to give herself another five minutes, then have a hot shower and get into bed with her laptop. Dad wasn't going to be home from his meeting for another hour or two and it was silly to heat the flat when she was the only one in it. Not that they needed to worry all that much. The café was doing well with all the extra trade the breakfast club had brought in. Membership was still quite low, but overall numbers were up. Mr Cardew – it still felt wrong to call him Jonny – was pleased. The last figures he'd taken to his board of directors were well above what they had predicted and numbers, he was sure, would pick up even more. People were dropping in to see what it was all about and to sample the menu, just as he had done himself. Once they discovered how well it was working, they'd join in droves. Mr Cardew knew about things like that. He should do; he had a lifetime of experience.

But this evening Jasmine planned to put everything to do with the café to one side and concentrate on finding out more about the pendant in the tree. She already had a file of facts she'd collected about Raymond Pierce. Not that she'd found anything very inter-

esting about him. From what she'd discovered, it looked like he had
led a very ordinary life. A few mentions on a Facebook page for
people who played bridge, a local paper announcement that he'd
been nominated for an award for some charity work he'd done, a
discovery that he'd lived in the same house since it had been built
eight years earlier, and a letter he'd written to the local parish magazine about setting up a neighbourhood watch scheme in his community. Nothing that suggested he was the type someone would want to
murder. She read through the file, then closed it and opened up
Google to search for Herne the Hunter pendants.

There was plenty of Herne-related stuff out there; figurines, t-
shirts, keyrings, even a green spell bottle containing mugwort and
frankincense, and adorned with a Herne medallion. She couldn't
imagine why anyone would need to cast spells involving mugwort
and frankincense, but buyers had left excellent reviews so it must
have its uses. Herne was clearly a popular, if sinister, chap. Jasmine,
who had lived in the area all her life, was surprised that she knew so
little about him. What she didn't find was a medallion like the one in
the tree. It was all very well knowing that all this stuff was available.
What she really needed to discover was who had owned this particular example.

Then she had a brainwave. She logged into eBay, uploaded the
photo and began the process of selling it. She wouldn't actually
launch it for sale but along the way she'd be given an opportunity to
look at *similar items*. This was a facility offered by eBay to price match
things people wanted to sell, and Jasmine hoped that it would come
up with people who had bought or sold them in the past. She would
be able to check out sellers and find any who operated locally. She
might be able to contact people who actually owned them and find
out what they were used for. It might well be against eBay's terms and
conditions, but she'd take a chance and if it solved a mystery, well,
what was the worst that could happen? A lifetime ban from eBay?
She could live with that.

She was in luck. There were no pendants that matched the one
Ivo had found. But she did find a seller who operated under the

slightly sinister-sounding name of Darkjeweller and who made quite similar things. She sent them a message and a copy of the photo, saying she'd found a pendant like the one in the image and asking if it was likely to be worth anything.

Jasmine had done all she could for this evening. She logged out of eBay and opened Netflix to search for a nice feel-good romcom. She was about to start watching a film about an artist who went to Italy and fell in love with a chef, when there was a ping and an alert on her screen. A message from Darkjeweller. She clicked it open. Yes, Darkjeweller had seen one of those. Several had been made but Darkjeweller's advice was to leave well alone. There are some unpleasant people out there, Jasmine was told. Don't even think about trying to sell it. *Or what?* Jasmine wondered. Not that she was in any position to put it up for sale. All she'd wanted was to know more about it. So what was she going to do now? Did what she had been told suggest that Mr Raymond Pierce was one of these *unpleasant people?* Or was he just a blameless person who had somehow or other upset one of them and nailing the pendant to the tree had been a way of leaving a message? A pretty stupid message, since Raymond Pierce was dead and not in a position to appreciate the gesture. And since the body had been removed, the only people who knew what it meant were probably more of the unpleasant lot.

She tried to return to her film but was unable to concentrate on it. Instead, she clicked out of Netflix and typed *Darkjeweller* into Google. He, or possibly she, had a Facebook page, a TikTok account, stuff on Instagram and several Pinterest boards. Darkjeweller was *happy to cater for all your pagan, witchcraft and occult needs.* Scary stuff. Scarier still if it involved groups of unpleasant people and a body in the Long Walk.

There was not much more she could do this evening. She imagined the rest of the breakfast club detectives would find it interesting. And with luck they'd have some ideas about what they could do about it. Hopefully down to earth, sensible ideas. Not ones that would have them trekking around seances and pagan events. Getting Katya to talk to her police friend would be a good place to start.

Wandering around Windsor Forest at night looking for demons, ghouls and witches was, she hoped, an idea that would be firmly rejected. She imagined Katya might actually be up for something like that, but she was fairly certain Mr Cardew wouldn't. She wasn't sure about Ivo. He didn't look like a fearless hunter of the dark arts, but who knew? And he was good at climbing trees, although Jasmine thought that was not really much help, except that it had led them to the pendant in the first place.

Jasmine made some notes about her evening's discoveries and then heard her dad come home. She went downstairs to make him a cup of tea. They'd have a chat about his evening, and she could put all thoughts of the pendant and its spooky connections out of her mind until the morning.

10

Weekends were the hardest. It reminded Ivo of lockdown, when he'd either been shut in his hotel room with no one to talk to, or he'd been at work where he was also in a room on his own. Social distancing, he was told. Hand-washing whenever he entered or left the building, wearing a mask when his supervisor dropped in, and the canteen closed. Ivo would have enjoyed the canteen. There'd have been hot meals and people to chat to, but during lockdown it was sandwiches only. A sign-up sheet and then pick them up at the door. There was a good choice; he'd no complaints about that. And all free, thanks to a generous management. But no company. He'd never want to go back to living on the streets and sleeping rough, but at least he had friends there. Quite a little gang of them. Ivo wondered if they were all still there or had they, like him, been rehoused?

Weekends were when he missed Harold the most. But this morning, Saturday, he had a job regrouting a patio at a house in Arthur Road. He'd be done by lunchtime, and it was only a five-minute walk into town from there. He'd visit some old haunts and maybe catch up with some friends. And tomorrow he was meeting Jonny and Harold at *Jasmine's* so that they could all go for a walk together.

Katya had asked him to find out about anyone who'd bought the wire and screws to fix the pendant to the tree. A couple of days ago, he'd driven with his van-owning friend to stock up on what he needed for his next few jobs. He asked the bloke on the checkout, who had laughed at him. They sold stuff like that every day to an endless stream of customers. How could he be expected to remember any individual? Ivo didn't even have a description and he sympathised. It had been a stupid question. Katya would just have to find a different way to discover who it was.

He did a good job on the patio. The elderly woman who lived in the house was very pleased and promised to recommend him to her friends. She'd paid him in cash, which was unusual these days. Karim and one or two others still used cash, but these were mostly shop and café owners who were glad of a chance to empty their tills and not have cash readily available to any thieves who might chance their luck. This woman was in her eighties and didn't hold with online banking. She'd been to the Co-op, where there was a cash machine, to get his money. Ivo counted the notes she'd handed to him. 'You've overpaid me,' he said, handing back a ten-pound note.

'No, no,' she said, patting his hand. 'You keep it.'

'I couldn't,' said Ivo. 'It's too much.'

'Not at all,' she said. 'You're an honest lad and you've done a good job. You keep it and treat yourself.'

There didn't seem much point in arguing so Ivo tucked the note, along with the rest of the fifty pounds, into an inside pocket of his jacket. He didn't feel comfortable carrying cash around. He'd seen too many thefts in the town. But there wasn't much he could do about it. Insisting on bank payments would only upset the old lady and that was the last thing he wanted to do. It was safe enough in broad daylight and he'd be home before it got dark. He'd lock the money away in a box he kept in the wardrobe, hidden behind some spare blankets. It was a habit he'd started in the hotel where he'd been warned not to trust anyone who might wander into his room. Oddly, it had felt safer when he had no money at all. He'd had to rely on people's goodwill to keep him fed, but at least no one was going to rob him.

It was a chilly morning. The grouting job had kept him warm, but he'd soon need a coat for the winter. Perhaps he'd go to Oxfam and see if they had anything to fit him. He trotted up Arthur Road, twisted in and out of the multistorey car park and emerged at the lower end of Peascod Street just a short distance from Oxfam, where there was a disappointing selection of coats. Plenty of books and CDs, alongside ethically sourced gifts and Christmas cards, but no coats. 'We've had a run on them,' he was told. 'It's the cost of living crisis.' *No problem,* Ivo thought. There were other charity shops in the town, or he could catch a bus to Slough one day. Shops were cheaper there and with the way things were right now he might be able to afford a new coat. And it wasn't really cold. Not yet.

He emerged from the shop and walked up the hill towards the castle. Saturdays were lively in the town. There were buskers and stalls selling hot food. He bought himself an expensive burger. Made from organic grass-fed beef, he was told. *Didn't cows always eat grass?* The burger had cost him six pounds, an amount that would normally feed him for several days. But this was the tourist heart of the town, not Tesco. And besides, Ivo was an unexpected ten pounds better off. He could afford it.

Having finished his burger, Ivo continued up the hill, turning right in front of the castle and making his way to the parish church where he hoped to find Charlie Jones. Charlie had spent his whole life, as far as Ivo knew, living a hand-to-mouth existence around the town. He'd been good to Ivo in the past. It was Charlie who first introduced him to the parish soup kitchen, which opened up in a tent outside the church once a month. And now Ivo intended to return his kindness by suggesting that he might join the breakfast club.

He found Charlie sitting on a tombstone outside the church, sipping from a cardboard mug. 'Leek and potato,' he said, raising the mug as if giving a toast. 'You'll need to hurry. There's not much left.'

'It's okay,' said Ivo. 'I've just had a burger.' He sat down next to

Charlie, reached into his pocket and fished out one of Jasmine's leaflets. 'Thought you might like this,' he said, handing it to Charlie.

'Might give it a go,' said Charlie, folding it up and putting it in his own pocket. 'Had a bit of luck myself this week.' He fumbled into his pocket and pulled out a leather wallet. 'Found it up by the Cambridge Gate. Probably dropped by one of them who watched the funeral procession.'

'Was there anything in it?' Ivo asked.

'Nah,' said Charlie. 'I'd have handed it in if there was. I ain't no thief. Nice bit of leather work, though.' He handed the wallet to Ivo.

'Looks expensive,' said Ivo, opening it up and wondering what had happened to its contents.

'Got initials and all.' Charlie pointed to the initials RIP, embossed in gold on the wallet. 'Bit unfortunate that,' he chuckled. 'Reckon if I was RIP, I'd have dropped the I and just gone by RP.'

Something was nagging at Ivo's memory. Where had he heard a similar comment recently?

'You take it, lad,' said Charlie. 'You're in work now. You need somewhere to keep all that cash you're raking in.'

'No, I couldn't,' said Ivo, handing the wallet back.

'No use to me,' said Charlie. 'I never have two pence to rub together.'

Ivo wasn't going to offend the old man by refusing. He didn't often have anything to give away and he still needed some dignity. 'Okay,' said Ivo. 'But let me pop across the road and get you a coffee.'

'I wouldn't say no, but could you make that a hot chocolate?'

11

'**K**atya, old love, I thought it was you, sitting up there scribbling away in your notebook. Haven't seen you for years. How are you?'

Katya could do without this. She'd already had a trek to get there. Two trains and then a walk across town to the coroner's office for a pre-inquest hearing. She'd left home at half past seven that morning and all she'd had to eat was a piece of toast. She'd planned to walk back into the town and go to McDonalds or Subway before she got her train home again. She needed to be home to think over all she'd learnt this morning. Things that made her even more determined that Raymond Pierce had been murdered. And here was this little scrote of a journalist, Teddy Strang, standing in her way and greeting her like a long-lost cousin. He was right, though. They hadn't seen each other for years, not since the body parts in the post case. What would that be? Five years ago? They'd all got a bollocking for it. Lined up in the superintendent's office being yelled at. But even as the decibel level of the yelling rose, no one had admitted leaking the story to the press. It left the team grumbling and suspicious of each other. Even after the case was solved and the perp well and truly banged up, the ill feeling persisted. And not long after that, the team was broken up and went their separate ways. The only upside was that Katya was allocated to the same team as Lugs Lomax; the beginning of a long and comfortable partnership.

'What do you want, Teddy?' she said. 'I've not got the time to chat.'

'Just greeting an old friend,' he said. 'No need to sound so bad tempered. Are you staying for the afternoon sitting? I could buy you lunch.'

'I've a train to catch,' she said. 'Just time to pop into McDonalds.'

'Have you no thought for your cholesterol levels?' he asked. 'And anyway, what's the rush?'

'Just don't want to hang around here. Never know who I might have to rub shoulders with.'

Teddy laughed. 'Same old warm-hearted, frolicsome Katya, I see.'

Katya scowled at him.

'Look,' he said. 'I'm just off to the Crown for one of their steak pies and chips. Why don't you join me? My treat.'

Probably after a story. Doesn't know I've retired. She'd been to the Crown before. A nice old-fashioned coaching inn. It would be warm and the helpings generous. Could she put up with him for the sake of a hot meal? Maybe even a pint. All at his expense. Of course she could. 'Okay,' she said. 'Lead on.'

SHE HADN'T EXPECTED the roaring log fire. Today was definitely looking up. She even managed a smile as Teddy put a pint of the local brew down in front of her.

'How's tricks?' Teddy asked. 'Still at Windsor nick?'

'Retired two years ago,' she said, downing half her beer in a single gulp and sighing with pleasure as she put the glass down on the table and eyed the steaming plate of pie and chips that had arrived.

'What brings you to the coroner's office today?'

'Local interest,' she said, sprinkling salt on her chips. 'You?'

'Ever heard of Edwin Eastman? Councillor Eastman, I should say.'

'Don't think so,' said Katya. 'What's he done?'

'Where do I start? He's a slimy little character. We've had several tip-offs about him, ranging from fingers-in-the-till type things to activities that attract attention from *#MeToo*. Trouble is, he doesn't leave any kind of a trail. His social media's squeaky clean, a whiter-than-white record where council audits are concerned and no police record. Oh, I lie, he had a speeding ticket once.'

'So perhaps your tip-off is from someone who just doesn't like him. Perhaps he's as pure as the driven snow.'

Teddy tapped the side of his nose. 'Can't reveal my sources, but believe me, he's not. And one day I'm going to get him.'

'So why were you at Raymond Pierce's inquiry this morning? You don't think this Mr Eastman is a murderer, do you?'

Teddy took a thoughtful sip of his beer. 'Interesting use of the present tense there, Katya. Do you think the open verdict was wrong?'

Katya shook her head. 'No, a verdict of natural death would have been wrong. An open verdict supports my theory that he could have been murdered. It just leaves scope for more enquiries. But from what I know about our current super, that's not going to happen. The coroner doesn't seem to be going for a full inquest.'

'Time constraints, most likely,' said Teddy. 'There's a backlog following lockdown so they're pushing the more straightforward cases through as fast as possible.'

'More likely there's not enough cash to pursue it,' said Katya. 'I know the coroner is supposed to be independent but giving the police extra work won't make him popular.'

'What do *you* think, Katya? You're obviously leaning towards murder or you wouldn't have been there this morning.'

Katya was wondering if Teddy's largess would extend to a pudding. She fancied the fruit crumble and custard. 'You're not going to use what I think about this case as a story, are you?'

He managed a hurt, *what, me?* expression. 'Katya, how could you even think that?'

'You've got previous,' she said.

'I think,' he said, picking up the dessert menu and studying it, 'that we could work together. But for now, I promise that anything you tell me will be strictly off the record. You can trust me.'

He was one of the least trustworthy people she'd ever met, and in her job she had met quite a few dodgy characters. And what exactly did off the record mean? On the other hand, she had very little to go on and even if he did publish what she told him, she didn't see that it would do very much harm. It was hardly Official Secrets Act stuff. 'Okay,' she said. 'I'll tell you what I think. I had my doubts, but after this morning, I'm sure Raymond Pierce was murdered. But first, why do you think Eastman and Pierce are connected?'

'That was a bit of a long shot. I came across Pierce's name while asking questions about Eastman. All I know is that they used to play bridge together. They belonged to some team and met regularly. And now Pierce is dead and we know from the pre-inquest report that he was playing bridge the night he died. Chances are that Eastman was there as well. It wouldn't be hard to find out.'

'I learnt a lot from the woman whose evidence was read out this morning.' Katya flicked through her notes. 'Catherine Wallace,' she said, finding the name. 'The woman who confirmed that Raymond Pierce was one of a foursome at her house that evening, and that they'd all been drinking. Although she said that Pierce was definitely none the worse for drink when he left.'

'So Raymond, Catherine and two others were playing cards and drinking. One, I assume, was Mr Wallace. The other possibly Edwin Eastman.'

'Okay,' said Katya. 'I can probably find that out.' Jonny Cardew would be the person to do that. His wife was on the council and would know Eastman. A bit of a step to establishing where he was on the night Pierce died, but she'd think of a way around that.

'Your turn,' said Teddy. 'Why do you think Pierce was murdered?'

'Well,' said Katya, enjoying the sensation of being warm, well fed and the centre of someone's attention. She drew a rough map of Windsor on a paper napkin. 'The Pierces live here.' She drew a cross to mark the Saville Garden. 'We learnt today that the Wallaces live here.' She added another cross. 'The two addresses are only a mile or so away from each other. About three miles from where Pierce's body was found. He didn't drive that night, presumably because he knew they would be drinking, and Catherine Wallace called him a taxi at ten-thirty assuming it would take him home. So what was he doing in the middle of Windsor Great Park in the dark and several miles from where he lived?'

'A good point,' said Teddy.

'That's not all,' said Katya. 'Nothing was found on the body. No wallet or phone and nothing to identify him.'

'A robbery?'

'Possibly, but a bit extreme, don't you think? Then there's the postmortem report, which found not only alcohol but traces of propranolol.'

'Not that unusual,' said Teddy. 'A lot of men his age take beta blockers.'

'But not with alcohol,' said Katya. 'It can cause hallucinations.'

'Maybe he forgot, or hadn't read the warning.'

'Or someone gave it to him. Perhaps Eastman slipped it into his drink. Did he have a motive for killing Pierce?'

'No idea,' said Teddy. 'I was working on the assumption they were up to something dodgy together.'

'Well, maybe they were. And they fell out over it. Perhaps Pierce was going to rat on Eastman and had to be got out of the way.'

'But the cause of death was heart failure, not poisoning. A cocktail of alcohol and beta blockers is not pleasant, but I don't think it's lethal. Fancy a pud?'

Even contemplating what a mix of alcohol and beta blockers could do, Katya definitely fancied one. She nodded enthusiastically. 'And coffee?'

Teddy laughed. 'You don't change, Katya. But yes, lets push the boat out and get coffee as well.'

By the time they'd finished it was nearly four o'clock. Teddy, to Katya's relief, had settled the bill and collected a receipt. As she suspected, this lunch was going to be claimed for on expenses. Quite right too. She'd had more information about the case than Teddy. Although this Eastman character sounded interesting, so she had picked up something. She'd definitely find out more about him. All in all, she thought, as she sat in the train reading her notes and going over everything she'd discovered, it had been a profitable day. She'd listened to evidence that confirmed her opinion that they were looking at a murder. She even had a possible suspect. A tenuous one, but better than nothing. There was plenty for her team of breakfast detectives to get their teeth into. She'd call a meeting and allocate tasks.

Her train arrived at Slough and she heaved herself out, crossing the platform to the little train that would rattle her over the meadow to Windsor. Then only a ten-minute walk home. Best of all, she'd eaten well today and had no need for more than an egg sandwich for supper. She would sleep well tonight.

12

They were short staffed in the café on the morning of the meeting, so Jonny volunteered to help clear up the last of the breakfast tables, loading trays, carrying them into the kitchen and tossing the occasional scrap to Harold.

'You shouldn't be doing that,' said Karim, taking the tray from him and setting it down on a work surface where a number of similar trays were waiting.

'Not at all,' said Jonny. 'I'd hate to think the breakfast club was making a lot of extra work for you and I'm happy to volunteer myself.' The fact was Jonny actually enjoyed helping out there. At Cardew Packing he felt a bit spare. Marcus did his best. He was a good son and tactfully popped in to ask Jonny's advice now and then. But he didn't really need advice. Marcus was already doing a far better job than Jonny ever had, and it made him feel like a spare part. There were only so many canal boats one could watch without going insane with boredom, and he'd made no progress with his enquiries into Raymond Pierce's carpet company. The Axminster in the boardroom and management offices had been bought to last. It would be many years before it needed replacing, so there was no reason to make any enquiries about carpet companies.

Sponsorship of the breakfast club had helped. The board were impressed and since the company was flourishing, had agreed to increase the sponsorship budget. But it wasn't enough to keep him busy, even though he officially worked only two days a week. Not with his recently recovered energy levels. What Jasmine obviously needed now was not more money but more hands-on help. And Jonny really did enjoy clearing tables and washing up. He felt a lot more useful there than he did sitting in his office staring at the canal. Harold enjoyed being there as well. Jonny took him to the office with him and that helped to alleviate the boredom because Harold was popular and people dropped in to see him. But here in *Jasmine's*, Harold got titbits of food and a chance of being with Ivo. He was an easy-going, obliging kind of dog, but there was no question where he'd rather spend his time. Given the choice, *Jasmine's* would win every time.

The café was quiet in the hour between the late breakfasters and early lunchers. Jasmine could leave any customers who might drop in for coffee for Karim to attend to while the 'detectives' met to discuss the case. Jonny still found it hard to see himself as a detective, even though it had been his ambition for more years than he cared to count. He wondered if the others felt the same. Not Katya, obviously, because she had been a real one. But Jasmine, Ivo and Jonny himself had been unexpectedly drawn into the mystery and they were just amateurs. Harold had solved a crime once and detained a criminal, but that didn't really give him the status of a police dog. So was it just a bit of fun to pass the time or should he actually take it seriously? Yes, of course he should. And he was. This morning, he was excited by it all. He couldn't wait for the others to arrive so that he could tell them his theory. He might just be the one to have solved the case.

Jasmine made a pot of coffee and carried it to the window table where her laptop was already waiting. She sat down next to Jonny, slipped Harold a biscuit and looked at her watch. 'I hope Ivo and Katya won't be late,' she said. 'I can't leave Dad to do the lunches on his own.'

Jonny peered at Harold who sat under the table, his head on his paws, gazing expectantly towards the door. 'Harold's getting anxious as well,' said Jonny, patting him on the head.

'Oh, it's okay,' said Jasmine. 'I can see Katya now.'

They watched as Katya appeared at the end of the narrow lane, dressed as usual in her heavy boots and layers of mismatched clothes.

'I wonder how much more she'll wear when it gets really cold,' said Jasmine, watching her struggle through the door with a large carrier bag.

Katya arrived at their table, sat down and pulled a clipboard out of the bag. 'Getting organised,' she told them, diving back into the bag and eventually, after a lot of scrabbling, extracting a handful of pencils. 'Where's Ivo?' she said. 'We can't start without him.'

'He's here now,' said Jonny as Ivo appeared in the doorway and Harold began his usual ecstatic greeting, settling down as Ivo pulled up a chair and joined them.

'Shall I take the minutes again?' Jasmine asked. 'Or are you going to do it all on that clipboard?'

'This just has the notes I made after the hearing yesterday. You'll find them interesting, very interesting. You can take it all down and print copies for everyone.'

'Email it to me, if you like,' said Jonny, who was familiar with the cost of ink cartridges. 'I can print them at work.'

'You should all have a folder,' Katya added. 'We're collecting a lot of stuff. You need to keep it organised.'

'It's like being back at school,' Jasmine muttered.

Jonny was inclined to agree but didn't want to dampen Katya's obvious enthusiasm. He was getting quite enthusiastic himself.

'I trust you've all got something to report,' she said.

'I've got a suspect,' said Jonny, expecting looks of admiration from the rest of them.

'So have I,' said Jasmine.

'And me,' said Ivo.

'Sounds like you've all been busy,' said Katya. 'And as matter of fact, I have a suspect too. But you go first, Jonny. Tell us who you think did it.'

'Stella Pierce.'

Jasmine looked up from her typing in surprise. 'The victim's wife? But she was in Spain. She got back several days after he died.'

'That's what she *says*,' said Jonny. 'But how do we know she was telling the truth? All we know for sure is that she didn't report Raymond missing until she allegedly arrived back from Spain and he failed to meet her at the airport. They lived on their own. She could have been lying low at home.'

'Wouldn't someone have noticed she was there when she turned the lights on?' asked Ivo.

'That's a good point, Ivo,' said Katya. 'And anyway, what motive did she have for wanting him dead?'

'She didn't like him,' said Jonny.

'How do you know?' Jasmine asked.

'I remembered where we'd met. It was at a charity do a year or two back. I sat next to her at dinner and we got chatting. I went to see her a couple of days ago. It was Belinda's idea really. She said I should go and express my condolences and take some flowers. Anyway, Stella was very hospitable and asked me in for coffee. She didn't seem like a grieving widow at all. In fact, she told me it wasn't a happy marriage.'

'If you think she's a murderer, it's lucky she didn't poison your coffee,' said Ivo, laughing.

'Hear him out,' said Katya, frowning at him.

'Not everyone has a happy marriage,' said Jasmine. 'There's a thing called divorce. You don't need to murder your spouse.'

'But that would mean dividing up the assets,' said Jonny, reluctant to drop his theory. 'Raymond Pierce was obviously well off and I guess she inherits everything.'

'There's still the problem that she says she was out of the country at the time,' said Katya. 'But I can check that.'

'How?' asked Ivo.

'Lugs can ask for the passenger lists.'

'Who's Lugs?'

'Try to keep up, Ivo,' said Jasmine. 'He's the bloke that Katya used to work with.'

'Right,' said Katya. 'Make a note of all of that, Jasmine. Let's move on to the next suspect.'

'I don't have a name,' said Jasmine. She read them the notes she had made about the pendant and Darkjeweller's email. 'But if we can get this guy to tell us who he made the pendant for, we'd know where to look for the killer. Pierce could have belonged to some dark arts type secret society who had the pendants as a badge of membership.'

'Why would they kill one of their own members?' Ivo asked.

'Perhaps he upset them somehow,' said Jasmine.

'Stella did say Pierce belonged to a group who met at night, but then she clammed up and wouldn't say any more,' said Jonny.

'Okay,' said Katya. 'That's two possible suspects. Who's yours, Ivo?'

Ivo took the wallet out of his pocket and put it on the table. He told them how Charlie had found it and given it to him. 'Look at the initials,' he said. 'RIP. It took me a day or two to remember why they were familiar and then it came to me. Raymond Irving Pierce. The wallet was empty when Charlie found it. It would have been full of cash and bank cards. I think that whoever stole the wallet killed Pierce.'

'Which day did Charlie find the wallet?' asked Katya.

'Two days after the funeral. It was hidden in some bushes.'

'The timing works,' said Katya. 'That's another question for Lugs. They'll be able to check whether anyone tried to use the cards.'

Jasmine picked up the wallet and looked inside. 'There's a hidden pocket,' she said. The wallet had several pockets all stitched together apart from one, which had a strip of leather dividing it from the others. Jasmine eased it open and felt inside with the tip of her finger. 'There's something in there,' she said, gently easing out a small piece of card. She laid it on the table. The card was blank apart from three lines of letters and symbols written in ink.

'That doesn't mean anything,' said Ivo. 'It's just letters and numbers.'

Jonny picked it up and stared at it. 'It could be a code,' he said.

'Why would he need a code?' asked Ivo.

'Could be a lot of things,' said Katya. 'Passwords, perhaps. I'm always forgetting mine.'

'It can't be day-to-day stuff like bank accounts,' said Jasmine. 'He'd not keep those in his wallet. Most people tape them to the underside of their computer keyboard. This is either something he needed when he was out and about, or something he had to keep secret from his wife.'

'What should we do with it?' asked Jonny.

'Put it back inside the wallet. And then, I'm sorry, Ivo, but we should give it to the police.'

'That's okay,' said Ivo. 'I couldn't use it anyway, not with those initials.'

'But we'll take a photo first,' said Katya.

'So we're not going to stop searching?' said Jonny.

'Of course not. I don't expect the police to do much with it, but if Lugs knows I'm not withholding evidence, he's much more likely to keep me up to date with anything they've found out.'

That makes sense, Jonny thought. 'You told us you have a suspect as well.'

'I did,' said Katya, giving them a rundown of everything she'd discussed with Teddy Strang. 'I think this Edwin Eastman is our man.'

'He could have been blackmailing Pierce,' said Jonny, warming to Katya's theory and feeling relieved because he'd actually quite liked Stella Pierce.

'That would be a motive, certainly. But I can see Jasmine's worried about the time and we mustn't keep her from her work. We'll just make a quick action plan and meet again in a day or two. I'll arrange a meeting with Lugs and get him to check passenger lists. And I'll give him the wallet and mention the bank cards. Jonny, do you know Catherine Wallace? Could you find out if Eastman was one of the bridge players that night and what time he left?'

'I don't know her, but Belinda will.'

'And give Stella a call. Let's make sure the wallet really was her husband's.'

'Fine,' said Jonny, wondering how he was going to persuade Belinda to chat to Catherine Wallace about who was at her bridge evening.

'Jasmine, keep in touch with Darkjeweller. But only by email. Don't do anything risky and whatever you do, no face-to-face meetings.'

Jasmine nodded.

'Ivo, have another chat with Charlie. See if he knows anyone who might steal bank cards and chuck away an expensive leather wallet.' She pushed the clipboard back into her bag, tucked the wallet into her pocket and stood up. 'Well done, everyone. Keep it up.' She lumbered towards the door, and they watched as she made her way up the steps towards the town centre.

'I've got gutters to clear,' said Ivo, standing up and putting on his jacket. He gave Harold a hug and made his way to the door.

'And I need to go and make sandwiches,' said Jasmine. 'Thanks for offering to do the printing,' she said to Jonny. 'I'll email the stuff later today.'

Everyone has somewhere to be except me, thought Jonny, not sure whether he was pleased or sorry. But he had tasks for the next meeting. Stella first. He'd drop in and see if she needed any help with the funeral. And there was no time like the present.

He drove to the Pierce house, where he found Stella heaving black bin bags into the back of her car. 'Can I help with that?' he asked.

'Just packing up Raymond's clothes,' she said, shutting the tailgate. 'I'll take them to the charity shop later. Come in for a coffee. I could do with some company.' She led him into the lounge, which was untidier than Jonny remembered from his previous visit.

'Sorry about the mess. I never realised how much stuff Raymond had. Can't decide what to do with most of it. But I'm getting there,' she sighed. 'Have a seat. I'll go and make the coffee.'

Jonny sat down and stared at an assortment of things spread out on a coffee table: a wooden box containing cufflinks; a clothes brush shaped like a duck; a watch and some small change; and a pile of books. He was flicking through them when Stella returned with a tray of coffee and biscuits. She cleared a space on the table and put the tray down. 'No idea what to do with most of this,' she said. 'I suppose I'll just box it up and take it to the charity shop with all the clothes.'

'Nothing of sentimental value?' Jonny asked, wondering how on earth he'd cope in a similar situation. But it would be different for him. He had family to help.

'Not really,' she said. 'There's just one thing I would like to have kept but it's not here. Raymond must have lost it. He never liked it.'

'Something valuable?'

'Just something I gave him as joke, really.' She giggled. 'It was a wallet. An expensive one. I had it engraved with his initials, RIP. He didn't appreciate the humour.'

Well, that was proof that the wallet was Raymond's and Jonny didn't even have to ask. He must be getting the hang of this detective lark.

'But it's gone and there's nothing else I want to keep,' Stella continued. 'I'll just be glad to have it all cleared away so I can get on with selling the house.'

'Raymond had no family?'

'He was an only child. His parents both died years ago. I don't think he even had cousins. Not ones he mentioned, anyway. He had a floozy tucked away somewhere but I'll be damned if she gets anything.'

'A floozy?' Jonny said, suddenly alert. *Did the police know about that?* he wondered. 'Do you know who she was?'

'Preferred not to.'

'Not even her name?'

'Oh, it was something odd, Hermia, Hermione, something like that.'

She seemed oddly detached about it. The effect of bereavement? Or did she just not care what Raymond had got up to? 'If you don't mind me asking, how long had it been going on?'

'A year or two. But that wasn't the first. Raymond had always had a wandering eye. I preferred to turn a blind one.'

'You weren't worried he'd leave you?'

She laughed. 'Not in the least. You see, all of this is mine.' She waved her arms around. 'The house, the money...'

'But the carpet company?'

'All mine. He drew a salary but I'm the major shareholder. Inherited it from my father. If Raymond left me, he knew he'd be penniless and out of a job.'

Not a marriage made in heaven, then. But there must have been something that attracted them to each other. Probably best not to ask. He turned back to the books. 'I see he was interested in local history.' There were several books of stories and legends about the area, and one called *The Symbolism of the Black Arts.* He flicked through some of the illustrations, wondering if anyone actually believed in that kind of thing. Then one of the pictures caught his attention. He stared at it.

'Take those if you are interested,' said Stella.

'Maybe just this one,' said Jonny, holding the book up.

'Sure,' she said, barely looking at it.

Jonny slipped it into his pocket. It obviously meant nothing to Stella. He assumed she'd never looked inside the book. Least of all at the picture that had caught his eye.

13

'How well do you know Edwin Eastman?' Jonny cut down the last of the raspberry canes and dragged it onto the bonfire, where Harold was doing his best to sabotage any efforts Jonny and Belinda were making to tidy the garden. The next job was to rake up leaves and that was going to be fun with Harold charging into the carefully piled up heaps they made and scattering them around the garden again. Perhaps he could persuade Ivo to come and help. Two birds with one stone. Ivo would get to spend time with Harold and Jonny could forget about the leaves.

'I shouldn't speak ill of fellow councillors,' said Belinda, who was harvesting the last of the courgettes. It had been a bumper crop this year and they were both getting rather sick of them, but they were too good to waste, and they would freeze well in soup.

'Sounds like you're about to,' said Jonny, propping his tools against a fence and thinking it could be time for a cup of tea.

'He doesn't pull his weight on the council, misses too many meetings and doesn't do a lot for the people who live in his ward. And he's a creep. Why?'

'It's possible he was one of the last people to see Raymond Pierce alive.'

'The chap who died in the Long Walk? Do they know how he died?'

'It was heart failure, but the coroner suggested it would be an open verdict, which means there are doubts about what caused it. It may have to go to an inquest.'

'Isn't it up to the police to find out that sort of thing?'

'Looks like they don't have the funding for anything that isn't an obvious crime.'

Belinda laughed. 'So your little band of sleuths is going to do their work for them?'

'We're just trying to find evidence that might get the police to keep the case open.'

'I'd be careful involving Edwin Eastman. He's probably hand in glove with the commissioner. It's rumoured they are best buddies. Golf and all that.'

'Bridge players?'

'Quite possibly. I should think a lot of shady deals are clinched over a hand of cards.'

'The night Pierce died, he was playing bridge at the Wallaces' house. Catherine Wallace submitted a statement that said Pierce left her house at ten-thirty. She confirmed that they'd all had a drink or two, although not an excessive amount. But she didn't say who else was there.'

'And you think Eastman was?'

'He and Pierce were known to have been bridge partners in the past. But I can't very well knock on the Wallaces' door and ask.'

'It would seem a bit odd. And dangerous, if you're about to accuse Eastman of being involved in a death. Is he a suspect?'

'Katya thinks so. Apparently, there's a journalist sniffing around him. Katya didn't have details, but it seems he might be involved with some very dodgy stuff.'

'That doesn't surprise me, but he's a rich man. If he's up to something, he'll have covered his tracks well.'

'How did he make his money?' Jonny asked.

'Waste management. Probably not very ethical. It's rumoured he's exporting dangerous waste to places that aren't licensed to handle it. He's also doing a bit of greenwashing.'

'What's that?'

'He's set up a scheme for ethical waste disposal and is pushing it as environmentally friendly.'

'That's good, isn't it?'

'It is, but it's only a tiny fraction of what he does and yet it gets ninety per cent of his publicity.'

'If I could just confirm that he was at the Wallaces' that night...'

'And what? Accuse him of following Pierce home and bumping him off? It's not very likely. Eastman is the sort who'd employ someone to do that kind of dirty work for him. Anyway, how would he bring on heart failure?'

'Perhaps Eastman laced his drink with something. The post-mortem revealed traces of some drug he'd taken.'

'Jonny, love, do you think you might have been watching too many crime dramas?'

'It's not me,' said Jonny, feeling offended. 'Katya thinks Eastman is suspicious and she's been a real detective. If we know that he was there that night, she'll be able to pass it on to the guys she used to work with.'

Belinda cut the last courgette and started pulling out the hairy stems. A task she seemed to be enjoying. Jonny could see why. Courgette roots didn't grow deep. They were easy to pull out. A couple of sturdy plants on the bonfire and the bed would be clear and ready for whatever they decided to plant next year. After months of eating courgettes at every meal, Jonny hoped she'd decide to plant something else. Runner beans were nice.

'Tell you who would know,' said Belinda, pulling off her gardening gloves and heading, Jonny was pleased to see, towards the kitchen. He'd head her off and have the kettle on before she finished putting the tools away. 'Who?' he asked.

'Mrs Gage. I recommended her to Catherine years ago. I bet she still works for her and if that was the last time Pierce was seen before he died, she'll be very full of it and more than keen to gossip about it.'

Great idea, Jonny thought, wondering how he was going to get Mrs Gage to gossip to him. She complained if he 'got under her feet' when she was cleaning and she'd yet to meet Harold. Jonny was certain that as much as she didn't like men around while she was working, dogs would be ten times worse. But if she could tell him what he wanted to know, it might be worth trying to soften her up. He'd no idea how, but there must be something that would get her talking.

IT WAS EASIER than he expected. On Mrs Gage's next visit, Jonny decided, he would make sure all the bins were emptied. Dealing with other people's rubbish must be one of the less pleasant tasks of a cleaner. He shut Harold in Belinda's study and set about emptying every bin in the house. He washed them out and replaced the liners. He had just put the last one back in its correct place when Mrs Gage arrived. 'Good morning,' he said, smiling at her.

'You're still here, are you?' she said, looking less than thrilled by the idea of him hanging around. It was not a promising start. Not if he wanted to get her gossiping. Perhaps he should leave it for today and think up a better plan.

He was about to put his coat on and head for the office when Harold pushed open the door of the study and peered out at them. That was going to make matters worse. Not only was she not going to chat to him, he would have to explain Harold's presence as well. She didn't like Jonny very much. Goodness knew what she'd make of a dog. But he'd underestimated her. As Harold emerged from the study and wagged what was left of his tail at them, Mrs Gage sank to her knees and put her arms round him. 'Oh, doggie,' she said, as Harold licked her face. 'Where did you come from?'

'I'm looking after him for a friend,' said Jonny. 'He won't be staying long. And he won't be in your way today. I'll take him to work with me.'

'Oh, but he's such a sweetie, don't take him away.'

Jonny wasn't sure what Harold would make of being called a sweetie. This was probably the first time since he was a puppy. Even

Ivo, who adored Harold, never called him sweet. But Harold seemed to be taking it well, succumbing to Mrs Gage's attentions with an expression of fortitude.

'We could stay for a cup of tea,' said Jonny, heading for the kettle. 'If you have time. I wouldn't want to get in the way of your work.'

'I can always spare time for the little doggums,' she said, making Jonny cringe and deciding he'd not let that get back to Ivo. It was not doing anything for Harold's street cred.

Jonny made the tea and pushed the biscuit tin in Mrs Gage's direction.

'Can the nice doggy have one?' she asked.

'Just one,' said Jonny, hoping Harold wouldn't snatch it and possibly remove one of Mrs Gage's fingers at the same time.

'Trust,' she said, holding the biscuit in the air six inches above Harold's nose. Jonny looked on, lost for words as Mrs Gage lowered the biscuit and Harold took it gently out of her hand.

'You're very good with dogs,' said Jonny. 'Are many of your clients dog owners?'

'One or two,' she said, mentioning a few names.

'Do you still go to the Wallaces'?' he asked.

'Not regularly. I do occasional work when they need help with a dinner party or something like that. They've never had a dog.'

'Have you been there recently?' he asked, hoping she wouldn't ask why he wanted to know.

Her eyes lit up. 'Do you know,' she said, wrapping her hands around her mug of tea and giving him a conspiratorial look. 'I was there the very night that poor man died. The one they found in the Long Walk. And he was right there at the Wallaces'. I served him his sandwiches.'

'Really?' Jonny asked, doing his best to look impressed. 'What happened?'

'They were sitting around playing cards. I was there to serve the drinks and hand round snacks. Poor Mr Pierce was drinking a lot and getting very talkative. There was an argument with the other guest and then he asked Mrs Wallace to call him a taxi and when it came, he left.'

'Do you know who the other guest was?'

'I've seen him before at evenings like that. Local businessman, something to do with rubbish. Don't remember his name, but there was some talk about getting the council to do something or other, I wasn't listening, but you can't help picking things up, can you?'

'I suppose not.'

'Of course, your missus would know him, being on the council herself. But I can't sit here chatting all day,' she said, standing up and starting to unpack her cleaning things.

'Of course not,' said Jonny. 'Harold and I will get out of your way.'

'Harold?' she said. 'That's a daft name for a dog.'

Jonny didn't wait around for her to suggest a more suitable one.

He put on his coat, the first time he'd needed it since the summer, and clipped on Harold's lead. They usually walked into town first thing and had breakfast, driving into the office in the afternoon if it was a workday, strolling back through the park if it wasn't. But Mrs Gage had kept him talking. By the time they'd walked into town and back it would be mid-afternoon. No, they'd go straight to the factory and grab something to eat in the canteen.

14

I've done well for food this week, Katya thought. *First a pub lunch with Teddy Strang and now a fish and chip supper with Lugs Lomax.* The pub had been cosy and warm. If Katya had not been shovelling in her food, she could easily have nodded off. No chance of that here. Lugs' generosity didn't extend to sit down meals and Katya was perched, huddled into her coat and a knitted hat with ear flaps, on a seat close to the river. Lucky she'd worn her fingerless gloves. Greasy gloves would be nasty, and she didn't fancy going bare handed in this weather. But the parcel of fish and chips was keeping her lap warm, like a hot water bottle. It could have been a lot worse.

A few yards away, the kiosk that sold hot drinks was still open, even on a dank Autumn evening. Lugs had wandered over to buy them both mugs of hot chocolate to go with their fish and chips. 'My treat,' he'd told her when he knocked on her door and invited her out for a meal with him. She'd called him earlier in the week with some questions and with any luck, he was here to give her some answers.

Lugs returned from the kiosk and handed her a styrofoam mug. He sat down, placing his mug on the ground at his feet, and tucked into his fish and chips. Katya wrapped the mittened fingers of her left hand around her mug and ate with her right hand. They chomped in silence. They'd be better able to concentrate once they finished eating and Katya was in no hurry to get home.

Once finished, Lugs scrunched up the wrapping and threw it into a bin. Then he reached into his pocket and pulled out a scrap of paper. 'Right,' he said. 'I checked with the airline Mrs Pierce used and they confirmed that she left on a flight to Madrid ten days before her husband died and arrived back at Heathrow when she said she did. She took a taxi home to an empty house. It wasn't unusual for her husband to be out of an evening, so she didn't worry. She reported him missing the following morning.'

'So that all checks out,' said Katya. One suspect out of the way. Three to go.

'Now, this will interest you,' said Lugs, moving on to the next item on his list. 'We had a call from the bank that Pierce used. Mrs Pierce reported her husband's death to them and his accounts were closed.'

'That's normal, isn't it?'

'Absolutely. Mrs Pierce went to the bank with a copy of the death certificate. Banks don't just take people's word for it that someone's died.'

'Of course not,' said Katya. 'You can't go around closing down people's bank accounts willy-nilly. Even if you are married to them.'

'Particularly if you're married to them,' said Lugs, laughing. 'Imagine the havoc that could be caused. By a vengeful wife, for instance.'

'Okay,' said Katya. 'So Mrs Pierce works her way, quite correctly, through all the admin her husband's death caused. So why would the bank call you?'

'Because they noticed a discrepancy between the day and time of Pierce's death and the date of his last credit card transaction.'

'You mean his card was used after he was dead?'

'Precisely. There were several transactions. Small, contactless ones, not involving large sums. The cards have all been stopped now, but not before several payments went through. We're in the process of checking and hopefully some of the terminals will have had CCTV and we will get a look at whoever used them.'

'Then it was murder?'

'Possible, but unlikely. At least not murder with robbery. The cause of death was heart failure, possibly brought on by drug and alcohol use. If that was murder it would have to have been premeditated. If you kill someone to rob them, you'd hit them over the head or something. You don't drug them and wait around for it to take effect.'

'I suppose he could have died from fright,' said Katya. 'Being robbed at night in the park would be very frightening.'

'More likely someone came across his body and thought they'd go through his pockets. If we can find who it was, they'll be up on various charges, but not murder ones, probably not even manslaughter.' He reached into his pocket again and handed her the wallet Ivo had given her. 'You can have this back,' he said.

'No fingerprints or DNA?'

'Nothing forensics could make any use of. Been handled by too many people. But your lad's friend Charlie Jones is in the clear. Got himself arrested that evening. Drunk as a lord and spent fourteen hours in a cell, sobering up.'

That was good. Ivo had been worried. Not that Charlie had stolen the wallet but that he'd be accused of it. 'What about Pierce's phone?' she asked.

'Probably stolen at the same time as the wallet. No chance of tracing that. It will have been wiped and sold on within hours. What we could do is ask the phone company for a list of the calls Pierce made.'

'You might learn a lot from that,' said Katya. 'If the killer was someone he knew, they might have called him to arrange a meeting.'

'And we can see who Pierce called that night, which could also be significant.'

'How long will it take?'

'I should be able to get back to you in a couple of days. Not sure the guv would approve of me passing on the information, but to be honest he's not putting much effort into this inquiry so he probably won't give a toss.'

'He'll care if it leads to a conviction.'

'Yeah,' said Lugs. 'And take all the credit.'

15

Belinda was out for the evening, so Jonny took Harold for a quick walk in the rain, which neither of them enjoyed very much. Returning home, he rubbed Harold dry with a towel and fed him a bowl of dog food. Then he made a cheese and tomato sandwich and poured himself a glass of beer, putting them on a tray with a slice of salted caramel cheesecake he found in the fridge. Carrying his tray into the living room, he pulled the book he'd taken from Stella out of his pocket and placed it on a small bureau next to his laptop.

Having finished his meal, Jonny rooted around in one of the drawers in the bureau and fished out a magnifying glass. He opened the book and flicked through it until he found the page with the image that had caught his eye. It was a photograph of a pendant that was identical to the one they'd found in the tree. He aimed the magnifying glass at the caption below the picture and read the name of the photographer. The print was tiny, and he'd barely been able to make it out in Stella's living room. He'd not wanted to draw her attention to it while he was there so her offer had been timely. He'd just been debating whether or not to ask her if he could take the book without raising her suspicion. She'd played right into his hands. And now, reading the name with a magnifying glass and in the strong light from a desk lamp, he could see he had been right. Could this be a coincidence? It could, of course, but it was an unlikely one. He read the name again. *Hermia Rutherford.* And Stella had told him she suspected – no, not suspected, knew – that the woman she described as Raymond's *floozy* was called either Hermia or Hermione.

Hermia, he thought, connecting the facts like links in a chain. Raymond was interested in the black arts. Someone had left a Herne the Hunter pendant at the place where his body was found. The ghost of Herne made regular appearances in the park, rattling chains and apparently predicting deaths. A woman called Hermia had photographed this very pendant. And Raymond was having an affair with a woman called Hermia. There had to be a connection, didn't there? If the photographer had been a Sarah or a Catherine, he'd have thought no more about it. But how many women were called Hermia?

He pulled the laptop towards him, typed *Hermia Rutherford* into Google and, as he had suspected, there were very few of them. In fact, only one. A photographer who worked in a graphic design studio in Staines. He checked out the studio's website and discovered a small company that specialised in magazine and website commercials. Jonny was particularly taken with a sample of their work that depicted doughnuts floating out of the sky like snowflakes. The image was not attributed to anyone in particular, none of the images on the site were, and none were of anything remotely connected to black arts or magic. But Hermia could have been doing a bit of moon-lighting, couldn't she? He checked the black arts book for a date of publication and was surprised to find it was first published in 1997. He'd imagined Hermia, anyone working in graphic design, to be young. But he was probably being very ageist. And Raymond was in his fifties. Why wouldn't he be having an affair with someone of more or less his own age? Not all men went for women half their age, even when straying into extramarital territory. Hermia could have been a student when she took the photo. Perhaps she'd sold it to the author of the book to make a bit of pocket money. He typed the author's name, D.P. Stanford, into Google. *The Symbolism of the Black Arts* seemed to have been the only mark he'd left on the world. The book was no longer in print, but Jonny discovered it had been produced by a small publishing company called Kingfisher Press in Kingston-upon-Thames. And Kingston was a stone's throw from Staines. Surprisingly, Kingfisher Press was still in business, the possessor of a small and very dull website that gave little idea of what they actually did but Jonny jotted down their email and phone number.

Having done that, he searched social media for Hermia Rutherford. She was on the usual; Twitter, Instagram and Facebook, but was not a big user and none of them gave much information about her. Only what he knew already, that she was working in graphic design. He tried an image search and found a professional-looking head and shoulders shot of a woman called Hermia Rutherford, which in turn led him to a Facebook business page. Jonny was not good at guessing ages and he'd no idea when the photo was taken, but he was looking at an attractive woman with striking red hair. Younger than Belinda, he guessed, but not as young as Jasmine. From his comparison he estimated Hermia to be in her mid-forties. Which meant that she could have taken the photo in the book while around the age of twenty, and that confirmed his theory that she'd taken it to raise a bit of cash while she was a student.

He sat back in his chair and wondered what to do next. He could hardly turn up at Hermia's place of work and demand to know if she'd been having an affair with a man who was now dead, possibly murdered. He could telephone Kingfisher Press and ask what they knew about her. Or he could do nothing and tell Katya what he'd discovered at their next meeting. But that was a cop-out. Instead, he tapped the messenger icon on Hermia's Facebook page and sent her a message saying he'd seen her Herne photograph and would be interested in discussing it with her as he had recently found a similar pendant.

Hermia Rutherford replied more quickly than Jonny expected and they began an exchange of messages.

'I've not seen one of these for years,' she said, leafing through the book. 'I thought they were out of print.'

Jonny looked at the woman sitting opposite him. Hermia Rutherford was very like the photo he'd found on Google. What surprised him was that she suggested a meeting. It was after they'd exchanged a few messages and Jonny had sent her the photo Ivo had taken of the pendant hanging in the tree. Having established that they both lived in Windsor, Hermia suggested meeting for a coffee. He chose the café in a department store in the town. He didn't want her to think he was trying to date her, and this was the most un-datelike place he could think of where they actually served coffee. Jonny arrived first and stood up as Hermia came in through the door. He introduced himself and ordered coffee. Hermia sat across the table from him, noticing that he had placed D.P. Stanford's book on the table in front of him. Hermia picked it up and turned to the page with her photo. 'It was the first picture I ever sold,' she said. 'I must have been about nineteen. They paid me twenty-five pounds for it. My college tutor was horrified. She told me I should never have sold it outright. If it became popular, I could have claimed royalties.' She put the book down again and laughed. 'As far as I know only about six people ever read the book and absolutely no one has shown any interest in the photo. Until now.'

Jonny smiled. 'I promise I won't be using it to make anyone money.'

'You're not planning to make me famous? So what is your interest?'

Did she know Raymond Pierce was dead? He wouldn't want to upset her by being the bearer of bad news. But if she and Raymond had been as close as Stella suggested, surely she would already know, wouldn't she?

'Well,' he started cautiously. 'A friend and I found the pendant nailed to a tree near the Long Walk. It was close to where... where...'

'To where Raymond Pierce's body was found?'

So she did know. And she didn't seem all that upset about it. Either Stella had been mistaken or he should add Hermia Rutherford to his list of suspects.

'That's right,' he said. 'I gather you knew Raymond Pierce.'

'We met a few times,' she said vaguely. 'Like you, he contacted me wanting to know more about my photo. That's why I wanted to meet you. After twenty-five years of obscurity two people have shown an interest in it within months of each other. And you both had a copy of the book. One that's been unobtainable for years.'

'I'm sorry to disappoint you, but it's the same book. Raymond's widow gave it to me.'

'Oh, well,' she said. 'It was never going to be a bestseller. I suppose two of you reading it is better than nothing, even if it was the same copy. But I'm losing track a bit. You say you found the actual pendant and that Stella Pierce gave you Raymond's copy of the book. I don't see where you come into it. Why the interest?'

Jonny tapped his fingers on the table and drained his coffee cup. 'My wife would say it's because I have too much time on my hands. But I found the whole thing intriguing. People don't die in the Long Walk very often. Well, not these days. And why would someone nail a pendant to a tree? I told the police about it, but they weren't interested. Then I remembered I had met Stella at a charity do a few years ago. So I went to see her to express my condolences. She was turning out Raymond's things and I found the book. She was quite happy for me to keep it.'

'So you thought you'd do a bit of research about the photographer?'

'It was more than that.'

'Go on.'

'I'm not sure I should. It's rather personal.'

'Oh, come on. You can't say that and then leave me guessing.'

'Well, Stella told me Raymond was having an affair with someone called Hermione or Hermia. And then I saw your name in the book.'

'So you imagined we were having a steamy affair? And did you assume it was me that left the pendant in the tree? A memento to a dead lover. Very romantic.' Her lip curled in a way Jonny would describe as cynical.

Hermia didn't look like a tree climber, although one never knew. 'Did you leave it in the tree?' he asked.

Hermia sat back in her seat and roared with laughter. Not the reaction he'd expected and certainly not that of a grieving lover.

'So you didn't?'

'Didn't what?'

'Climb the tree and nail the pendant to it?'

'No, I didn't do that. And I didn't have an affair with Raymond either. He really wasn't my type.'

'But you met a few times?'

'First because of the photograph. He asked me a lot about where I'd taken the picture.'

'Where *did* you take the original picture?'

'At a house sale. A creepy old place just outside Sunningdale. I went with a friend who wanted to buy old furniture. This was hanging on a wall. I just thought it would make a good picture. It was printed in a student magazine and Kingfisher asked if they could buy it for a book they were publishing.'

'*The Symbolism of the Black Arts,*' he said. 'Was Raymond interested in the black arts?'

'Oh, yes. He'd heard of some secret society that used them as badges. Just a few blokes messing around, probably. You know, dressing up in silly clothes and prancing around in the moonlight chanting stuff about Herne the Hunter.' She stared at her coffee cup for a moment. 'I expect,' she added. 'Don't know anything about it really.'

'You don't know who they were or where they met?'

'No. I'm not interested in that sort of thing.'

And yet she seemed to know about the Herne connection.

'There's one thing that did interest me, though,' she said, changing the subject.

'About Raymond?'

'No, about Stella. Raymond wasn't having an affair. But he told me that Stella was.'

'Really? How did he know?'

'No idea.' she giggled. 'It wasn't you, was it?'

'Certainly not. I'm very happily married.'

'I believe you,' she said. 'You're obviously not the type to date women you're not married to, or you'd have chosen to meet somewhere far more discreet than this.'

She was right, of course. The coffee bar they were sitting in was right in the middle of the shop. A continuous flow of shoppers passed them on their way from the car park to the shops. They were surrounded on all sides by franchises: men's jackets and shirts; shoes; toys and stationery. It was a place to take tea with one's elderly mother, or for a sit down with a shopping companion. 'I didn't want you to get the wrong impression,' he told Hermia. 'I mean, you're very nice, but...' He could feel himself blushing. 'What I'm trying to say is that I'm not...'

Hermia sighed. 'It must be really difficult being a bloke,' she said. 'Having to be careful all the time that you are not being misunderstood. There you go having a nice chat and the next thing, you find yourself being outed on #MeToo.'

Jonny hadn't thought of it like that. Perhaps he should have brought Belinda with him. But he supposed that might have been open to misunderstanding as well. Hermia was right. Next time he planned on meeting someone he wanted to question, he'd get Katya to come with him. 'So you've no idea who Stella was having an affair with?' he asked, hoping to steer the subject back to the Pierces.

'No, sorry.' She finished her coffee and picked up her bag and coat ready to leave. 'Although, wait a minute. Raymond did say something interesting about it. Something that made me think it was a friend of his, or perhaps a colleague. He sounded a bit miffed about it.'

'Miffed? I suppose he would be angry if it was someone he'd introduced her to.'

'Wrong word. I'd say he was jealous rather than angry. Anyway, I need to get back to work.' She held out her hand. 'Nice to meet you,' she said. 'I hope you find answers to your questions. Sorry I wasn't much help.'

'Not at all,' said Jonny, standing up and holding her coat for her. 'You've given me some very interesting leads.'

Jonny watched as she left and headed for the car park. She'd given him a lot to think about and he needed to write it all down before he forgot the details. He searched his pockets and found a pen, but the only thing he had to write on was a scrunched-up Tesco receipt. He headed out into the street and towards a shop selling upmarket stationery. He needed to get properly equipped.

16

'What you got there?' Jasmine asked as she handed Jonny his coffee and surreptitiously passed a biscuit to Harold, who was in his usual place under the table.

'Been doing some research of my own,' said Jonny. He held up a notebook. 'I just bought this and now I'm making notes.'

Most people made notes electronically nowadays, on laptops or tablets; even phones had note-making apps. But Jonny was kind of old school, so Jasmine wasn't surprised that he preferred a note-book and pen. A bright red moleskin notebook and a set of coloured pens in a black case. He'd obviously treated himself so he must be taking their detective group seriously. She'd wondered about that. Katya, convinced that Pierce was murdered, was handling the case as if she was still in the force, while Jasmine and Ivo followed along enthusiastically. She wasn't so sure about Jonny, who seemed to think it was all a bit of a joke. But perhaps she was wrong. He'd been busy enough this morning. She glanced over his shoulder and saw the name *Stella*. 'Researching the Pierces?' she asked.

Jonny nodded and turned back to the first page of his notebook. 'It's interesting,' he said. 'Stella accused Raymond of having an affair, but the woman she was accusing told me that Stella was the one having an affair.'

'You met her? Raymond's lady friend?'

'Yes, although, as I say, she denied it.'

'Well, she would, wouldn't she? But how did you find her?'

He pulled Stanford's book out of his pocket. 'I went to visit Stella and she confirmed that the wallet did belong to Raymond. She'd given it to him herself and had his initials engraved on it because she knew it would irritate him.'

'Nice,' said Jasmine. 'I can see why you thought she might be a suspect. Pity she has an alibi.'

'She gave me this.' Jonny showed her the book and opened it at the page with Hermia's photograph. 'I checked out the name because Stella told me Raymond's lady friend was called Hermia and it's not a common name. I contacted her and we met for coffee.'

Jasmine was impressed. She took the book from him and studied the picture. 'That's the same as the pendant,' she said.

'I'm guessing this was the original and the pendant in the tree was copied from it. Hermia told me it was in an auction at an old house that was about to be demolished, somewhere near Sunningdale. She didn't know what had happened to the pendant. I suppose someone must have bought it. She also told me that Raymond belonged to some secret society. Something to do with the Herne legend.'

Jasmine looked around. The café was quiet with no customers waiting to be served. She could take a few moments off, so she sat down next to Jonny. 'That's very interesting. We should find out more about this secret society. Perhaps they are the unpleasant people Darkjeweller warned me about.'

'Unpleasant enough to kill one of their own?'

'Well, someone was.' And members of secret societies came high on her list of those capable of doing it. 'And it might account for why he was wandering around on his own at night. Perhaps they met in the forest that night and Raymond had done something to upset them, so he left to walk home and one of them followed him.'

'But he was playing bridge that night and went home in a taxi.'

'But he didn't go home, did he?'

'We need to find out where the taxi dropped him,' said Jonny.

'How?' she asked. 'Call all the local taxi companies?'

'Mrs Wallace would know. She called the taxi for him that night.'

'How well do you know her?'

'Not at all. My wife does, but I'm not sure they see each other very often.'

'It would look a bit odd, wouldn't it? Just calling round to ask about taxis.'

'It's possible Mrs Gage would know.'

'Who's Mrs Gage?'

'She does our cleaning, and she was there that night, serving sandwiches.'

All right for some. Jasmine could do with someone here to help with the cleaning. But she supposed the Cardews could afford it. They probably lived in a massive house and they'd worked hard all their lives. 'Can you ask her?'

'I suppose I could. But I'd need to think of a reason why I'm asking. I've lived here all my life. I know how to call a taxi.'

'You could say the company you usually use have not been very reliable recently and you're looking for a new one to try.'

'And if she knows, what then?'

'You can call them and ask where Raymond was dropped off. And if he was going home but suddenly changed his mind. Perhaps he had a phone call. The police could trace that.'

'Or we could ask Katya,' Jonny suggested.

A couple came in and were waiting at the counter. 'I'd better go,' said Jasmine. 'Can't keep customers waiting.'

'Take this,' said Jonny, handing her his notebook. 'I've written down everything I know. It might give you some ideas about what to do next.'

'Thanks,' said Jasmine, tucking it into the pocket of her apron.

'Do you want to copy the photo in the book?'

'Yeah, but I've not time now. Can you do it and text it to me?'

Jasmine returned to the counter and served her customers. She

heard the ping of a message on her phone and watched as Jonny left
with a cheery wave.

LATER THAT EVENING, Jasmine left her dad watching football on the
telly and took her laptop and Jonny's notebook to her room. She was
determined to find the Herne society, or whatever it was called. If she
could find out more about it, then she might be able to discover
something about its members and that could shorten their list of
suspects.

She considered herself good at finding things on the Internet but
on this occasion drew a blank. There was a lot about Herne the
Hunter, much of it very creepy, but there was nothing about groups of
people forming societies about it. Herne had been associated with
witchcraft and Jasmine discovered that witch sightings were still
reported in the forest and near the castle. Herne was also a spectral
huntsman who led something called Wild Hunt, nocturnal proces-
sions of the dead which, further searching told her, occurred at the
full moon and on stormy nights. A retinue of ghostly huntsmen raced
around followed by a pack of baying hounds and anyone who spoke
to a huntsman was doomed to die. Jasmine checked the weather and
the phase of the moon and found that the night after the Queen's
funeral had not been stormy and the moon was in its waning crescent
phase. Whatever that meant, Jasmine didn't think it was a full moon.
Anyway, it was all a long way from normal life in a small town and
Jasmine didn't believe a word of it. She couldn't imagine that
Raymond Pierce came across many witches while selling carpets, so
his interest must have been more of a hobby. A dangerous one that
had let his imagination run away with him. Perhaps poor old
Raymond, full of alcohol and drugs, and roaming the forest on a dark
night, believed it was all real. Was he the victim of a trick? Members
of this society, possibly annoyed by something he'd done, scaring
him, literally to death?

If only she could find out more about who they were. She sat back in her chair and stared at the screen. She had hit a brick wall. She should return to real life and work on food orders and menus for next week. And then she remembered her searches of a few nights ago. Darkjeweller. He must know who the pendants were made for. She opened her email and started typing. Then she deleted it. Much better to go and see him. He might never reply to an email, but face to face he'd have to tell her what she wanted to know. She checked his website and found that he had a stall at Kingston Market every Friday. She checked Google Maps. It was only twenty miles away. Dad and Stevie would cover for her in the café. Dad was always telling her she needed to take more time off. She could borrow his car and be there and back in a couple of hours. Katya had told her there were to be no face-to-face meetings. But that was with actual scary people. Darkjeweller had been the one to warn her. He was hardly going to do anything to her in a busy market, was he?

JASMINE HADN'T BEEN to Kingston before, but she was definitely coming again. It was shopping heaven. She parked in a multistorey car park and found herself in a big shopping mall. No time to shop now, but she made a mental note of where all her favourite stores were. She descended an escalator and made her way out into the main shopping street, and after a walk of a few minutes she was in the market square. The huge number of food stalls was making her mouth water, but she'd no time for that right now. First she must find Darkjeweller, and if that went well, she'd treat herself to a hot meal. *Possibly Thai,* she thought. A nice change from finishing up what was left in the café at the end of the day.

She found Darkjeweller's stall, a small wooden hut, mostly by the smell. A not unpleasant mix of patchouli, incense and lavender oil. Possibly a lot more that she couldn't identify. Behind the counter was a woman who was maybe ten years older than Jasmine. She was dressed in black with a collection of piercings. Several in her ears and two in her nose. Her black hair, tinged purple, was tied in a plait that hung down her back, reaching well below her waist. She was serving a customer who was trying to choose an anklet with jingling bells. Jasmine was happy to wait and spent the time rifling through a rack of clothes: new age stuff in Indian cotton; tie-dyed shirts; patterned leggings and bright coloured jumpers knitted, so a sign claimed, at a Peruvian women's collective.

Eventually the customer made her choice, paid and left with her purchase in a small brown paper bag decorated with what Jasmine suspected was a hand-painted cannabis plant.

'Can I help you?' asked the woman with long hair.

Jasmine assumed she must be Darkjeweller's assistant. She'd expected him to be here, which was stupid really. Why wouldn't he employ someone to run his stall for him? Was this a wasted journey? *No,* Jasmine thought. Even if she discovered nothing about the Herne pendant, she was still enjoying her day out. And she'd not told Katya or either of the others that she was coming, so no one would be disappointed if she had nothing to report. 'I'm looking for Darkjeweller,' she said.

'That's me,' said the woman. 'My name is Diane James. Most people just call me DJ. Does for both names, see.'

'Oh,' said Jasmine, wondering why she should be surprised. 'I don't suppose you remember but I emailed you about this.' She opened her phone and showed DJ the photo of the pendant.

'Yeah, I remember.'

'You kind of warned me off finding out any more.'

'And yet here you are.' DJ smirked at her. 'Persistent type, are you?'

'Guess I am,' said Jasmine.

'So what's important about this thing?' She looked again at the photo. 'Nailed to a tree, is it?'

'Yes, just above where a man was found dead. We think he might have been murdered.'

'Not the police, are you?'

'Not exactly,' said Jasmine, not wanting to go into more detail. 'We really want to know who these pendants are made for. It seems they're for some kind of secret society. It could be very important for our enquiries.'

'Look,' said DJ. 'I can't tell you much. I know the guy who makes the pendants. He works for me and I pay him good money for them. I sell them on, but the people I sell them to are not a nice crowd. You'd best leave them well alone.'

'Why? What do they do?'

'They dress up in black and prance around in the middle of the night wearing antlers.'

'That doesn't sound too bad. Weird, but not exactly dangerous. What do they call themselves?'

'Can't remember.'

Would she really forget something like that? 'Was it something to do with Herne the Hunter?' she asked.

DJ sighed. 'You weren't wrong about being persistent, were you? I can't tell you what they're called. And you need to keep away from them.'

Just then a small white van drew up in the road at the side of the square. A man got out and waved at DJ. 'Excuse me,' she said. 'My supplier. I need to help him carry stuff.'

'No problem,' said Jasmine. 'Thanks for your help.' She watched as DJ crossed the square and started talking to the van driver. It seemed like a complicated discussion involving a lot of arm waving and peering into the back of the van. DJ wasn't going to be back for a few minutes. Jasmine slipped into a small room at the back of the hut and looked around. There was a corkboard to which were pinned a number of cards with the names of suppliers and makers of jewellery. She glanced over at the van where the discussion was still going on, got her phone out of her pocket and took a photo of the board, hoping it would enlarge enough for her to read the cards. Then she went round to the front of the shop and out into the square. She waved to DJ with what she hoped was a jaunty, guilt-free smile and made her way over to a stall selling Thai curries.

· · ·

AFTER HER MEAL, Jasmine returned to her car feeling well fed and pleased with herself. She opened her phone and scrolled to the photo she'd taken. She used her fingers to enlarge the image and found that she could easily read the text on the cards. One of them, she was sure, would be about the pendants. She drove home planning her next move. She'd spend the evening making up a story that sounded like a convincing reason for asking questions about secret societies who got up to who knew what at night dressed all in black. There couldn't be all that many who did that. All she needed was a name. They'd be somewhere on the Internet and once she found a website, she'd be able to find out who belonged to it.

17

I vo's phone pinged. A message from Katya with a picture. He clicked on the picture and stared at it. He enlarged it as much as he could, but it meant nothing to him. She had to be joking. A man he had never seen before, wearing a hoodie and leaving a well-known coffee chain. He was clutching a cardboard mug and something in a paper bag. It could be anyone. There must be hundreds of people in town dressed in hoodies.

He saved the photo and read Katya's message.

Got this from Lugs taken by a CCTV camera sited high on a wall at the end of the Windsor Yards shopping centre. Used mostly to monitor the cash machine next to the post office, but it also covers various shop entrances including Caffé Nero. This still was taken from footage two days after the funeral. The time coincides with the use of Pierce's card at the café to pay for a takeaway cappuccino and a lemon muffin, which fits the description of items carried by the man caught in the doorway. Can you ask around and see if anyone recognises him?

What did she think he did all day? Today and tomorrow were full with people wanting last-minute repairs done before winter set in: clogged gutters; cracked window panes; garden paths made slippery by leaves and replacing a warped cat flap. And what did Katya do all day? To be fair, he wasn't sure what she did. She was retired, yes, but that didn't mean she had no way to fill her time. And in a way, she was right to ask him to do this. She was an ex-copper and it showed. If she walked around asking questions, people would be suspicious and clam up. But he was one of them, well known around the town and with a reputation for always being ready for a chat. He should be flattered that she'd given him this task. And the gutters could wait a day or two. He had a mate with a van and a ladder who could help him and that was best done at the weekend. The friend was also giving him driving lessons in the hope that one day he might be able to afford his own van. If he kept working hard it might not be all that long, but it was obviously not going to be in the next day or two. So yes, he could spare a morning for Katya. The rest of the team as well. It would be great if he was able to tell them he'd found the guy who'd stolen the cards. Assuming it was a guy. He clicked on the picture again and enlarged it. The face was partially obscured, but he was able to make out angular features, a pointed nose and wisps of hair escaping from the hoodie. *A bloke,* he thought. Or a very skinny, sharp-faced girl.

He dropped a text to the owner of the gutter, assuring her that he'd be there first thing on Saturday with a ladder. He'd set off right away and spend the morning wandering round town and chatting to people. He'd start off at *Jasmine's* and pick up a bacon roll. With any luck Jonny would be there and Ivo could take Harold with him. Everyone was fond of Harold and usually happy to stop for a chat.

He walked to *Jasmine's* and found Jonny in his usual place by the window, and Harold in his usual place under the table, bounding out as soon as he saw Ivo. He ordered his bacon roll and asked for it to be put in a box, explaining that he was going to be walking round town asking questions.

'Shall I come with you?' Jonny offered, as Ivo picked up Harold's lead.

'Probably better if you don't,' said Ivo. Jonny was a posh bloke and might put people off. The trouble was Ivo didn't know how to explain that to Jonny without hurting his feelings.

'You're probably right,' said Jonny, to Ivo's relief. 'You know your way around much better than I do. Just text me when you want me to pick Harold up again.' He patted Ivo on the shoulder and ordered himself another coffee.

Ivo felt guilty as he left. Jonny practically lived at *Jasmine's*. Since he'd cut down his working hours, he probably didn't have much to do with his time. But it couldn't be helped, and Jonny did have Harold for company most of the time, which was more than Ivo did.

He decided to start with Alexandra Gardens, where there would be other dog walkers and Harold could have a run around. Then they'd walk along the river path. Some of his friends would be down there. Some had dogs so they wouldn't be likely suspects, but they might just recognise the person in the photo.

He had no luck in the park, although there was plenty of friendly chat about dogs. Funny how much less reserved dog owners were than people walking on their own. In the past, people would cross the road to avoid Ivo. Nothing personal, just that young men on their own could be threatening, particularly to women. But with Harold at his side everyone wanted to stop and chat. Asking what had happened to his ear (a run-in with an evil cat) and to half his tail? Ivo didn't know. That was before his time, when Harold lived with a grumpy, dog-hating pensioner. But not a single person recognised the photo Ivo showed them. Probably if he was going around with a picture of a dog, they'd all know exactly who the owner was. As well as both their life histories. But people? Nothing. Not a flicker of recognition.

Time for a hot drink. Ivo made his way to the kiosk close to where the tourist boats were moored. He bought himself a hot chocolate and showed the picture to the woman behind the counter. She shook her head. Ivo paid for his drink and walked over to a bench near the river. Harold growled at a group of swans and Ivo pulled him closer. 'No barking at them,' he said. 'They belong to the Queen. She'll have you locked up in the castle if you don't watch it.' But of course, it was the King now. Were the swans part of his inheritance? Ivo supposed they must be. Strange that the swans had an owner. None of the other birds did.

Someone sat down next to him. Charlie. Ivo had wondered if he'd bump into him. He might be hard of hearing and poor of eyesight, but if anyone knew who was wandering around town, Charlie did. 'Fancy a hot chocolate?' Ivo asked.

'Don't ask stupid questions, lad. 'Course I do.'

Ivo passed him Harold's lead to hold while he went back to the kiosk. When he returned, Harold had jumped up onto the bench and was lying with his head in Charlie's lap.

'What you up to then?' Charlie asked, taking the mug from Ivo and pushing Harold gently back onto the path. 'No work today?'

'Taking the morning off to do a bit of detecting.' Ivo pulled his phone out of his pocket, clicked on the photo and passed it to Charlie. 'Seen this person recently?'

Charlie took the phone, stared at the screen then handed it back to Ivo. 'Why? Who is he?'

'Might have been using a stolen credit card,' said Ivo.

'Joined the fuzz now, have you?'

'Just helping,' said Ivo.

"Oh yeah?'

'New friend, used to be a detective sergeant. She thinks that bloke they found in the Long Walk was murdered.'

'What's that got to do with him in the photo?'

'Looks like he was using the bloke's credit card after he died.'

'So this woman, she thinks he was murdered for his credit card?'

'Dunno. Bit of a coincidence, though.'

'Wait a mo. That's why that policeman was asking about the wallet and where I was the night the body was found. Stupid pillock. He only had to check the records to know I was in the nick all that night. But he didn't think to do that until I told him to. Shouldn't have to tell them how to do their job, should I?' Charlie drained his drink and ran his finger round the inside of the mug, scooping out the last of the chocolate. 'They brought me a pizza and Coke though. It's worth getting drunk and disorderly just for that. Do they think the wallet belonged to the dead bloke?'

'Probably. It was his initials on it.'

Charlie chuckled. 'Yeah, RIP. Must've been fate.'

'They gave the wallet back to me. Not good for fingerprints, they said. Too many people had touched it.'

'Let me have another look at that photo.'

Ivo handed the phone back to him.

'I've seen him before,' said Charlie. 'Weasley-faced little bloke. Seen him with those buskers playing the banjo. Three of them there were. One on drums and a girl playing accordion.'

That was promising. Charlie, when sober, didn't miss much. 'When did you see them?' Ivo asked.

'Couple of times. They've a regular slot outside Boots on a Saturday morning.'

'Can you remember what they were called?'

Charlie scratched his head. 'Something stupid. Farmhands? Cowmen? Can't remember.'

It shouldn't be too hard to find out. Street performers probably needed some kind of permit, and that sounded like something Katya would know about. There wasn't much more Ivo could do about it right now. 'Better be getting on,' he said. 'Good to see you, Charlie. Take care.'

Charlie nodded and handed him Harold's lead. Ivo sent Jonny a text then headed back to *Jasmine's*.

18

Katya tapped an app on her phone and checked the weather forecast. Sunny but cold, she discovered. She now had to decide whether to stay in or go out. She could stay at home and clean the oven, which would warm her up and give her a nice feeling of satisfaction. It would also mean that when she heated up tonight's shepherd's pie, she'd no longer have to put up with the smell of burning cheese – the result of her over-enthusiasm with the grated cheese when putting together a do-it-yourself pizza a couple of weeks ago. She read the instructions on the tin of oven cleaner and discovered she'd need to run the oven for an hour with the stuff inside it standing in a dish of water. Had it always been that complicated? She couldn't remember. It was a long time, a very long time, since she'd last cleaned it. So she rejected oven cleaning. What was the point of paying to heat an oven that wasn't about to provide her with a nice hot meal. It would warm her up, of course, but just doing the cleaning would warm her up. There was no point in paying twice for the same result.

So how was she going to pass the day? She could just stay in, wrap herself in a blanket and watch DVDs. She had a good supply of those. No one wanted them these days and Oxfam were practically giving them away. But really she should go out. She became stiff in the legs from too much sitting. She should lose some weight, she supposed. But she'd never managed that before. Why would now be any different?

No, she must get out and enjoy the sun. It was cold but she'd wrap up well and go for a brisk walk. She checked the jam jar in the kitchen. Not enough for a meal, but enough for a coffee. And if she went to *Jasmine's* she might get one for nothing. Jasmine was generous with her complimentary coffees since they'd started detecting together. She should join the breakfast club, but the cost of membership horrified her. She'd fallen into the gap between not being well off enough to join and not being hard up enough to qualify for free membership. Jonny and Jasmine had not thought of that when they set the thing up, had they? Perhaps there was a way she could pay in instalments. She might suggest it to them.

She gathered up an array of warm clothes. Not her very warmest. She'd keep those for when the winter frosts set in. For that morning she chose a long-sleeved thermal vest, one of a pack of three that had been on offer in Tesco at the height of the summer heatwaves. Not many people had thought of that, had they? She'd wager they were regretting it now. She added a pair of baggy corduroy trousers – a bit worn at the knees, but comfortable and warm – a heavy knit jumper in bright red that would clash with the maroon trousers, but who cared? And thick socks picked out of a bag of rejects behind Trespass in Peascod Street. Brand new they were, just a tiny hole in one of the heels. She completed the ensemble with a red bobble hat she'd owned for years, and which had seen her through plenty of cold outings.

She was just lacing up her boots, now thankfully worn in, when there was a ring on the doorbell. *Could be the postman,* she thought, *with a parcel.* But she wasn't expecting one. Couldn't afford online shopping these days. She now had a smart meter, so meter readers were a thing of the past. She heaved herself out of her chair and opened the door to find possibly the last person she expected. 'Teddy,' she said. 'This is a surprise. Don't get many journalists turning up on my doorstep. Not since I retired and not this early in the morning.'

'My God, Katya,' said Teddy, laughing. 'Why are you all dressed up like Santa Claus?'

''How did you know where I lived?' she asked, ignoring his question. Not very gentlemanly, being rude about what she chose to wear. But he was a journalist. She couldn't expect good manners.

'A nice desk sergeant down the road told me.'

'You've been to the police station?' she asked. 'Why?'

'Just checking in on the off chance of a story. Nothing doing though. Thought there might be an update on the body in the Long Walk, but they're not interested, are they?'

'It's a disgrace,' said Katya. 'The only one who's shown any interest in the case is DI Lomax. You should have asked for him.'

'Well, to be honest, I thought I'd probably get more from you. I've found something that will interest you. But if you're going out...'

'Just going for some fresh air,' she said. 'And maybe some breakfast,' she added, hoping Teddy might be willing to flash his expenses again. 'Fancy joining me?' She hoped it didn't sound as if she was offering to treat him. Maybe she'd get away with the offer of a coffee.

'THIS IS NICE,' said Teddy as he and Katya settled into one of the comfortable sofas at *Jasmine's*. 'What's it to be?' he asked, studying the menu.

'Well... a coffee?'

'Oh, Katya, you can be such a disappointment sometimes. I thought you'd be more of a full English type. Go on. You know you want it. All on expenses again.'

That was a relief. 'Well, if you insist,' she said, as if the idea had only just occurred to her.

'That's more like it.' He smiled at Jasmine as she came over to take their order.

'You a regular here?' he asked Katya.

'She is,' said Jasmine. 'She's leading our detective enquiries.'

'Jasmine,' said Katya. 'I'm not sure you should've said that. Teddy is a journalist. We don't know if he's to be trusted.'

'I thought we'd agreed to work together,' said Teddy. 'And you'll regret it if you don't hear what I've discovered.' He winked at Jasmine.

'Katya told us about you,' said Jasmine. 'The man you're trying to uncover is now one of our suspects.'

'One of them? You have others?'

'We've got one each,' said Jasmine.

'And how many of you are there?'

'Four. But like I said, it's Katya's case really.'

'So Katya's now leading a team of amateur sleuths, is she?'

'That's strictly off the record,' said Katya.

'Of course,' said Teddy. 'As long as you let me help. Like I said, I've got something you may be interested in. Are the other two about?' he asked, looking around.

'Jonny usually pops in around now,' said Jasmine. 'Not sure what Ivo's up to today.'

'We'll have our breakfast and then a meeting,' said Katya, hoping Teddy wasn't about to upstage her and take over. Or Jasmine, for that matter.

'RIGHT,' said Katya half an hour later, feeling pleasantly well fed. They'd finished eating and had moved to one of the larger tables. Jonny had joined them and was tucking into a plate of toast. 'Let me introduce you all to Teddy Strang,' said Katya. 'He's a journalist but everything we say today is strictly off the record and he has some information for us.' She smiled at Teddy. 'Jasmine you've already met. And this is Jonathan Cardew.'

'Pleased to meet you,' said Jonny. 'This is Harold,' he added.

'Bloodhound?' Teddy asked. 'Only joking,' he added as the door was flung open and Ivo came in looking flushed and excited.

Ivo pulled up a chair. 'I'm Ivo,' he said, staring at Teddy. 'Who are you?'

'This is Teddy Strang,' said Katya. 'He's got some info for us.'

'Me too,' said Ivo. 'I might have found the murderer.' He dug into a cloth bag that had MICK'S TOOLS stencilled onto it in green letters. Mick had now progressed to a fully fitted-out van and Ivo had grabbed the bag on its way to the council tip. He pulled out a handful of papers. 'I went to the library to use the Internet and printed all this.'

Jonny looked through the sheets of paper. 'It's about a band,' he said. Unnecessarily, Katya thought, since there were pages with pictures of people playing instruments. Although on close inspection, the same three people on multiple pages.

'This one,' said Ivo, pointing to a skinny young man holding a banjo. 'He's called Tommy Brooke and the band is called the Cowpokes. And this is him.' He pulled out the photo from the CCTV taken outside Caffè Nero.

They all stared at the two pictures. 'I think he's right,' said Jonny. 'They do look like the same person.'

'I'm not sure,' said Katya. 'You can't see the man in the hoodie very well. But we should tell the police.'

'And if they just tell us we're wasting their time again?' Jonny asked.

'I'll take it to Lugs myself,' said Katya. 'And if he says they're not interested then we'll go and watch the band next time they're in town and—'

'And what?' said Teddy. 'Accuse the bloke of murder?'

Put like that, Katya thought, it didn't sound like a very good idea. 'We can decide when I've spoken to Lugs,' she said. Hopefully Tommy Brooke would already be on the police radar and Lugs would pull him in to question him about the credit cards, if nothing else. 'So what's this info you've got for us?' she asked Teddy.

'I've been digging into the press archive looking for signs of dirt on Edwin Eastman,' he said. 'And I found this photo.' He handed it to Katya.

'This is Edwin Eastman?' she asked. 'There's no caption.'

'Yes, it was taken at a do in London last year. I assume he wanted to remain anonymous because the lady he's draped all over probably isn't Mrs Eastman.'

Katya turned to the only one of them that might just recognise Mrs Eastman. 'Jonny,' she said. 'Have you ever met Mrs Eastman?'

'No,' said Jonny. 'I haven't, but this isn't her.'

'How do you know?' asked Katya. 'Perhaps you should check with your wife. She might have met her at a council do.'

'I know it isn't her,' said Jonny, tapping on the photo with his finger. 'Because that is Stella Pierce.'

'You're joking,' said Katya. 'You know what that means, don't you?' She looked round to see if they had worked it out.

'If they are having an affair,' said Jasmine. 'It means that both Edwin Eastman and Stella Pierce had a motive for getting rid of Raymond Pierce. They could have been in it together.'

'But Stella was in Spain when Raymond died, and Eastman was playing bridge,' said Jonny.

'We don't know what time Eastman left that evening. We do know that Raymond got a taxi at around ten-thirty and you need four people to play bridge, so perhaps he left soon after that.'

'And what?' said Katya. 'Hauled him out of his taxi and down the Long Walk?'

'If Eastman had wanted Raymond dead,' said Teddy, 'he'd have paid someone to do it for him. Most likely he'd have stayed where he was for a nightcap so he had an alibi.'

'We've got this Brooke bloke, Stella and Eastman all looking suspicious,' said Katya. 'Anyone else?'

'I may have got more on the secret group Raymond belonged to,' said Jasmine, opening her laptop and turning the screen so they could all see the picture she'd taken of the cards in Darkjeweller's shop. 'I'm sure one of these cards is connected to both the maker of the pendant and the group. I've checked out some of them but so far, I can't find a connection. None of them do Herne the Hunter stuff and the others don't have websites so I can't check them.'

'What about this one?' asked Teddy, pointing to a card tucked into a corner at the bottom. There was a small logo of a tree and the letters F and H wound into its branches. There was also a web address.

'I wondered about that one,' said Jasmine. 'But it's a restricted site. All you get is a login page. I tried making up some passwords but none of them worked.'

'Did you try googling FH?' asked Ivo.

'Yes, but it didn't come up with anything interesting. It's too vague.'

'So where do we go from here?' Jonny asked.

'I don't know right now,' admitted Katya. 'We need to think about it.'

'I'm making a table of suspects,' said Jasmine. 'First row – Stella Pierce has a motive but also an alibi. Next is Edwin Eastman – motive but no alibi. Then Tommy Brooke – no alibi but also no motive, except to steal a wallet.'

'People have been convicted on less,' said Teddy. 'But I agree. The circumstances of the death don't suggest murder for robbery.'

'I'm starting a fourth row,' said Jasmine. 'Unknown suspect linked to secret society which we know from Darkjeweller has some very nasty members.'

'What about Darkjeweller herself?' Teddy asked. 'Could she have a motive?'

'Or Hermia Rutherford,' Jonny added.

'Okay,' said Jasmine, adding two more rows.

It felt to Katya that they had suspects queuing up. She yawned. 'We are making progress,' she said. 'So don't look so downhearted.' Were they looking downhearted or was she just projecting how she felt? Was it time to let it go? But then what? Get back to watching daytime TV and trying to exist in a cold flat on a pittance? No, she was on to something, she knew she was. And they knew a lot now that they hadn't known before. She was still convinced that Raymond Pierce had been murdered and she was going to keep digging until she proved it. Somehow, she had to produce enough evidence for the police to open up a murder enquiry.

'Haven't you got tasks for us?' Ivo asked.

'What?' said Katya, realising she had been staring out of the window and probably looking glum.

'Tasks. You know. You always give us stuff to do.'

'Of course,' she said, managing a smile. These people were counting on her, weren't they? How could she lose interest now? 'Jonny, carry on watching Stella. She may let something drop about Eastman and what he's up to. Jasmine, keep searching for this mysterious group. Ivo, see if you can find out when the band, the Cow-whatsits are next in town. I'll talk to Lugs again. He was going to get a call log for Raymond's phone. It would be helpful to know about his final calls even if we don't have the phone itself.' And what about Teddy? He seemed interested in their case as well as his own research into Edwin Eastman, and now it looked as if the two were connected. Stella Pierce and Edwin Eastman. Who'd have thought it? He'd be even more interested now. 'Are you staying with us, Teddy?' she asked. He'd be a fool not to. He could have a story about corrupt businessmen and a murder. She'd never, in a million years, have thought she'd be sharing info with Teddy. He was a smooth operator with no scruples, but on further acquaintance, she found she rather liked him.

'Of course,' he said. 'I'd be honoured. And I'll keep up my Eastman research.'

'Just don't publish anything about us.'

'You don't want all the glory of uncovering a murderer?'

'When we have, you can shower all the glory you want on us, but right now don't blow our cover.'

19

Jasmine was woken by something rattling against her bedroom window. She looked at the clock by the bed. It was just after midnight. She should go back to sleep. It was probably just tree branches in the wind. There was a plane tree in the road outside the café that was overdue for a trim. Then she heard it again. No, not the tree. Someone was throwing something at the glass. She dragged herself out of bed and, without turning the light on, looked down at the street just as the next handful of pebbles arrived.

For God's sake, she thought, opening the window and sticking her head out. 'Ivo, what the hell?'

'Can you come down and let me in?' Ivo called up to her. 'I've got something to ask you and the door's locked.'

'Of course it is. It's the middle of the bloody night. The café closes at eight.' She supposed Ivo might not know that. He was only here at breakfast time and occasionally for lunch. All the same, midnight? She hoped he wasn't drunk, but Ivo rarely drank so that was unlikely. Perhaps he'd been thrown out of his flat. But would even the most hard-hearted of landlords do that in the middle of the night? 'Hang on,' she said. 'I'll come down and let you in. It had better be something important.'

She scrambled into some jeans and a sweater and ran down the stairs. She slid back two bolts, unlocked a double set of deadlocks and opened the door. Ivo was standing on the step, shivering. 'Come in,' she said. 'I'll put the kettle on. Looks like you could do with a hot drink.'

'Thanks,' said Ivo. 'I suddenly thought of something and couldn't get back to sleep again.'

'You couldn't have phoned?'

'I did, but you weren't answering.'

Jasmine looked at her phone. It was on vibrate only, with a missed call from Ivo. She must have slept through that. 'So what is it that's so urgent?'

'That card you found in Pierce's wallet. You took a photo of it, didn't you?'

Jasmine nodded.

'And you still have the photo of all those cards on your laptop?'

'Yes, it's still there, although they weren't much use.'

'Have you got your laptop handy?'

'It's upstairs. I'll just pour your tea and you can bring it up with you. It's warmer up there.'

Ivo took the mug from her and wrapped his fingers around it. He took a sip of tea and followed her up the stairs.

Jasmine switched on the electric heater. Ivo put his tea down and sat in front of it, rubbing his hands.

'Why didn't you wear a coat?' Jasmine asked.

Ivo shrugged.

'Ivo, you have got a coat, haven't you?'

'I usually just wear a thick jumper, but I forgot tonight. I wanted to get here as soon as I could.'

She'd never actually seen him wearing a coat. He was always on the go, and she supposed that kept him warm. She'd trawl through Stevie's dad's trove of stuff he kept behind the vestry. Boxes of blankets, sweaters and thick socks. She was pretty sure she'd seen coats there as well. But that wasn't why he was here now. 'What did you want to tell me?' she asked, waking up the laptop and opening the photo.

'That website, the one we talked about earlier, with the tree thing and the letters. Can you open it now?'

'I couldn't get beyond the sign-in page. It won't have changed.'

'Just open it,' said Ivo.

Jasmine did so and once again was faced with a blank page asking for a username and password. 'What now?'

'Find the card that was in the wallet.'

'Got it right here,' she said, clicking it open.

'Okay,' said Ivo. 'See if that's the username and password.'

'There are three lines on the card and only two spaces on the webpage.'

Ivo thought about that for a moment. 'Try the top one as the username and the second line for the password. That's usually the order people save them. The third one could be a double security one.'

Jasmine carefully copied the letters and numbers from the card and clicked enter. Another page opened, showing an irritating captcha screen asking her to tap on pictures of fire hydrants. Then another, which asked her for bicycles. And then another page opened and, as Ivo had suggested, it asked for a second password. Jasmine typed in the third line from the card in the wallet and the screen came to life with a picture of an oak tree with antlers. 'Ivo, you're a genius,' she said. 'It's the same design as the pendant. But what do we do now? There's no menu. I can't see how we get any further.'

'Try clicking on the picture,' Ivo suggested.

Jasmine did so, but nothing happened. Then she moved the cursor and clicked on the two initials – FH. Another page loaded, this time with a message:

Welcome to true Followers of Herne

Next meeting Stir up Sunday 0.00 dog.mouse.moon

'What does that mean?' Jasmine asked.

'It's the details of the next meeting.'

'But it doesn't say where and when. It must be a code.' She sat back, feeling disappointed. They'd seemed to be getting somewhere and had just hit another brick wall.

'When I was little and before my mum got ill, we used to go to church, regular like.'

'Very nice,' said Jasmine. 'But I don't see—'

'Stir-up Sunday,' said Ivo. 'Sunday before Advent. It's when people made their Christmas puddings.'

'Your mum made Christmas pudding?'

Ivo shook his head. 'She didn't, but we used to go round Aunty Ida's for tea and help her stir hers.'

'You've got an aunty?'

'Not a real one. She was a friend until Mum started swigging her cooking sherry and passing out in her lounge. They had a big row about it and we never saw her after that.'

'Oh, Ivo,' said Jasmine. She'd lost her mum too, but her dad had always been there for her. Ivo had no one. She put a sisterly arm around his shoulder.

''S okay,' said Ivo. 'Got friends of my own now.'

Advent, Jasmine thought. She didn't know much about the church calendar, but Stevie had talked about Advent because he played the organ for some of the services, and Advent was when he started to play Christmas carols. 'Stir-up Sunday must be quite soon,' she said.

'It's this coming Sunday,' said Ivo, checking it out on Google.

'Okay,' said Jasmine. 'Their next meeting is on Sunday. But the park is enormous. How do they know where to meet? What does this mouse stuff mean?'

'I think I know how it might work,' said Ivo. 'Have you heard of an app called what3words?'

Jasmine shook her head.

'It's a GPS system that divides the whole world into three-metre squares and names them using three words.'

'You're joking,' said Jasmine.

'There's an app you can download, and it will give you the three words for wherever you are. Emergency services use it, so it must work the other way around as well. If you know the three words you can type them in, and it will give you a location.'

'Let's try it,' said Jasmine, reaching for her phone. Within minutes she'd downloaded the app, signed herself in and tapped to find the three words for the café. 'Wow,' she said. 'I never knew about this.'

'Try these words,' said Ivo, pointing to the webpage.

Jasmine typed them in, and a map popped up with a triangle in the middle of the Deer Park.

'There,' said Ivo. 'That's where the next meeting is.'

'But we don't know what time,' said Jasmine.

'0.00? I'm guessing midnight.'

'Do you think there was a meeting the night Raymond died?'

'It's quite likely, isn't it? We know he was in the park that night.'

'And if he left the Wallaces' at ten-thirty, he would have been in the park too early for a midnight meeting. But unless we are planning to go, it doesn't really matter, does it?' Ivo fiddled with a loose thread on the sleeve of his jumper and grinned at her.

'Oh, don't tell me you're trying to work it out so you can pop along to it,' she said.

'Well,' said Ivo. 'We can tell Katya what we found, or even go straight to the police, but there's no evidence that there's anything sinister about it. It's just a few people meeting in the Deer Park. We need to go and spy on them and find out what they do.'

'We?'

'Yeah.'

'When you say *we*, do you mean you and me, or all four of us?'

'Just you and me. We can creep up on them without them knowing we're there and watch what they do.'

'And risk getting ourselves murdered?'

'Not if we're careful.'

It was a crazy idea. Ivo was just getting carried away. 'We've no idea how many of them will be there,' she said. 'There might be hundreds of them.'

Ivo was looking closely at the tree and antler motif in the centre of the web page. 'Those deer in the park,' he said. 'Don't they usually have the same number of spiky bits on both sides of their antlers?'

'No idea,' said Jasmine, opening a new tab, tapping it into Google and finding plenty of information about the deer in the park. They were red deer, she discovered. 'They're called points,' she said, pointing to the antlers. 'Not spikes. And yes, they usually have the same on both antlers although sometimes they get damaged in fights.'

'Go back to the other page,' said Ivo. He tapped on the image. 'Look, one of these has an extra one. Six on one side and seven on the other. It looks unnatural, doesn't it? Was it like that on the pendant?'

Jasmine opened the photo of the pendant. 'Yep, the same.' She checked her history for the sites she'd found on Herne the Hunter regalia. All the antlers in those had even numbers of points. And Ivo was right. The extra one on the pendant looked contrived. As if it had been photoshopped in or soldered on by the pendant maker.

'Six and seven,' said Ivo. 'Thirteen. That's significant, isn't it?'

'Unlucky thirteen. That would appeal to secret groups, I suppose.'

'It might mean they have thirteen members.'

Ivo clearly wasn't going to let this go. 'Pierce died on the twentieth, not the thirteenth,' she said.

'Perhaps they meet every thirteen days.'

Jasmine had to admit that Ivo might be on to something. 'What are you planning to do about it?'

Ivo opened the calendar on his phone. 'The thirteen days thing doesn't work if there was a meeting the night Pierce died. But it doesn't matter, we're not planning to go regularly. If there are thirteen in the group and Pierce was one of them, they'll be one short now. They'd need to meet and choose a new one.'

'Won't they have done that already?'

'Doesn't matter if they have. We can still go and see what they do. You busy on Sunday night?'

Jasmine sighed. She could hardly let Ivo go on his own. And he was probably way off the mark. It would just be them and a few deer strolling around in the dark.

Ivo was still tapping on his phone. 'It's a waning gibbous moon that night. A full moon would be better but there should be light enough to see by. We can hardly use a torch.'

'What does waning gibbous mean?' Jasmine asked.

'It's the face after the full moon. That means—'

'Yeah, I get it. But what if it's raining?'

He handed her his phone, which was open at a weather app. 'No rain forecast,' he said.

'Okay,' said Jasmine reluctantly. 'What's the plan?'

'We need a map,' said Ivo. 'We'll find the nearest car park and walk from there. We should dress in dark colours.'

'That's it? Not much of a plan. Shall we take Harold? Then if we're spotted, we can say we were just out for a walk.'

'We could,' said Ivo. 'But there are too many problems with that. He might bark and give us away. And if we take him, we'd need to tell Jonny what we are planning, and he might want to come with us. And he might tell Katya and she'd want to come and probably bring that journalist bloke with her. And there might not be anything going on and then we'd look stupid.'

Jasmine tended to agree with the looking stupid bit. The fewer people that knew, the better. 'Okay, no Harold. We'll just have to be lovers out for a bit of moonlight smooching.'

'I don't think—'

'Just pretending to be smooching,' she said.

'And it's not a full moon.'

'Okay, gibbous-light smooching. Is that a thing?' What the hell had she just let herself in for? And just supposing Ivo was right and they witnessed some kind of ritual, what then? They could hardly take photos. Even if they did, there was nothing illegal about people meeting in the Deer Park at night, was there? But there was one thing Jasmine was certain about. She couldn't let Ivo go alone.

20

Katya sat on a bench outside Marks and Spencer and bit into a jam doughnut. The town was bustling that afternoon with Saturday shoppers and colourful stalls selling food. Expensive food. She'd no time for olive oil at fifteen pounds a litre, French cheese that you could smell half a mile away or chocolates which, besides costing four pounds for something you could swallow in a single bite, were so dark in colour they were no more than a particularly bitter way of bankrupting oneself. One hundred per cent cocoa and no added sugar, they claimed. What was the point of that? Just to set your teeth on edge. Give her a nice bar of Cadbury's milk any time. But the bakery stall, that had been okay. She wasn't sure about focaccia baked with olives and rosemary, or sourdough with pine nuts, but good down-to-earth doughnuts were fine. She'd hesitated when she saw the price. She could buy a bag of four at Tesco for the cost of one here. But Tesco was way out of town and she'd no plans to go there unless someone gave her a lift. A couple of quid on the bus just to buy a cheaper doughnut was a non-starter. And this one that she had just taken a second bite of was delicious; the dough fresh and soft, a generous dollop of jam – some of which was currently making its way down her chin — and a crunchy, sugary coating. Scrumptious.

Finishing her doughnut, she chucked the paper bag into a litter bin and licked some sugar from her fingers. Then she sat back and paid attention to what she had come for, which was to listen to the music. Well, not so much to listen as to watch the band who were playing it. In particular the banjo player, young Mr Tommy Brooke, who right now was looking like the cat who had stolen the cream and got away with it. Which, in a way, he was. Not cream in this case, and not actually a cat. In fact, his thin face and whiskery chin reminded Katya more of a mouse. But he had apparently got away with the theft of one or more credit cards, which had provided him with several days' worth of snacks and drinks.

They'd let him go. Lugs had been almost apologetic when he told her. Ivo had done an excellent job of tracking him down and the lazy so-and-sos, her ex-colleagues, so-called upholders of law and order in the area, had done nothing. Well, almost nothing. Brooke had been arrested and questioned. He'd spent all of half an hour at the police station proclaiming his innocence. Not him on the CCTV – Katya was convinced it was. Never been to the Long Walk – tell that to the marines. And he didn't drink coffee. Oh yeah, what was in that cardboard cup he was taking sips from between numbers?

No evidence, Lugs had told her. He'd rounded up Brooke and marched him off to the nick, only to be told someone else would now handle the case. Next thing he knew, Mr Brooke was a free man. Not enough evidence to charge him with the theft of the credit cards or their fraudulent use. Definitely nothing to suggest he was guilty of murder. Lugs thought they'd probably not even asked about that. She'd not said so to Lugs, but Katya thought it all sounded very dodgy. Since when did arresting officers not get to question their suspects? And who had made that decision?

'Enjoying the music?' Katya looked up and saw Jonny and Harold standing next to her.

Jonny squeezed onto the bench and sat down. 'Didn't expect to see you today. Want one?' he asked, holding out a brown paper bag. 'Miniature vegan sausage rolls.'

Katya peered into the bag. Vegan sausage rolls? Whatever next? But they did smell good. She took one and bit into it. 'Not bad,' she said. 'What's it made of?'

'No idea,' said Jonny. 'But it tastes the same as real sausage, doesn't it?'

Katya agreed that it did. 'But what's the point? Why not just use real sausages?'

'Better for the planet,' he said. 'Plant based food.'

'What about the pigs?'

'I suppose they appreciate not being eaten,' said Jonny, with a laugh.

'But if no one eats them they'll go extinct, won't they?'

Jonny appeared not to know how to answer that.

'Anyway,' Katya continued. 'Are you here to watch the band?'

Jonny nodded. 'I expected them to be one short. Weren't they going to arrest the banjo player?'

'They did,' said Katya. 'And let him go without charge half an hour later. Idiots.'

'Do you think perhaps Ivo was mistaken?'

'No.' She helped herself to another sausage roll, wondering if they were cheaper than the real thing. 'Either my ex-colleagues are even more useless than I remember, or there's someone hushing something up.'

'Police corruption? Surely not.'

'I've no reason to think so, not really, but a quiet word over a game of golf, the odd slap-up meal, and you'd be amazed what can be overlooked.'

Jonny stared at the band, who had now launched into *Stand By Your Man*. 'Or across a bridge table?' he asked.

'You're right,' she said. 'We might just be starting to join the dots. A clandestine club, Eastman, Pierce...'

'Stella Pierce? She could be an accessory even if she was out of the country.'

'I wouldn't rule her out.'

'Where does Brooke the banjo player come into it?'

'I don't know yet. But I'm sure he's involved somehow. Just look at the smug git.'

'That hat looks new,' said Jonny, looking at Tommy Brooke. 'I've seen them in that shop on the corner by the castle. They cost over a hundred quid.'

Katya grabbed Jonny's arm in excitement. 'My God, Jonny. I think you might be on to something.'

'Really?' he said, freeing himself from her grasp. 'What?'

'How much do you suppose they get busking here?'

'I've seen quite a lot of people dropping money into that banjo case,' he said. 'And there are some tracks you can download for a small fee.'

'Hardly superstar money, though,' said Katya.

'We don't know what they do during the week. Perhaps they've all got well-paid jobs in the city.'

'Nah,' she said. 'Jobs like that don't give you time to be in a band. And the others haven't got any expensive kit. No, I think someone's paying him off.'

'What for?'

She was silent for a moment, trying to work it out. 'I think we could be wrong looking for a murderer,' she said, helping herself to another sausage roll. She could get to like these, but she probably shouldn't get too used to them. They'd be way out of her budget and they weren't that good.

Jonny fished out the last one and broke a bit off for Harold, who snatched it out of his fingers, seeming to have forgotten the good manners he'd displayed to Mrs Gage. 'You don't think Pierce was murdered after all?' he asked Katya.

'Oh, I do,' she said, brushing some pastry crumbs from her lap. 'I'm more convinced than ever that he was murdered. But I think we could be looking for a team rather than a single person.'

'And the motive?'

'Money, I suppose. It's nearly always about money one way or another.'

'If Stella and Eastman are involved with each other,' said Jonny, 'it could be a crime of passion.'

Could he be right? It was possible, she supposed. But even if it was, it still came back to money. Both Eastman and Stella were rich. Raymond Pierce relied on Stella for his money. Something he'd be reluctant to give up. Could they have planned to make the death appear to have been a heart attack, and paid Brooke to cover their tracks and make it look like a robbery?

'We need to find out more about all three of them,' she said. 'Stella, Eastman and Brooke.'

'Where do we start?' Jonny asked.

'*You* could start by finding out about that taxi. Where did it drop Pierce off that night?'

'You want me to call every taxi company in the area and ask?'

Katya laughed. 'Don't look so horrified. I bet there's a short cut.'

'How do you mean?'

'Networking,' she said, noticing that Jonny still looked puzzled. Did networking not happen in the world of cardboard packing? Possibly not. She'd need to explain. Sometimes Jonny Cardew, in spite of his long years earning pots of money as a factory owner, was strangely unaware of what went on in the real world. Katya knew all about networking. Even Ivo and Jasmine, young as they were, caught on more quickly. She'd become quite fond of Jonny and he was keen enough to help, but really it felt like explaining things to a child. A dreamy kind of child who knew little about the world around him. 'It's like me and Lugs,' she said. 'Teddy as well. We share things, information, places to eat, odd-job men, whatever. I bet if you ask that cleaner of yours, she'll know all about which taxi was called that night. If you know which company it was, you can just call them and find out who did the pick-up from the Wallace address.'

'I can do that,' said Jonny, swallowing the last of his sausage roll and standing up. 'Mrs Gage has taken a fancy to Harold. I'll make her a cup of tea and chat to her when she comes on Monday.'

'Excellent,' said Katya, remaining seated. 'I'll hang on here for a bit and see where our Mr Brooke goes when they've finished their set.'

J onny sat in the front seat of the taxi to make it easier to chat to the driver. Once again, Mrs Gage had turned out to be a mine of useful information. Jonny had misjudged her, or rather he had underestimated the power of dog. Who would have guessed that she had a soft spot for them? More than a soft spot. She turned into a regular marshmallow of softness whenever she set eyes on Harold. They'd sat at the kitchen table earlier that day with cups of tea and the biscuit tin as Mrs Gage fed Hobnobs to Harold and chatted about taxis.

Katya had been right. It turned out there was a regular *you scratch my back, I'll scratch yours* kind of economy going on locally. Cleaners, childminders, car washers, hedge trimmers, taxi drivers, even handymen Jonny supposed, all recommending each other to their clients. And yes, Mrs Gage not only remembered who had driven the taxi that night, she had actually recommended him. She had been very proud of it. She'd thought ahead. She was serving refreshments to a group of bridge players. They'd need to drink with their sand- wiches, wouldn't they? And the chances were that at least some of the drinks would be alcoholic ones. Respectable bridge players didn't drink and drive, although they sometimes didn't plan ahead and would swallow the odd beer or whiskey before realising that somehow they'd need to get home. And it just happened that Mrs Gage's husband's pal, the one he went to the pub with on a Thursday night, drove a taxi and was always up for a bit of moonlighting on his evenings off. He'd had cards printed and distributed among friends, one of whom was Mrs Gage. Mr Pierce had become a little the worse for drink and Mrs Wallace was concerned. Ever willing to oblige, Mrs Gage just happened to have the number of a very reliable taxi driver in her apron pocket. And then Jonny, too, had a card in his pocket. He also had a very nice Maison Louis Jadot Beaujolais that he'd been saving for a suitable occasion. His daughter-in-law, he knew, had a yoga class that evening and Marcus would be at home with Justin, watching something on Sky Sports. What better than a boys' night in with a bottle of Beaujolais? The only thing that had prevented him doing this on other yoga nights was the thought of how he would get home. Marcus didn't live far away. Too far away while Jonny had been suffering the extreme fatigue of long covid, but nothing now he had his energy back. He'd walk there and book Mrs Gage's taxi-driving friend to pick him up, when the wine was finished and they'd had enough of whatever sport they chose to watch.

The sudden death of a customer has a way of getting people talking. Mrs Gage's friend, Cliff, was no exception. He was happy to gossip about Raymond Pierce and the short time they had spent together.

'Was he very drunk?' Jonny asked.

'A bit unsteady on his feet,' said Cliff. 'But he seemed more distracted than drunk. At least, he did after he got the phone call.'

'I don't suppose you heard what the call was about?' Could he ask that? He doubted if Cliff would admit to eavesdropping.

'He was sat in the back, and I couldn't hear what he was saying. But that was when he changed his mind about where he wanted to go.'

'Really?' So he had planned to go home to sleep off the evening's booze when a phone call changed his mind. A call from a lover? Or a murderer? Possibly one and the same person.

'Yeah,' Cliff continued. 'The lady that called me gave me an address near Virginia Water. We were almost there when Mr Pierce changed his mind.'

'So where did you drop him?'

'Said he was meeting someone near the Copper Horse so I dropped him off on the A332. Close as I could get, but he said he could walk from there. Sorry I did now. Should have driven the poor bloke to the hospital. But I swear he didn't seem that ill, just a bit worse for wear.'

'You weren't to know,' said Jonny. The Copper Horse would have been within walking distance across the park, but only for someone who knew the park well and who wasn't groggy from alcohol. 'Did you see anyone else when you dropped him off?'

'Not a soul. I had another call come in, so I did a quick turn around and left him there.' Cliff shook his head. 'Poor bloke,' he said. 'When I heard he'd been found dead, well, you can imagine how I felt.'

They'd arrived outside Jonny's house and he paid Cliff, adding a generous tip. 'Thanks,' he said. 'That was very helpful.'

'Any time,' said Cliff. 'You have my number.'

JONNY LET himself in and was greeted by an excited Harold. Jonny patted him on the head. 'Belinda not back yet?' he asked. Harold didn't know where she was. Why would he? He was a dog. *I've had too much to drink,* Jonny thought. Probably just as well Belinda wasn't back yet. He went into the kitchen and put the kettle on. Then he sat down with his notebook and wrote down everything he'd discovered. Pierce was on his way home when someone had called him. He then changed his mind and was dropped off in the park three quarters of a mile or so from the Copper Horse. Meeting someone, he had told Cliff. Near the Copper Horse but not actually at it, and there was no one there when they arrived. There were plenty of trees in the park, even in the more open areas, where someone could have been hiding in wait for him. Jonny checked a map of the park. It was quite a long way from where Cliff had dropped him to where the body had been found. Could he have been running away from someone, or something? After an evening of booze, medication and fright, he could have dropped dead from exhaustion. Had anyone asked if he'd died at the place he was found? Presumably not, or there'd be no question that it wasn't a natural death. Katya was probably right. Dragging him across the park to where he was found would take more than one person. But why bother? From what he'd read, there had been no attempt to conceal the body. But since the various authorities concerned accepted that this was a natural death, there would have been no one asking that question. Perhaps in his groggy state, Raymond had staggered into the park, got lost and then collapsed from exhaustion. He might have met up with the person who'd called him. Or they might have missed each other. The first would mean that Katya's theory was valid. The second leaned towards the natural death assumption.

Jonny was confused by it all, so he opened a file on his computer and created a table with all the possible scenarios. He decided it was not something he could unravel on his own and emailed the document to Katya. Once sent, he saved it and closed the laptop. *Time for a cup of tea,* he thought, wandering into the kitchen where he re-boiled the kettle and made a pot of tea just as he heard Belinda opening the front door and letting herself in.

He watched as she hung her coat up and came to see what he was doing.

'How was the libraries meeting?' he asked.

Belinda reached into a cupboard for a wine glass and poured herself a drink from a bottle in the fridge. Obviously it was the kind of meeting that required alcohol rather than a cup of tea to get over. 'It was car parks this evening, not libraries. Riveting as ever.'

Belinda was locked in an everlasting battle, mediating between those who wanted to extend free parking rights for residents and others who wanted to keep all the libraries open. In the current financial climate Jonny suspected it was only a matter of time before they both lost out.

'How was your evening?' she asked. 'Marcus and Justin okay?'

'They're both fine,' he said. 'And I had an interesting taxi ride home.'

22

Katya woke early. She always woke up at half past five these days and could never get back to sleep again. Before she'd retired, she could only wake up in time for work with the help of two alarm clocks. Now she could stay in bed for as long as she liked, she was unable to sleep. Sometimes life was unfair.

On the other hand, if she got up now, she could set about doing some housework. A thing she'd never had much time for before. And she hadn't needed to because she was rarely at home. Now she spent more time in her flat, she had started to notice things like cobwebs and dust. And that stain on the kitchen floor where she'd spilt half a bottle of ketchup trying to shake it onto last night's beefburgers – cheap ones from Tesco that needed all the extra flavour they could get. She'd given it a cursory wipe and had then gone to bed. But this was her opportunity. Get up now and she'd get it all done by breakfast time.

She was just admiring the cleanliness of the floor and thinking it was a shame to spoil it by risking the chance of a Weetabix incident, when her doorbell rang. She opened it and found Lugs standing there with a large box.

'Brought you a present,' he said, staggering through Katya's door into the kitchen. Katya was too intrigued to waste time worrying about the cleanliness of his boots. She stared at the box. 'What the hell is it?' she asked.

'It's an air fryer. Me and the wife won it in a prize draw. We've already got one so we thought you could use it.'

'Why did you enter the draw if you have one already?'

'It was second prize. We were hoping to win the holiday in Tenerife.' He opened the box, lifted out a large, round, black object and sat it on Katya's kitchen table. 'There you are,' said Lugs. 'Just plug it in and you're good to go.'

'But what does it do?' said Katya, who thought her kitchen was already cluttered enough and really didn't need anything else, particularly, she thought as she spotted the flex attached to it, something that was going to use electricity.

'It cooks stuff.' He pulled on a handle and slid out a bucket-shaped drawer. 'Pop your food in here and it cooks in half the time it would take in the oven. Take my word for it. Ours has saved us a fortune.'

Katya walked round it suspiciously. 'What does it cook?'

'Anything you want. It makes excellent chips.'

She was beginning to warm to it. 'Well, thank you,' she said. 'And thank your wife. It's very kind of you. But can I give you anything for it?' She'd no idea what these things cost, but they could have put it on eBay and made themselves some money.

'Wouldn't hear of it,' said Lugs. 'It's what friends are for.'

'At least stay for a coffee.' Lugs nodded and Katya turned on the kettle. Opening the fridge for some milk, she spotted the remains of a shepherd's pie she'd bought as a BOGOF at the Co-op. She could heat it up in this contraption tonight.

Lugs pulled up a chair and sat down at the kitchen table. He removed a sheet of paper from his pocket and handed it to Katya. 'Pierce's call log for the week before he died,' he said. 'Calls from his company phone. He must have had his call redirect on. Incoming calls are mostly from phones registered with other companies, so probably work related. There's one from his wife's phone the morning of the day he died.'

'Really?' said Katya. 'But she said she was in Spain then.'

'Doesn't mean she wasn't. The log just shows the number the call came from. It could be from anywhere in the world.'

'Is there any way of checking?'

'No. Even if we could get the phone company to release the information, it would only tell us which mast pinged it to Pierce's phone.'

Katya remembered the email Jonny had sent her. Pierce had taken a call in the taxi on the night of his death. He'd been picked up soon after ten-thirty and looking down the list she saw one that had called in at ten-forty-five. She pointed to the number. Do you know who this is registered to?'

Lugs checked his list. 'It's another company contract,' he said. 'Global Graphics.'

'Any idea who they are?'

'Something to do with advertising, so I suppose it's another work call.'

'An odd time to be getting work calls,' she said.

'Could be from abroad. Perhaps he advertised carpets in America.'

They'd hardly be arranging to meet him at the Copper Horse to discuss carpet adverts. Katya kept that thought to herself. For now. She was damned if she was going to tell the police about that unless they showed some interest in the case. 'Any progress on the likelihood of an inquest?'

'The open verdict? None at all. The super's not enquiring any further. Says there's not enough evidence. And not enough in the budget unless he can guarantee a conviction.'

'Hmph,' said Katya. She'd been right to retire. If anyone was going to get justice for poor old Raymond Pierce, it was going to be her. If she'd stayed in the police, her hands would have been tied and however much her suspicions were justified, she'd have had to keep them to herself. Thank God for Lugs. She hoped he wasn't risking his own career by passing on information.

He must have guessed what she was thinking. 'Don't look so worried,' he said. 'It's not as if I'm disclosing anything that's part of an ongoing enquiry. Anyway,' he said, standing up and rinsing out his coffee cup at the sink. 'I'd better be on my way. Good luck with the air fryer.'

'I'll try it tonight,' said Katya. 'And thanks again.'

She showed him out then sat down at the kitchen table to collect her thoughts. She snapped a fresh sheet of paper onto her clipboard and wrote:

Tasks for the team. She underlined it in red. It was good having a team to run. She'd never have got that far by staying in her job. She would always have been Katya the dogsbody. Left to make the tea and do the photocopying. Not so bad when she was younger and more active, but even then, women coppers got the grunt work. And as they got older it was even worse. They became invisible. It was the younger, brasher coppers who got all the fun stuff. And if they noticed her at all, it was for some unpleasant banter about her weight or her wrinkles or the way she dressed. No, she was having a far better time now. She returned to her list and wrote:

Jasmine – research Global Graphics

Ivo – keep an eye on Brooke

Jonny – stay in touch with Stella Pierce. Try to find out more about Raymond's work. Was it unusual to get work calls late at night?

And for herself, she would update Teddy on where they had got to and find out if he had anything new on Edwin Eastman. She delved into a drawer and pulled out an ancient iPad. Emailing from her phone was too fiddly. Reading emails was okay but typing them with chubby cold fingers was a pain. She dug back into the drawer for a charger and plugged it in. The wretched thing was too old to hold a charge for more than ten minutes at a time. Something Apple did, she suspected, to force people to buy new ones.

It took her half an hour to write three emails. Her phone and iPad didn't speak to each other, so she had to copy the email addresses by hand. And once written she couldn't send them. She usually piggy-backed onto the WiFi belonging to her neighbour in the flat upstairs, but now the rotter had added a password. Sometimes people could be very selfish. She'd have to go to the library, a fifteen-minute walk away but where WiFi was free. If she'd realised that earlier, she could have logged on to one of their computers and done it all in proper-sized print on a keyboard that was the right size for her fingers. And saved herself half an hour of wasted time.

23

The congregation were belting out *Dear Lord and Father of Mankind* when Jasmine crept into the hall behind the church, using a key she had wheedled from Stevie with a promise that she would return it within the hour and that no one would be any the wiser. She'd told Stevie that she needed to find a warm hoodie for Ivo. This was quite true, but she hadn't told Stevie why she wanted it. He hadn't asked and the fewer people who knew about tonight's exploit the better. She must have been mad to agree to this, but the least she could do was make sure they were properly prepared. First, they needed to dress in black, so they were less likely to be seen. Ivo told her the only black clothes he had were a beanie and some very old jeans that he wore when he knew he would be getting dirty; clearing out fireplaces or rodding drains. Jasmine had only ever seen him in a denim jacket with a mock shearling collar. He'd probably get away with the jacket, but the collar was a pale cream colour. No, it didn't detach, Ivo complained, hugging it around him as if he was afraid she was about to attack it with scissors. Jasmine herself was well supplied with black clothes. She had black leggings that she wore for aerobics and a black fleece jacket with a hood. But there was no way she could ask Ivo to go and buy something. Even Oxfam was probably beyond his means. Then she remembered the bags of clothes at the back of the food bank. These were things people had donated, usually, Jasmine decided, because they were too far gone for any other purpose. Even the charity shops were likely to reject them. The volunteers sifted through the clothes picking out anything they could wash and mend, bagging up the rest for recycling. The clean, repaired clothes were hung on a rail at the back of the church hall, and anyone could help themselves. Coats were popular, and children's clothes. There was less interest in flimsy party clothes. Not surprising. Jasmine wondered why people even bothered to donate them. Too lazy to drive to a recycling bin, she supposed.

The hymn was one she remembered from when she was little, and her mum had taken her to a few church services. She didn't remember her mother as a religious person, but she'd liked the rituals and the music, and they went to church every Christmas and Easter. Her mum had had a church funeral. Karim had been lost in a fog of grief until Jasmine remembered that her mum had liked church services and they'd decided to approach the local vicar, Stevie's dad as it happened, to arrange it for them. None of the Christmas carols or Easter hymns seemed suitable and Stevie's dad had recommended this particular hymn, the one they were singing right now. One of his own favourites, he told her. He'd sat down and played through the tune and Jasmine thought she recognised it. Listening to it now, she wiped away a tear and turned her mind to the bags of clothes.

She flicked through the hangers on the rail but didn't see what she was looking for. There was a grey jumper that looked about Ivo's size and might do if there was nothing better. Then she spotted a bag that must have only recently arrived. It had been left just inside the door and was tied with a knot at the top. It looked as if no one had had time to sort it yet. Jasmine untied it and tipped the contents out onto the floor. Someone had taken some trouble with this, Jasmine thought as a waft of fabric conditioner reached her nostrils. She pulled out some brushed flannel shirts. They were going to be very popular. And they were clean and in good condition. She reached for some hangers and added them to the rail. Next were some thick socks, also clean and carefully bundled into pairs. She put those into a box under one of the tables. A few pairs of corduroy trousers were added to the rail along with a nearly new dressing gown. It struck Jasmine that these were clothes that had been loved and cherished. This bag must have come from a grieving relative. Someone had lost a father or grandfather and had lovingly packed away their clothes, hoping perhaps that they would give someone else some warmth and comfort. There was no note to say who had donated them and Jasmine wished she could thank whoever it was.

The final item was a black anorak with a fur-trimmed hood and was exactly what Jasmine had hoped to find. It was a bit big for Ivo, but he was only going to wear it for an hour or two and he could roll up the sleeves. She struggled for a moment with her conscience. Was this stealing? And worse, was it stealing from someone who really needed it? But she was only going to borrow it. She could return it first thing the next morning and no one would notice. All the same, it didn't feel right. She found a slip of paper and wrote *Did a bit of sorting, nice shirts and trousers now on rail. I have borrowed a coat for a friend and will return it tomorrow. Hope that's okay. Jasmine.*

She slipped the note under a box they used for donations of small change, locked the door behind her, slipped the key into the pocket of Stevie's coat that he'd left hanging in the vestry and went home.

24

———————

Around the same time that Jasmine was sorting through the bag of clothes in the church hall, Jonny was parking his car in Stella Pierce's drive. She'd called him asking if he could help her sort some papers. Raymond, Stella told him, had at one time developed an interest in his family's history and had left boxes full of old photographs, copies of birth and death certificates, school reports that had belonged to an aunt, and some personal letters from various grandparents and cousins. She'd appealed to Jonny for help to sort it and weed out anything important. How would he know? If she disliked Raymond, why not just heave the whole lot onto a bonfire? The last thing he wanted to do was sift through Pierce family history. That wasn't going to reveal who had murdered him.

But Belinda had been unsympathetic. 'The poor dear is on her own. A bereft widow who wants a bit of company,' she told Jonny impatiently. 'Surely you can spare her an hour or two. It's not as if you're busy these days.'

Yes, she didn't have to remind him about that. He might not be working full time any more but that didn't mean he was at the beck and call of all and sundry. And he was busy. He had a murder to solve. Just because he didn't spend every day at the office, it didn't mean he hadn't found a way to fill his time. And then his conscience took over and he realised that, as usual, Belinda was right. He also remembered that Katya had tasked him with keeping up to date with what Stella was up to. They no longer suspected her of actually murdering her husband, but there was still a chance she could be involved in some way, namely in conspiring with Edwin Eastman.

Jonny sent Katya a text to say he was going to see Stella and was there anything in particular he should ask her? Katya replied telling him to find out if Raymond often took work calls late at night. He should be able to manage that. Stella didn't seem the type to dissolve into tears at any mention of her late husband's name. Jonny disagreed with Belinda about Stella's degree of bereftness. She seemed to him the essence of a merry widow. He also realised that while they might have cleared Stella on account of her alibi, they were still treating Edwin Eastman as a suspect and he was intrigued to know more about his involvement with Stella. The photo Teddy had found was taken over a year ago. Perhaps it was now all over, done and dusted. He doubted if Eastman went in for long-term affairs. He was probably more of a quick grope in the stationery cupboard type. Jonny had worked with plenty of those and got the impression that a year-long affair was unheard of. Two months was more like it. And even that was unusual. One-night stands were more popular.

It had occurred to Jonny that Stella might be after more than just a sympathetic shoulder to cry on. She'd only been widowed a couple of weeks and he was hardly the type to take advantage. He hoped he hadn't come across that way. Had his sympathetic offer of help been completely misunderstood? Was Stella looking for someone to console her in a way that involved something more intimate than house clearing? Was she hoping Jonny might fill a Raymond-shaped gap in her life? Surely not. The idea made Jonny shudder. He'd said as much to Belinda but she'd told him not to be silly. A remark he'd not found wholly flattering. He'd never for one moment considered the possibility of straying from a long and happy marriage, but that didn't mean there weren't women who found him attractive. He knew he was being pathetic, but just in case, he decided to take Harold with him. Although just what a dog could do if Stella went into all-out seduction mode, he wasn't sure. A quick nip in a sensitive part of the anatomy would probably solve the problem, but he and Harold didn't have that kind of relationship. They'd just about cracked *sit* and *stay*. They'd yet to tackle the *rescue me from this lecherous woman* module, even if such a module existed in the *Train Your Dog* handbook.

WHEN HE ARRIVED, Stella had made coffee and was staring glumly into a collection of cardboard boxes lined up in the living room and stuffed with papers. She was dressed in a grimy set of workman's overalls with her hair scraped back from her face and fastened with an elastic band. Jonny immediately felt safer. There was no way he'd been invited here for anything other than paper sorting.

Stella pushed the coffee table to one side and upended the boxes, scattering papers the full length of the living room. Jonny would have taken them out one by one and arranged them in orderly piles. But they were Stella's boxes and it was her choice how they set about sorting them.

'I thought I'd keep the photos,' she said, pulling out the first few that she could see and piling them up on the coffee table. 'Could you do the same with the letters?'

They worked in silence and were gradually able to see the carpet once more. Perhaps it was not such a bad system after all. He might be home by lunchtime. Stella began tidying up the coffee things, piling mugs, a plate of biscuits, milk jug and sugar bowl onto the tray. 'Let me do that,' Jonny offered, standing up suddenly to take the tray from her and knocking a magazine from the arm of the sofa onto the floor.

'Don't worry,' said Stella. 'You carry on sorting the letters. I'll just take this lot into the kitchen to give us a bit more space.'

Jonny picked up the magazine – a Spanish edition, he noticed – and as he placed it back on the table something fell out onto the floor. He picked it up and read it. It was an airline boarding card for a flight leaving Madrid early on the morning of Raymond's death. Still grasping it, Jonny sat down, feeling breathless and wondering if she'd just inadvertently blown her alibi. What else could it mean? Had Stella lied about the day she travelled home? She travelled regularly to Spain to visit her cousin. Could this have been from another flight? He checked the date and time again to see if he'd misread it. He hadn't. This was definitely a boarding card for that day and with Stella's name on it. He glanced towards the kitchen, where he could hear the rattle of china and cutlery. Then he got out his phone, took a picture of the card and tucked it back into the magazine.

As Stella returned from the kitchen, Jonny pushed the few remaining papers they had earmarked as trash into a black bin bag. 'I'll take this out to the bin,' he said. 'I think we're about done, aren't we?' He hoped he didn't seem to be leaving too hastily, but Stella agreed that they'd finished and thanked him for his help. She showed Jonny and Harold to the door and waved to them as Jonny stuffed the black bag into the bin and led Harold towards the car.

Jonny drove away, relieved to be out of the house and thinking that Stella had once more jumped to the top of their list of suspects. He needed to tell Katya about it as soon as possible.

25

I t could all be a complete waste of time, and in a way Jasmine
hoped it would be. It would be less dangerous, and they'd be
unlikely to stumble across a load of weirdos, possibly
murderous ones. But then they'd learn nothing about the Followers
of Herne. And besides, Ivo was so set on the idea. If the two of them
could uncover some useful information that might help solve the
mystery of Pierce's death, then they had to do this. And if they really
were going to do it, they should be as prepared as possible.

Obviously, they couldn't just wander around the park on the off
chance of finding the correct place. Pinpointing it on Google Maps
was one thing, actually being able to head straight there in the dark
and possibly away from the footpaths was another. They needed to
plan it out from the start; where to park, how far it was to the meeting
place, was it on a footpath? In trees? Would there be hiding places
where they could observe without being seen?

Jasmine's mum and dad had been keen ramblers. Jasmine was
less enthusiastic, although she remembered a few occasions when
she had unwillingly tagged along. She didn't remember why she
didn't enjoy it. She supposed it wasn't something teenagers did very
often, and any interest she might have had was extinguished when

she took part in the Duke of Edinburgh's Award scheme, which had involved trekking around inhospitable bits of the English countryside with tired feet and wet hair – it invariably rained – and sleeping in tents under the watchful eye of the gym mistress from school. However, it had left her with the ability to map read. And she was fairly sure that one or other of her parents had maps of the park. Not the flimsy illustrated ones they gave away at the tourist office in town, but old-fashioned Ordnance Survey walkers' maps. Big ones that folded into pocket-shaped rectangles or which could be clipped to a lanyard and worn around the neck.

Jasmine and Ivo met on Sunday afternoon to plan exactly what they were going to do, and Ivo was strutting around the living room in his borrowed coat as Jasmine sifted through the contents of her dad's bookshelf. The lower shelves contained only books and a few magazines, so she climbed on a stool to explore the upper shelves. 'Ah,' she said, pulling out a handful of heavy-duty maps that had probably not been touched since around the time of the millennium celebrations. 'I'm sure it's here somewhere.' She jumped down and searched for the one she wanted. Her parents had certainly got around. There were maps of the New Forest, the South Downs, the Isle of Wight and finally, at the bottom of the pile, one of Windsor and the Great Park. She opened it up and spread it out on the table. 'Stop preening yourself and come and look at this,' she said to Ivo. 'And take that coat off or you won't appreciate it tonight in the cold.'

'Pity it's so big,' he said, peeling off the coat and hanging it on the back of a chair. 'I could do with a warm coat.'

'It's only borrowed,' said Jasmine. 'If one comes in that's the right size I'll ask if you can have it.' She could donate something to the food bank so they wouldn't lose out. 'Come and look at this so we can plan our route.'

Ivo stared at the map. 'It's enormous,' he said. 'How did people use them when they were out walking?'

'I suppose they had to keep refolding them,' said Jasmine, trying to remember if she'd ever seen her parents using one on a walk. For the D of E they'd made laminated copies of the area and carried them in plastic pouches. That was all part of the skills they recorded to prove they hadn't just been larking around.

'Wouldn't it be easier to use the maps on our phones?' Ivo asked.

'I wanted to get an idea of the whole area before we go. And our phone maps won't help much once we're off the road. I don't suppose they show footpaths.' She picked up a pencil and drew a small square on the map. 'This is where we're going. I've marked the coordinates from what3words and checked it on Google Earth. It looks like there's a clump of trees there.'

'That makes sense,' said Ivo. 'They wouldn't meet out in the open, would they? How far is it from here?'

'It's just over three miles. We'll go by car and park here.' She pointed to a small car park.

'Is your dad okay with you borrowing his car?'

'Of course. I often use it.'

'But not in the middle of the night to spy on potential murderers.'

That was true. She hadn't mentioned the murderers to her dad. It was most likely a wild goose chase anyway and she didn't want to worry him. She'd told him she and Ivo felt like getting out for a bit and they might drive through the park and then get a bite to eat. Which was true. They were going to set off at eight and take a look at the area before there was any likelihood of the Followers of Herne being there. Then they would pop into the Duke's Arms, which was just a mile or two down the road, and get a meal. She took a screen shot of the small area of the map that they needed, and saved it on her phone. A map like this would be useful for the detectives. She wondered if Katya had any maps. She'd not mentioned any. She picked up the pencil again and marked places of interest in their case: a cross where Pierce's body had been found; another for where Charlie said he'd found the wallet; a circle around Pierce's house and another for the Wallaces'. 'Any other places we should mark?' she asked Ivo.

'What about Darkjeweller's shop?'

'That's a good idea,' said Jasmine, 'but it's off the map. I'll make a note of it though.' She worked out the distance using Google and then drew an arrow on the southwestern edge of the map and wrote *Darkjeweller, Kingston 15 miles.*

'Do you know where Jonny lives?' Ivo asked.

'It's out here,' she said, moving to the other side of the map and pointing to a road south of the town centre.

Ivo tapped the name of the road into his phone. 'Looks okay,' he said. 'A bit posh.'

He was right. The houses were detached, red-brick Victorian villas, most of them quite large. 'Jonny is a bit posh,' she said. 'I don't know which house is his, but it looks as if Harold gets plenty of garden to run around in. Not that he wouldn't rather be with you,' she added, noticing Ivo's expression darken. 'Don't worry. You'll get him back. Everyone's on the lookout for somewhere you can go. Even Teddy said he was making enquiries and he must know loads of people.'

'Did he say that?' Ivo asked, looking a bit brighter.

'Yeah, he did. It'll just take time and at least you didn't have to give Harold away or make yourself homeless again.'

SEVERAL HOURS LATER, having driven through the park, earmarked the car park they would use and noted the footpath that would lead them to the clump of trees that was dog.mouse.moon, they were sitting in the Duke's Arms tucking into a meal of chicken and chips and trying to forget why they were there. 'We can still back out if you want,' said Ivo, reluctantly swallowing the last of his chips.

'Is that what you want?' Jasmine asked.

Ivo paused, the final chip speared by his fork. 'Yes, and no,' he said.

'Very helpful,' said Jasmine. 'But I know what you mean. It's like going to the dentist. You know you need to go but you also know you won't like what happens there.'

'We have to do it,' said Ivo. 'We could discover something really important and if we don't go, we'll just feel like wimps and wonder what we might have missed.'

Jasmine looked at her watch. 'Let's do it then,' she said, standing up and putting her coat on. They high-fived each other and left the warmth and security of the pub for... neither of them knew that.

Jasmine drove them back to the car park. On their earlier visit she had chosen a spot under a tree, close to the footpath into the park and she steered the car into it. They zipped up their coats and pulled on the black hats she had brought. Then they climbed out of the car and looked around. Earlier in the evening there had been no other cars parked there. Not a surprise. It was too late for dog walking or picnicking, which is what most people used that area of the park for. On their return from the pub there were half a dozen other cars.

'Do you think it's them?' she asked, wondering whether to be excited or scared.

'Bound to be,' said Ivo, looking at the cars. 'I told you they'd be here.'

'You can't be sure they belong to the Followers,' she said.

'Who else would they belong to? They can't all be dog walkers, or even doggers.'

She couldn't answer that. 'We'll take photos of the number plates,' she said. 'If there are people here doing weird stuff, we can pass them on to Katya's police friend and he'll be able to find out who they are.'

As they worked along the row of cars, Jasmine noticed they were all expensive makes; BMWs, Mercs, even a Porsche. 'Looks like you need to be rich to join the Followers,' she said.

'Makes sense,' said Ivo. 'They're probably all dodgy financiers stashing away pots of money in offshore banks.'

That was one idea, although why they should meet outdoors in the middle of the night, she couldn't imagine.

'Or drug dealers,' Ivo continued. 'Exchanging clandestine packages.'

'You don't go for the black magic idea?'

'With creepy pendants and black cloaks? That might make more sense. But would that just be well-off people?'

'More exclusive, I suppose.' Jasmine checked that the number plates in the photos she'd taken were legible, then put the phone in her coat pocket. She glanced across at a group of trees a hundred yards or so ahead of them across an open expanse of meadow. If anyone was watching from the trees, they'd be spotted. 'Don't turn your flashlight on,' she said. 'There's enough light to see where we're going, and we don't want to attract attention to ourselves. We'll keep to the outer fence and slip into the trees when we're nearer.'

Ivo nodded.

As they drew closer, Jasmine thought she saw a glint of light. She grabbed Ivo and pulled him to a halt. 'Look,' she said, pointing to a dim red glow ahead of them.

'It's not a torch light,' said Ivo in a whisper. 'Could be a bonfire.'

'Not enough smoke,' Jasmine whispered back. 'A lantern, perhaps?'

They crept on and a few feet further in they could hear a murmur of voices and the scent of something sweet and sickly.

'What's the smell?' Ivo hissed.

'Incense, I think,' said Jasmine. Whatever it was, she had smelt something similar in Darkjeweller's shop.

They were coming close to the three-metre square she had identified on the map, where Google Earth had shown a small clearing. The voices were clearer now, and Jasmine stopped in the shelter of an oak tree to turn on the voice recorder on her phone. 'We'll go from tree to tree,' she whispered to Ivo. 'See how close we can get to the clearing.'

'Should we take photos?' Ivo asked.

'Too dark,' she said. 'And we can't risk the flash.'

They had gone as far as Jasmine felt was safe. Peering out from behind a tree, she could see a circle of people dressed in black. She was somewhere between pleased that they had been correct about that night, and terrified of what they might be stepping into.

'We shouldn't go any further,' she whispered to Ivo. 'Stay hidden behind that tree, and try to listen to what they are saying.' She was looking at a group of people all dressed in black cloaks with hoods over their faces. Sinister hoods, tall and pointed like witches' hats with holes for the eyes. It was impossible to tell whether they were men or women. She guessed from their height and build that they were mostly men, although there were one or two slighter figures. Twelve were standing in a circle and one more was sitting on a block of wood in the centre. *Thirteen*, Jasmine thought. *We were right about that.* Next to the block was an iron fire pot, glowing red and emitting a smell of incense.

Then one of them spoke; a tall man standing to the right of the circle. And it was definitely a man's voice. 'Welcome, faithful Followers of Herne,' he intoned. 'Tonight we meet to put the past behind us. Brother Raven betrayed us, but that has been dealt with and now we meet to initiate our new member. Stand up, Brother Loki,' he said, and the person seated in the middle stood and faced him. The leader snapped his fingers. 'Sister Hestia,' he beckoned, and one of the others stepped forward. Jasmine realised that, apart from the man in the centre of the circle, they were all wearing pendants. The antlers and oak tree that Ivo had found in the tree. Sister Hestia was wearing two.

The tall man turned to look at Brother Loki. Were these their real names? Jasmine wondered. Probably not. Perhaps the names had some mystic relevance. So it looked as if they didn't even identify themselves to each other. But how had they come together if no one knew who anyone else was?

'Now,' said the man. 'You must swear the oath. Sister Hestia has the honour of investing you.'

Hestia bent down and picked up an oak branch that was lying at her feet. As she stepped into the middle of the circle, she laid the branch on top of the fire pot and it began to splutter. Then she removed one of her pendants and placed it around Loki's neck.

Sister *Hestia*, thought Jasmine. *So there are women as well as men.* Stella, she remembered, had told Jonny that Raymond belonged to a group of men, but perhaps she had just assumed that. Or perhaps Raymond didn't want his wife to know it was a mixed gathering. A lot of wives, she supposed, would be suspicious about husbands who attended mixed gatherings in the middle of the night.

The circle then began to chant, each one walking forward and tapping Loki on the shoulder and telling him he was welcome. Once everyone had done this, Loki raised his arms and looked up into the sky. He said something Jasmine couldn't make out and she wondered if her phone had been able to pick it up.

That seemed to be the end of the ceremony. The circle broke up, a bottle was brought out and something poured into small glasses, which were handed round. Hoods were pulled back, although it was too dark for Jasmine to distinguish individuals. They stood around in small groups, chatting. *Like a spooky cocktail party,* Jasmine thought, suppressing a giggle.

Had they seen enough? Jasmine wondered. They should probably leave before they were discovered. And now the main part of the meeting was over, and it had turned into a social event, there wasn't any reason to stay. They had found the Followers of Herne, which was what they came for, but hadn't really learnt much more about them. Apart from the hoods, they didn't seem particularly evil. Although one of them having been *dealt with* didn't sound good. How did they deal with people? A quick letter of dismissal, or quick death on a dark night? The idea of being dealt with, replaced by whatever means, made her shiver. What would Katya make of it? Jasmine thought she'd probably lean towards the more sinister scenario, but really there was no proof that the Followers were in any way connected to Raymond's death. There were no names that she recognised, but could Brother Raven have been Raymond? Same first two letters. She thought about the other names they'd heard. Loki? Hestia? People whose names began LO and HE? Perhaps they'd learn something when they discovered who the cars belonged to.

Ivo was mouthing something at her and nodding towards the car park. He was probably right. They were not going to learn anything more and it was getting cold. She was about to turn and agree with Ivo but then the leader clapped his hands for silence. 'Before we depart,' he said, 'I have to tell you that someone has breached our security. It will be necessary to change all our passwords. You will be notified before our next meeting and I must warn you that a breach of this type is very serious. Passwords must never be disclosed to anyone and if I discover who has entered our site without authorisation the consequences will be extremely serious.'

Jasmine gasped. Did he know that she had used Raymond's password? Would he be able to trace it to her laptop? She should have covered her tracks, used a different computer or public WiFi. She wondered if there was anything she could do now to cover up what she and Ivo had done. But if they were changing all the login details, perhaps that meant they wouldn't go any further to find out who it was. And people were in and out of the café all the time hooking up to the WiFi. All the same, she'd had enough and it was time they left.

She waved to Ivo to follow her and turned to leave the way they had come. Then she heard a sound close by, not a loud sound, the crackle of a twig maybe, as someone stood on it. Could it have been an animal? A deer, perhaps. Or something smaller; a rabbit or even a badger. She peered through the trees and thought she saw eyes staring at her. Human or animal? She couldn't tell, but suspected they were human. She and Ivo were not on their own hiding in the trees and they'd been seen. They needed to get out of there and quickly. 'Run, Ivo,' she whispered, relieved to find he was following close behind her. She tugged his sleeve, and they pelted towards the car. She didn't dare look back, but couldn't hear anyone behind them. As they approached, she clicked on the key fob and breathed a sigh of relief when she heard the system unlocking. They hurled themselves into the car and Jasmine drove off, skidding on the gravel. Ivo looked back the way they had come.

'That was close,' he said.

'Were we followed?'

'Yes, someone saw us in the woods but they stopped as soon as we were in the open away from the trees. I suppose running in one of those long robes can't be easy. We were way faster.'

'How many of them?'

'Just one.'

'And was it one of the Followers or someone watching, like us?'

'I don't know,' said Ivo. 'She was dressed in the same long, black cloak but I didn't see anyone leave the group.'

'She? Are you sure?'

'Fairly sure. I got a look at her feet and they looked like a woman's boots.'

Well, there were women in the group so it could have been one of them. 'Could it have been the one they called Hestia?'

'I don't think so. The one that followed us wasn't wearing a pendant.'

'She could have taken it off.'

'I suppose,' said Ivo. 'Can we just get out of here?'

Jasmine looked in the rear-view mirror. There were no cars behind them and they were almost out of the park on the road that went towards the town centre. There was more traffic and Jasmine felt safer. They were just a short distance from home. All the same, she was relieved to get there. She pulled the car into the lane behind the café and parked in Karim's space. It was deserted. They hadn't been followed, but she hoped that the woman who'd chased them had not made a note of the registration number. Her father was not going to be pleased about angry, pagan type people turning up on his doorstep and accusing his daughter of being a spy. *Don't be so dramatic,* she told herself. *Why would anyone bother to do that?* She and Ivo were just a harmless couple enjoying a night in the park.

They let themselves in through the kitchen door, which Jasmine locked thankfully behind them. She had an early start in the morning and should get to bed, but neither she nor Ivo thought they'd be able to sleep, and she didn't like the idea of Ivo walking home on his own. 'I'll make some tea,' she said. 'And then you can kip on the sofa.'

Ivo didn't object. In fact, he looked relieved. He had been as spooked as she had.

JASMINE DIDN'T SLEEP WELL. She couldn't get rid of the unsettling image of a hooded figure staring at her from the edge of the clump of trees. She and Ivo had been very quiet, but someone had noticed they were there. Why didn't they raise the alarm? Or follow them to the car? But it was a relief that they hadn't. Even though they'd prepared an answer for anyone who questioned them about why they were there, she was glad they hadn't had to use it. Being out with a boyfriend and just happening to stumble across a group of people in hoods was lame and not very believable. But being spotted and called to account felt a lot less sinister than being stared at. Had they been recognised? She wondered. She couldn't imagine that they had. Unless some of the Followers of Herne were also members of the breakfast club or had employed Ivo to fix something in their houses. How likely was that? She had no way of knowing and it worried her. Ivo had tried to reassure her. Okay, they'd been spying on a group of strangely dressed people who chose to meet in the middle of the night. But they'd been in a public space. Jasmine and Ivo had as much right to be there as they had. And if the Followers of Herne wanted to keep their existence a secret, they were hardly likely to turn up and interrogate the two of them even if they had been able to identify them. That would be a dead giveaway. Their cover would be well and truly blown. Ivo was right, of course, although Jasmine still had this uneasy feeling that someone had recognised one or both of them. But like Ivo said, what could they do about it?

They decided to tell the others what they'd seen at their next meeting. Katya would probably shout at them for not discussing it with her first. She'd warned Jasmine not to meet anyone they suspected face to face, and she'd not done as she was told – twice if you counted her trip to the market in Kingston and her meeting with Darkjeweller. But they had made some important discoveries. Surely Katya would approve of that.

Why did the time go so slowly when you couldn't sleep? Jasmine checked the time on her phone, expecting half an hour to have passed since she'd last looked and finding it was only ten minutes. Five-thirty and she wasn't going to get back to sleep. She might just as well forget about it, get up and make a start on some of the kitchen jobs that needed doing before the café opened. There would be deliveries to see to and she could get ahead with breakfast preparations before the kitchen staff arrived. She dressed quickly and went downstairs to make herself some coffee. Ivo had left a note on the table. *Customer texted – blocked drain – better go and fix it – see you later – Ivo.* Either he hadn't been sleeping either or he was very dedicated to his work. Who responded to calls about blocked drains at five a.m.? Who even noticed they had a blocked drain at that hour, never mind texting someone about it? But perhaps the text had come the day before and Ivo had failed to notice it.

Jasmine filled the kettle and plugged it in. As she waited for it to boil she bustled around, emptying the dishwasher, spooning coffee into a mug and sniffing the milk to check it hadn't gone off. She felt surprisingly wide awake considering she'd had practically no sleep. It would probably hit her later. She'd be overcome by sleepiness during the lunchtime rush, or worse, fall asleep in the middle of Katya's meeting.

Just as the kettle boiled there was a tap on the door. *Probably the bread delivery,* she thought. It was a bit earlier than usual so it was just as well she was already up. She unbolted the door and looked out, expecting to see the bread man with his plastic tray of loaves and rolls, a clipboard balanced under one arm and a pen behind his ear ready for her to sign the receipt. But the street was empty. No bread man in sight. In fact, no one in sight at all. It was still dark, but the streetlights were on and she'd have seen if there was anyone out there. *Strange,* she thought. Who would knock on the door and then disappear? It was far too early for passing schoolchildren, who still sometimes played the knock and run game.

She was about to shut the door again when she glanced down at the step and spotted an envelope. She'd heard of unpleasant things being delivered to people, but there was no reason she could think of why anyone should do it to her, or her father. They were part of a small community of people who both lived and worked in the town centre. They looked out for each other, and she'd not heard of it ever happening to anyone else. Why would it start now? They'd lived here for years and never felt they didn't belong. Even when her dad first came, he'd been made to feel welcome.

Jasmine stared down at the envelope. It looked harmless enough.

It was just tiredness making her feel edgy. She picked it up and felt it carefully, prodding and sniffing it just to make sure it didn't contain anything unpleasant. But it was just a thin, plain white envelope that felt stiff like a birthday card and with her name handwritten in blue ink. It was nowhere near her birthday, but it could be an invitation. An odd time to deliver it, but she supposed it could be a friend dropping it off on their way to work. She carried it into the kitchen, sat down at the table and carefully slit it open. She pulled out a card; not an invitation, but nevertheless a rather beautiful card. It was cream coloured with a gold edge and it had just six words printed on it:

I TOLD YOU TO KEEP AWAY

She felt her heart race and her hands were shaking. Someone had recognised her. Even in the dark, dressed in black and with her hat covering her hair. But who? And were they now threatening her? It was a scary feeling that someone knew who she was and where she lived. She read it again and calmed down a little. It was more of a reprimand than a threat. No *keep away or else*. Nothing to tell her what might happen if she didn't *keep away*. It didn't even tell her what she was to keep away from, although after the events of the night it was probably obvious. She'd done nothing else recently that she'd been warned to keep away from. So someone she knew had been there, had known she was there deliberately and had not just stumbled upon them when she was out for a walk. And what was more, this someone had already warned her to keep away. Keep away from what? It had to be the Followers of Herne. There was nothing else in her life that she should keep away from. She had no current boyfriend so there were no jealous girlfriends hanging around waiting to threaten her. Katya had warned her about meeting strange people, but she was far more likely to come and shout at her about that face to face. Jasmine didn't see her as a person who left scary notes in the early hours. Apart from anything else, Katya would never use such upmarket stationery. Recycled brown envelopes were more her style. Could it be Ivo teasing her? She didn't think so. Unless she was a very bad judge of character, Ivo was far too soft-hearted to play a cruel trick like that. The same went for Jonny, although he would no doubt have access to posh envelopes and cards with gold edges. There was just one other person who knew she was interested in the Followers of Herne. Diane James, AKA Darkjeweller. Was she one of the group? Was she the one who'd stood at the edge of the wood staring at them?

26

Katya couldn't face another session of alternately raging at and coaxing her ancient iPad into action, so she'd decided to spend the morning in a public library. It was nice in there. Warm and not too busy. It was a small, out of town library with limited opening hours. The library in the town centre was closer to where she lived but bigger and busier, and in Katya's experience full of noisy children being read stories or making things with papier mâché and old yogurt pots. What had happened to reading quietly? Bespectacled librarians enforcing strict silence. If libraries were now more lenient about silence, Katya suspected they had shifted their strictness to computer use and online time. She'd only get half an hour, forty-five minutes if she could prove she lived in the area, and then she'd be told to make way for someone else. The town was always bustling with tourists and those who didn't have smartphones, and those who did but who also had podgy fingers, like Katya's, dropped into the library to book tickets for castle tours, or train tickets to London, or to check the time of the next changing of the guard ceremony. There should be more concessions for residents. An hour at least. They were the ones who needed to pay their council tax online, or complain about unemptied bins, or check that their neighbours weren't planning to block out their light with house extensions. Perhaps she'd have a word with Jonny and ask if his wife could do something about it. What was her name? Belinda. That was it. She was in charge of leisure, wasn't she?

In the meantime, a short bus ride had brought her to this much smaller and more informal library, and Katya had been lucky that she'd arrived just as they opened. No one else was waiting to use the computers and the only other activity in the library was a group of elderly ladies gossiping over their knitting.

Katya typed in her library card number and PIN and logged into her email. She'd expected confirmation of a dentist appointment, an invoice from the plumber who had unblocked her sink and a payslip from the police pension people, to which she hoped might have been added a fuel supplement payment. All three were there, although the plumber's bill was more than she'd expected and the fuel payment less. In fact, they just about balanced each other out. Her upcoming dental treatment, she was pleased to see, remained in band one, so she was now no better or worse off than she had been the previous month. She cleared out a lot of spam emails about Black Friday deals. Wasn't Black Friday at the end of November? It seemed, like Christmas, to start earlier every year. Her inbox now looking pleasantly uncluttered, she was surprised to see the one remaining email was from Teddy Strang. She clicked it open and read it.

Sorry if this is bad news but we now have to eliminate Edwin Eastman from our list of suspects. On the night of Raymond Pierce's death, he was involved in a car accident. He was taken to hospital where he was found to have a broken leg, concussion and was over the alcohol limit. How he managed to keep this out of the press I don't know. I almost missed it myself, but his name popped up in a police record for that night. I suspect he blagged a private room for himself and probably persuaded his golf buddy police superintendent to keep schtum about the alcohol. Anyway, I chatted to a particularly charming receptionist who confirmed the time of his admission and told me that he was kept in for several days while his leg stabilised in traction (no idea what that means). So I'm afraid he has a watertight alibi. A pity. I'd like to have seen him defending himself on a murder charge. I did call at his home to ask for comments from his wife, but she appears to have gone to ground. A neighbour told me she had left some months ago and I understand divorce proceedings are under way.

*Having seen a photo of her in a compromising position with Eastman, I'm wondering what, if anything, Stella Pierce knows. I could contact her myself, but perhaps your nice Mr Cardew might be a better person for that. He seems to have struck up a friendship with her and she might be more forthcoming with him. People are strangely suspicious of journalists. (Usu-*ally with good reason, thought Katya.) *Eastman might not be a murderer, but I'm convinced he's up to something and I'm not ready to let it go yet. And with your police experience you would be the best person to help me nail him. Let me know what you think. Nice if we could expose the bastard. And when we do, I'll buy you a slap-up dinner. Tata for now.*

Katya read it twice. On the whole, it was good news, she thought. Okay, Eastman might not have been at the scene of Pierce's murder, but that didn't mean he wasn't implicated in some way. Teddy was sure he was up to no good and he was asking for her help, so in fact she might have two cases on the go. And rather more exciting ones than when she was actually in the police. She tapped in a reply. *Happy to do more digging into Eastman's activities,* she typed. *He could still be an accessory to the murder, but we'll keep working on other suspects as well.*

A very pleasant library volunteer appeared and offered her a cup of coffee and a chocolate biscuit. They didn't do that in the town centre library. A small clock at the bottom of her computer screen told her she only had five minutes left online and she wondered if she'd have time to drink her coffee before she had to leave. She could sit and chat to the knitters, she supposed, but the woman who brought her the coffee told her not to worry about it. They were not busy so she could have as long as she wanted. All that was needed was for the librarian to add on extra time. 'Makes me sound like a football match,' Katya said with a laugh. She'd definitely come here again, she thought, wondering if the chocolate biscuit was a regular feature or a one-off and they would be down to plain digestives, or worse, rich tea, next time she came. She was checking out online supermarket shopping when another email arrived. This one from Jasmine, with a photo attached. It was a list of car registration numbers.

Don't be cross, Jasmine wrote, *but Ivo and I did a bit of surveillance of our own. We've lots to tell you at our meeting this afternoon, but could you ask your police friend to check out these numbers? We have a theory about the Followers of Herne and their part in Raymond Pierce's death.*

Why would Katya be cross? What the hell had Jasmine and Ivo been up to? She'd assumed Jasmine had taken her words to heart about not getting into danger, but she was young and headstrong, and possibly reckless. And Ivo was no better. They could have blundered into anything, put themselves in danger and given away details of their enquiries. Good job they were meeting later. She needed to lay down a few ground rules. But car registrations were always interesting. One never knew who was where and what they were getting up to. A car parked where it shouldn't have been could take a case in a very interesting direction. And if these were people with connections to the Followers of Herne, she shouldn't be too hard on Jasmine and Ivo, even if they had gone free range without mentioning it to her. She forwarded the picture to Lugs, asking him to text the reply to her. She couldn't wait here, nice as it was, on the off chance that Lugs would reply instantly. She needed to head home and put together an agenda for the meeting.

It had been a good day. She had struck lucky with the library, and she was lucky again with the bus. One pulled up just as she arrived at the bus stop. She'd be home in time for a late lunch and then she'd have half an hour or so to plan her – and the team's – next steps.

Once home, she made herself a bacon and egg sandwich and a cup of tea. It had been a mild day, but even though she hadn't needed her usual layers of clothing, dragging herself on and off buses was tiring. She settled herself in a comfortable chair in a spot of sun near her window and shut her eyes. Just for a moment or two, she promised herself.

She was woken half an hour later by a buzz from her phone. It was a text from Lugs with details of the car registrations she had asked for. The text was tiny, but Katya shone her brightest light on it and carefully, with a lot of squinting, swearing and dogged determination, managed to copy the names onto a sheet of paper, which she fixed to her clipboard. It was an interesting list, she realised. A mix of private owners and upmarket-sounding companies, the kind whose names gave one very little information about themselves. It was like price tickets, or rather the lack of them. Displays in shop windows with no prices on show meant one thing. They were way too expensive for the average shopper. Companies with obscure names usually meant something similar. That they were not prepared to deal with the average man or woman in the street and probably diverted their profits into offshore accounts. Which, if these car numbers were significant for their case, was going to make it very difficult to identify potential suspects. The names were not much help either. None she recognised and her eyes were too tired to start googling them on her phone. She'd get Jasmine onto it. It would keep her out of mischief and might just reveal something useful. Two birds – one stone.

27

'Right,' said Katya, scooping up a few remaining crumbs of raspberry and chocolate chip muffin and sucking them off her finger. 'There's quite a lot to report.'

She reached for her shopping bag and cleared a space on the table for her clipboard and pens. First on her list was Edwin Eastman. 'He has an alibi for the night of Pierce's death,' she said, reading the details Teddy had sent her about his accident.

'Does that mean he's no longer a suspect?' Jonny asked.

'Couldn't he have killed Pierce before he was in the accident?' Ivo asked. 'Perhaps he was in a hurry to get away and didn't drive carefully.'

Katya shook her head. 'The accident was called in from Beaconsfield at eleven-fifteen. I checked it on Google Maps. It's a half-hour drive from where the Wallaces live so he must have left Windsor at ten forty-five at the latest. We know Pierce left at ten-thirty and the taxi dropped him off on the A332 at a spot that's about ten minutes' walk from the Copper Horse. That would have been at around ten-forty. If Eastman left at the same time and followed him to the Copper Horse, he'd have had five minutes to kill him, heave him down to where his body was found and return to his car, which is not possible. Besides, we've no reason to think he had anything against Pierce. So no motive.'

'We know they had an argument that evening,' said Ivo.

'And he was having an affair with Stella Pierce,' Jonny added.

'So you think after the argument Eastman decided to belt over to the Copper Horse and kill Pierce? And what about the phone call? Remember, Pierce was being driven home until he took the call and diverted the driver to the Copper Horse instead. Unless we can show that he paid someone to do it for him, I think we can forget about Eastman as a suspect for the moment. Teddy's still digging stuff up about him, but it doesn't look as if his activities involve killing anyone. It's more about money so we'll leave it to Teddy for now.'

'What's next?' asked Jasmine, looking up from her laptop where she'd been typing notes about Eastman.

'You'd better tell us what you and Ivo have been up to,' said Katya.

'What?' said Jonny, looking up in surprise.

'Seems they've been doing some detecting on their own.'

'Yes,' said Jasmine, looking up nervously. 'Kind of.'

'Without discussing it first,' said Katya, giving them the kind of look she rehearsed back in the day when there was still a chance of promotion to inspector.

'What did you do?' Jonny asked, looking, Katya thought, impressed. Not something to be encouraged.

'We found the Followers of Herne,' said Jasmine. 'And eavesdropped on one of their meetings.'

'Really?' said Jonny. 'Very impressive. How did you do it?'

Katya sighed. 'It was a stupid thing to do,' she said. 'Didn't either of you realise how dangerous that could have been?'

'Of course we did,' said Ivo. 'But we were very careful. And we're okay, aren't we?'

'We worked out the code for the website from the card in Raymond Pierce's wallet,' said Jasmine. 'That gave us the time and place for the meeting, so we went and listened in for a bit. They were initiating a new member taking the place of someone who had been *dealt with*. We wondered if it was a replacement for Raymond Pierce.'

'And we took a picture of their cars,' said Ivo. 'We can find out who they are now.'

'Can you be sure that the cars all belonged to people who were at this meeting?' Jonny asked. 'We don't want to be harassing them if they had nothing to do with it.'

'What else would they be doing in the park that late at night?' Ivo asked.

'People go for midnight walks,' said Jonny. 'Or badger spotting, or for elicit trysts.'

Jasmine giggled. 'Elicit trysts? We're not in an Agatha Christie novel.'

Jonny looked offended. 'Lovers still meet in car parks, don't they?'

'I suppose so,' said Jasmine. 'It's just that trysts sound a bit...'

'Old fashioned?' suggested Ivo.

'I suppose I am a bit,' said Jonny. 'But I'm not completely out of touch.'

They were getting off track. Katya needed to focus them on the matter in hand. 'There's no suggestion of harassing anyone,' she said. 'But it was good thinking to get the car registrations. It might give us a clue about who we are dealing with.' They had been enterprising, Katya had to allow them that. And it was impressive the way they had worked out the code for the website. 'But,' she said severely, 'if we are going to work as a team you mustn't do anything like that again without consulting me first.'

'Without consulting *us*,' said Jonny. 'I'm part of the team too.'

'Should we consult Harold as well?' asked Ivo with a derisive snort.

'Come on,' said Katya, starting to feel annoyed. 'There's serious stuff to discuss.' She rummaged through her pockets and found the list she had made from Lugs' text message. The names registered to the cars Jasmine had photographed. 'Did you recognise anyone?' she asked, handing Jasmine the piece of paper. 'Anyone on this list?'

Jasmine read it and shook her head. 'They were wearing long cloaks and hoods. It would have been hard to recognise them even if we knew who they were.' She handed it to Ivo.

'Only two actual names,' he said. 'The others look like company cars. Do you recognise any of them, Jonny?'

Jonny read the list and looked at Jasmine's photo of the cars. 'They're all quite upmarket,' he said. 'They'll be senior members of the companies, on the board or top salespeople perhaps. The names don't look familiar at all. I can check them out if you like.'

'Yes, do that,' said Katya. 'But do it discreetly. We don't want to make them suspicious.' She tapped her pencil on the table. 'Do we have any idea what the Followers of Herne actually do? And what poor old Raymond had done, assuming he was this brother who had been dealt with?'

'No,' said Jasmine. 'They were just doing a sort of ceremony for the new member. They chatted a bit and then they all had a drink.'

'That's when we left,' said Ivo.

'Well,' Katya said thoughtfully, 'if Jonny can get us some details, we might be able to find out a bit more. Right now, it just sounds like some club for senior businesspeople. I can't imagine why they need to meet in the middle of the night, though.'

'Darkjeweller told me they were unpleasant people,' said Jasmine. 'She warned me not to have anything to do with them. Perhaps they're involved in drugs or money laundering. Something illegal, if they have to meet in secret.'

'And with dire consequences for anyone who breaks the rules,' Jonny added. 'But we don't know for sure that they had anything to do with Pierce's death.'

He was right. It all depended on whether or not Raymond Pierce was the member who had been accused of betraying them, if he was indeed a member at all. If he was, they would be looking for a suspect within the group. If he wasn't, then it was back to Eastman and the possibility of a contract killing. And those were always the hardest to pin down.

It was time for a break, Katya decided, standing up to stretch her legs. She opened the door for a breath of air, shrugged her shoulders to relieve the stiffness in her back and then returned to her seat, where she found Jonny looking fidgety and excited. She was becoming fond of Jonny. Anyone else would have been impatient and bad-tempered about being interrupted. Jonny just smiled at them.

'Sorry,' said Katya. 'Sudden stiffness in the back. Needed to stretch. Didn't mean to interrupt you. You've something to tell us?'

Jonny nodded, then paused dramatically, waiting until he had all their attention. 'I still think Stella was involved.'

'But we've cleared Stella. She was in Spain when it happened,' said Katya, wondering why Jonny was looking so pleased with himself. Had he found some new evidence? She continued to watch as he picked up his phone, handed it to her and showed her a picture of a boarding card for a flight leaving Madrid on the day Pierce had died, complete with Stella Pierce's name and seat allocation.

Wow, she thought. *I didn't see that coming.* 'Now this certainly changes things,' she said, passing it across the table for Jasmine and Ivo to look at. 'Where did you find it?'

'Stella asked me to help sort out some papers, mostly dull family history stuff, but this fell out of a magazine that was on the coffee table.'

'Does she know you saw it?'

'No, she was in the kitchen making coffee. I thought it was best not to say anything about it.'

'Quite right,' said Katya. 'If she did kill her husband, she might be dangerous.'

'We know she was on a similar flight a few days later,' said Jonny. 'So she must have flown home and then back to Madrid almost immediately. We should pass it on to the police, shouldn't we?'

'We should,' said Katya. 'Send me a copy and I'll let Lugs have it. They need to check car hire companies. If she hired a car at Heathrow she could easily have driven to the park, called Raymond on the way, killed him and then returned to Heathrow for a flight back to Madrid. They can check that as well.'

'Some of the Followers of Herne were women,' said Jasmine. 'Perhaps she was one of them. She could have been the one who *dealt with him.*'

'Would she have been strong enough? Whoever killed Raymond

must have dragged his body from the Copper Horse down the Long Walk to where he was found.'

'Not necessarily,' said Katya. 'He might have been killed where they found the body.'

'It all sounds very weird,' said Ivo. 'Raymond is sitting in a taxi minding his own business when he gets a call from his wife, asking him to meet her in the park and go for a walk with him in the opposite direction from their house. Then she kills him, walks back to wherever she left her hire car and heads back to Spain. Wouldn't it have been easier to put poison on his cornflakes and bury him under the patio?'

'And she still doesn't have much of a motive,' said Jasmine.

'Perhaps he refused to divorce her,' Jonny suggested. 'And she might have had an accomplice. She calls Raymond and tells him to meet her in the park, where whatever hefty thug she's employed is waiting for him. A professional assassin wouldn't leave any evidence.'

'Couldn't she have done all of that from Spain?' Jasmine asked.

'I suppose so,' said Jonny.

'So where do we go from here?' asked Ivo.

Katya scratched her head. She really didn't know. 'I need to get my head around all of this,' she said. 'I'll go over everything that's come up today and have a chat to Lugs. He'll probably say there's still not enough evidence for a murder case. The local police are very reluctant to open up enquiries unless they think they'll get a conviction.'

'So we don't do any more?' Ivo looked disappointed. 'Just abandon it all?'

'Absolutely not,' said Katya. 'We keep collecting evidence. I'm still not convinced banjo man is as innocent as he claims. You could keep an eye on him, Ivo.'

Ivo nodded. 'I can do that.'

'Jonny, you've got plenty to do checking out the company cars. And perhaps keeping in touch with Stella. But don't challenge her about the boarding card. We don't want her bunking off again. And, Jasmine,' she paused, 'I'd really like to know more about the Followers of Herne, but the only source you've got for that is their website, and you've probably been locked out of it now, and this Darkjeweller, but I'm worried he might be dangerous.'

'She,' said Jasmine. 'Darkjeweller is a woman. I... I think she may have tried to contact me.' She explained about the delivery of the card. 'I think it would be safe to email her and maybe tell her who we are.'

'I'm not sure,' said Katya. 'It might be better to get Teddy involved with that. Leave it with me for now.'

28

J asmine read a text on her phone that simply said: *Meet me in the River Street car park 7.30 this evening – Teddy.* She'd missed a couple of calls while she was serving breakfasts but hadn't recognised the number and hadn't bothered to return them. Unknown numbers were usually people wanting her to update her phone contract. If it was an important call they'd have left a message. There were no messages, but at least the text had told her who had been trying to call her. She couldn't work out why, though. If he'd wanted to meet her, he could have dropped into the café and talked to her. But the café was in a narrow road with severe parking restrictions so dropping in was difficult. Customers either walked or parked in one of the town car parks. And there was always the chance of being overheard, so meeting in a car park to chat, or exchange info or whatever, made sense. Or was this a date? Probably not. They'd only met once before when Teddy came to a detective meeting. He'd been friendly enough, but there was no kind of a spark between them. They'd barely made eye contact and he'd seemed entirely focussed on the investigation. He probably wanted to talk about the case, and she was flattered that he might want her help. But why not involve the others?

The car park was a short walk from the café. It was big and covered the area from the station right down to the river. Theatre-goers parked there, and people going out for meals in the town. Jasmine had no idea what kind of car Teddy drove and wondered how she was going to spot him. She hoped she wasn't going to be wandering around staring into car windows and that he'd be there before she was. She didn't want to stand around in the cold waiting for him. But she needn't have worried, he'd parked right by the entrance and was leaning against the bonnet of his car, looking at his phone. She couldn't remember what he'd worn when they met before, but this evening he was wearing a leather jacket, jeans and a long, knitted scarf. He looked all set for an evening in a jazz club. The kind that was held in a dingy basement populated by real ale drinkers. If that was where they were going, she'd fit right in with her black rollneck jumper and jeans tucked into Chelsea boots.

As Jasmine approached, he put the phone in his pocket and opened the door for her. 'So tell me why I'm here,' said Jasmine, climbing into the car, buckling the seatbelt and watching as he got in next to her.

'We're going on a short road trip.'

'Where to?'

'Kingston. To meet up with an acquaintance of yours.'

There was only one person she knew in Kingston, and she'd been pretty much forbidden from meeting her, both by Katya and the person herself. 'Really?' she said. 'Does Katya know?'

'Yes,' said Teddy. 'She asked me to check out Darkjeweller, but she doesn't know I'm taking you with me.'

'So why are you?' And how would Katya react when she knew? 'She told me not to contact her.'

'Don't worry about Katya,' he said, with a wink. 'If we're successful she won't mind, and if we're not we won't tell her about it.'

Fair enough. At least if she got an earful from Katya, she had Teddy to blame. 'But Darkjeweller's shop won't be open this late, will it?'

'We're not going to the shop. I did a bit of snooping and discovered she spends her evenings in a folk club that rehearses in the cellar of a pub called the Six Bells.'

Not far off the mark with the jazz club scenario then. 'How did you find that out?' Jasmine asked.

'You don't need to know,' said Teddy, tapping the side of his nose. 'Can't reveal my sources.'

That was what journalists always said, wasn't it? Probably just an excuse for some dodgy snooping.

'Before we get there,' said Teddy, switching on the engine and pulling out into the road, 'tell me all you know about Darkjeweller.'

That was a bit unfair. She didn't see why she should tell him, when he clearly wasn't going to tell her anything in return. But then he was taking her with him, so she supposed she owed him something. 'Her real name is Diane James and people know her as DJ. But I expect you knew that already.'

Teddy nodded.

'She's tall and has got very long hair which she dyes an odd shade of purple and she dresses like something out of the Addams Family. I didn't know she was into folk music, but it kind of makes sense. And you should probably see this.' Jasmine fished into her bag and pulled out the card she had been sent, still in its envelope. She kept it in her bag because she didn't want to leave it lying around for anyone to see, but neither did she want to throw it away. She waved it in Teddy's direction.

He pulled over, stopping in a layby, and looked at both the envelope and the card. Then he sniffed the card. 'Patchouli,' he said. 'And recycled paper. Very new age. And you think DJ sent it?'

'It was pushed through our letterbox very early the morning after we'd spied on the Followers in the park. When I met her before, she'd warned me not to interfere with them. It can't have been from anyone else because she's the only person to have warned me, and probably the only one who knew I was interested in them. And...' She paused, recalling the figure they'd seen standing by the trees. She'd not told Katya about that, but if they were on their way to challenge DJ, Teddy should probably know about it.

'What?' he asked.

'Well, when we spied on the Followers that night, someone was watching us from the edge of the wood. They stared at us until we drove away.'

'You think that was DJ?'

'I didn't think about it at the time, but it might have been her. All we saw was someone tall wearing a cloak. DJ had warned me to keep away from them and I'd told her I worked in a café in the town centre. It wouldn't have been hard for her to work out which one, so she knew where to deliver the card.'

'Do you think she belongs to FH?'

'I don't know. I suppose she must, or she wouldn't have been there, would she?'

'Hmm,' he said, starting the car again and pulling out into the road. 'I have my suspicions about that.'

'But if it was her, then she must be a member.'

'We'll see,' he said. 'You and Ivo were there and you're not members.' He laughed. 'At least I hope you're not. You've not been double-crossing us all this time, have you?'

'Of course not,' said Jasmine indignantly, and then realised he'd been teasing her.

'Only joking,' he said. 'Although Katya's reaction would be interesting if she discovered she had double agents in her team.'

'She's taking it very seriously,' said Jasmine.

'And she's right to. There are some seriously nasty people out there.'

'So you agree with DJ?'

'I'll let you know when we've met her, but I suspect she's on to something and it's good that you are with me this evening.'

'It's exciting for me, but I don't see how it helps you.'

'Because from what I've discovered, DJ has a lot of useful information. If she knows you and I are working together, she'll be more likely to share it with us.'

'Do you think we'll be in any danger?'

'And end up like poor old Raymond?' He laughed. 'No. We're not in any danger from DJ. If my theory is correct, it's quite the opposite.'

He was losing her. How did he know who was dangerous and who wasn't?

'Trust me,' he said, with a grin.

She didn't have much choice, did she?

TEDDY SEEMED to know where he was going, and Jasmine wondered if he'd already been to check it out. He pulled into the car park, and they walked into the pub. 'Folk club?' Teddy asked a man standing behind the bar.

The man jerked his head towards a door at the end of the bar. 'Downstairs,' he said.

They made their way down a flight of creaky wooden steps and into a gloomy room where some young men were sorting cables, tapping on microphones and tuning various instruments. Jasmine's attention was caught by one of them lifting a banjo from its case, but then she was distracted as she noticed DJ, who was sitting on a stool on the far side of the room trying to fix her hair into an untidy bun with hairpins. 'She's over there,' Jasmine hissed at Teddy, nodding towards her.

As they approached, DJ looked up and scowled at them. 'You,' she said, pointing at Jasmine. 'I told you—'

'We know that,' said Teddy. 'But hear us out. You might be glad of our help.'

'Oh, yeah? What makes you think that? Anyway, I've got a gig to rehearse.'

Teddy looked around at the mess of cables, untidy heaps of chairs and piles of sheet music. 'Doesn't look like anything's going to happen down here any time soon. Join us for a drink upstairs and we can discuss it.'

DJ followed them, reluctantly Jasmine thought, back to the bar, where she ordered a pint and settled herself at a table in a dark corner. Teddy bought a pint for himself and an orange juice for Jasmine, all of which he paid for with a credit card.

'Right,' said DJ as he and Jasmine joined her at the table. 'What's this all about?'

'We want to know all about the Followers of Herne,' said Teddy.

Nothing like jumping in with both feet, Jasmine thought. She didn't think she'd have been that direct, but then, unlike her, Teddy hadn't been warned by DJ not to have anything to do with them.

'What makes you think I know anything?' said DJ. 'And if I do, why would I tell you?'

Teddy started counting on his fingers. 'First, you warned Jasmine about them. Why would you do that if you don't know who they are and what they do? Second, I believe you have infiltrated them and that would take a lot of doing. You must have more than a passing interest in them.'

That was risky, Jasmine thought. What if DJ was an actual member and was about to leap at them with a knife? But that was hardly likely in a crowded pub. Teddy, she hoped, knew a lot more than he'd told her.

DJ sighed and tapped a black painted fingernail against her glass. 'How do you know I'm not one of them?' she asked. 'And how do I know I can trust you?'

'So are you admitting you were there in the park with them the other night?' Teddy asked, not answering her question. 'And you then sent Jasmine a warning. Either of those tell me you are not one of them and that somehow you got yourself in there, presumably with none of them suspecting anything. So that answers your first question.'

'And your second point?'

'Did you infiltrate them?'

'No, I didn't, but I admit I was there that night. I'm not saying any more unless I know I can trust you.'

'You can, and you'll have to take our word for that. We're just interested in how Raymond Pierce was *dealt with* and why. We're really not bothered about people prancing around in the park in the middle of the night if that's all they're doing.'

DJ shrugged and pushed a strand of hair behind her ear. 'You think I can help with that?'

'I think we can help each other.'

DJ stared into her drink for a moment. 'You could be right. I just don't want to see Jasmine in any danger.'

'But you've no objection to me being in danger,' said Teddy with a grin.

'I guess you can take care of yourself.' She smiled back at him. The first time Jasmine had seen her smile.

'And who,' Teddy continued, 'is looking after you?'

'Good point,' she said. 'I suppose I'd better tell you why I got involved. But you have to promise to be very, very careful who you talk to. After what happened to Pierce, you could be putting my own life in danger. That is, if I haven't already done that myself.'

'You really can trust us,' said Jasmine, reaching across the table for her hand.

DJ nodded and gave Jasmine's hand a squeeze. 'Okay,' she said, taking a deep breath. 'You've already worked out that the Followers of Herne are a secret group of thirteen members who meet regularly at night and in different locations within the park. They communicate through a heavily secure website. By the way, I don't know how you managed to breach that to discover the meeting place.'

Teddy shook his head. 'Nothing to do with me,' he said. 'I only heard about it afterwards.'

DJ turned to Jasmine. 'Want to elaborate?'

Jasmine opened the photo she'd taken at the back of DJ's shop and showed it to her.

'Okay,' said DJ. 'That was careless of me. But it doesn't explain how you knew the passwords.'

'They were on a card hidden in the lining of Pierce's wallet. The one that was stolen from him the night he died. The person who stole it took the bank cards and threw the wallet into the bushes, where it was found by Ivo's friend.'

'Ivo?'

'He's another member of our group.'

'Oh yeah, breakfast club people. I've watched you at your café.'

'You've been to *Jasmines*? I've never seen you there.'

'I was intrigued after you told me about finding the pendant. You told me a bit about who you were when we met before. It wasn't too hard to work out where your café was. I didn't come in, just watched you through the window.'

'And that's how you knew where to deliver the card.'

'Ladies,' said Teddy. 'This is all very interesting, but we came to find out more about the Followers of Herne and why you are spying on them.'

'Like I said, they are a group of thirteen, all high-powered businesspeople who meet for what they describe as 'protection of mutual interests'. *Protection* in this case being a rather loaded word.'

'Like a protection racket?' Teddy asked.

'Something like that,' said DJ. 'But instead of extorting money to protect a business, they take care of rivals. And when I say take care of, I mean get rid of.'

'You mean they kill them?'

'I wouldn't put it past them. But they are usually more subtle than that. They can hack into records and make it look as if there are financial irregularities, they set up honey traps with a view to blackmail, they have all kinds of underhand means of destroying blameless companies.'

'But why?' Jasmine asked. 'What's in it for them?'

'Usually a chance to take them over at a bargain price, or cash in by poaching their customers.'

'And your interest in them?'

'I had a friend, a very close friend, who was in the jewellery trade. He was targeted by them. First with an offer to buy him out, and when he refused, they began a relentless attack on him which lasted for months. I won't go into details, but about a year after it all began, he was found hanging from a beam in his parents' garage. That's when I started plotting their downfall.' She wiped away a tear. 'I felt partly responsible,' she said. 'I took the commission to make the pendants from a colleague a few years ago. I had my suspicions about who they were. I should have warned him.'

'Couldn't you have gone to the police?' Jasmine asked.

'The Followers of Herne have long tentacles. I couldn't be sure they didn't have someone high up in the police working for them.'

'And you knew Raymond Pierce?'

'I met him when he came to order his pendant soon after he'd been recruited. He wasn't supposed to do that. New recruits are given a special online order form and it's all done electronically. The pendants are collected from me by a courier and delivered to an anonymous postbox. Anyway, Pierce was quite chatty. He was never going to be a model member of the group. He let slip that he belonged to them and even at that stage he was having doubts about what they did. But once you're in, there's no getting out again. They have ways of keeping you, information you don't want made public, unpaid debts, tax fraud, that type of thing. Anyone recruited will have been vetted extremely carefully. There's nothing they don't know about you.'

'So if you want to leave, they kill you?' said Jasmine, finding it hard to believe.

'I don't think they were going to kill Raymond,' said DJ. 'They just planned to make his life a misery because he was threatening to leave. I haven't discovered what happened yet, but I think that the member assigned to scare him that night decided to do rather more than that. It looks like one of them had a personal grudge against him and volunteered to do the dirty work when the group said it was time to target him. But I decided to join one of their meetings to try to find out.'

'How?' asked Teddy. 'There are thirteen members. I assume they can count, so even with black cloaks and hoods they would probably notice if there was one extra.'

'I wasn't actually part of the ceremony. I hid in the tress and watched, just like you and Ivo did.'

'But you were dressed like they were.'

'For protection. If I had been spotted, I could have passed for one of them, hopefully before they did any counting.'

'So how did you know where the meeting was?' Jasmine asked. 'We had the passwords from the wallet. How did you get them?'

'Raymond let slip that for initiation of new members they always went to that part of the park. I knew they always met on Sundays, so I took a chance on it being there that night. I hoped I would recognise some of the members.'

'And did you?'

'Only one of them. I recognised the leader from when he first visited me about making the pendants. He's head of an investment bank in the city.'

'Do you know a man called Edwin Eastman?' asked Teddy. 'We think he might be a member.' He showed her a photo on his phone.

'Doesn't look familiar,' she said. 'But it was a dark night and I didn't get to see many of their faces even when they took their hoods off.'

'He can't have been there that night,' said Jasmine. 'He was in hospital.'

'Yes, of course,' said Teddy. 'What would happen if one of them couldn't make the meeting? Can they send a substitute?'

'No idea,' said DJ. 'But I shouldn't think they'd risk it. They'd just be one short. They probably have a way of passing on what went on at the meeting.'

'And there were thirteen of them there that night?' he asked.

DJ and Jasmine both nodded.

'Looks like we can rule out Eastman, then,' said Teddy.

Jasmine felt sorry for him. Eastman had an alibi for the night of the murder and now it looked like he wasn't involved in the Followers of Herne either.

'Doesn't matter,' said Teddy. 'I've plenty more leads to follow.'

'There was a woman,' said Jasmine. 'They called her Hestia.'

'There are a couple of women. Hestia was chosen to do the initiation ritual that night. It's a big honour, apparently. I think she may have been one of Pierce's sponsors when he joined. He said she'd been involved in the design of the pendants when the group first started.'

'Pierce seems to have been a mine of useful information,' said Teddy. 'Ironic, really, since that's given us the only clue we have about why he was killed.'

'He was a real blabbermouth,' said DJ. 'I'm guessing that's what got him into trouble and why he had to be got rid of.'

'And the leader was the only one you recognised that night?' Teddy asked.

'It was a disappointment,' she admitted. 'I'd hoped to be able to name a few more of them.'

'And do what?' asked Teddy.

'Build a portfolio of who they are and what they've done and then expose them.'

'To the police?'

'Maybe, or in the press.'

'Well,' said Jasmine. 'You're in luck. Teddy's a journalist.'

DJ gave her a withering look. 'I know that,' she said. 'Why do you think I agreed to have a drink with you?'

'You two knew each other already?' said Jasmine. How come Teddy hadn't told her earlier?

'Our paths have crossed before,' said Teddy.

'An incident I prefer to forget,' said DJ.

'Don't worry,' said Teddy with a grin. 'Your secret's safe with me.'

'What are we going to do next?' Jasmine asked, not wanting to be drawn into their murky past, whatever it was.

'First, I'm going to wring the neck of Tommy Brooke, the banjo player,' said DJ.

'Why?' asked Teddy. 'Does he play out of tune?'

'Tommy has a van and we use it to drive our equipment around when we've got a gig. We were playing at a pub near Ascot and he was supposed to collect an amp we were borrowing from a guy who lives in a grace and favour house in the lower ward. You can't park there so he and a mate were going to carry it down to the Queen Victoria statue. Tommy was supposed to park there and wait for them. But he didn't turn up and the next thing I knew, the little twerp had got himself arrested for using stolen credit cards. He said he'd been there, but it turns out he was waiting in the road near the King George statue that you can see from the road at the Long Walk instead of the Queen Vic one in town. He went for a bit of a wander down the Long Walk while he was waiting and found a wallet. He kept the bank cards that were in it and threw the wallet into the bushes.'

'Pierce's wallet?'

'As it turned out, yes. And to make it worse, it seems he chucked away the only really useful clue there was. Now it feels like I haven't made any progress at all. Lucky he wasn't arrested for murder. The police believed him when he said he'd found the wallet in the bushes. But now a man's dead and I'm no nearer exposing who these people are.'

'We took photos of the car number plates the night of the meeting,' said Jasmine, hoping to cheer her up.

'I don't see how that can help. You don't know who owns the cars.'

'Katya's police friend traced them for us. They are mostly company cars.'

'Figures,' said DJ, not looking any more cheerful.

'Jonny's going to check them out. He knows people who work for them.'

'Loads of people have company cars. Doesn't mean they're all evil.'

'It's a start,' said Teddy. 'Once I have names, I can do a bit of digging. That usually turns up some suspicious types.'

That seemed to cheer DJ a little. 'I can let you have names of people who were intimidating my friend. He kept evidence of threatening letters and stuff like that. His parents gave them to me when I told them I wanted to help.'

'That would be great,' said Teddy. 'I can feel a story coming together.'

'We should be ready to name all thirteen of them,' said Jasmine. 'Otherwise there could be more deaths.'

'How do you work that out?' asked DJ.

'Because once people are named in the press, others are going to start feeling vulnerable. They might think the named people are whistle-blowers or being paid by the press, and silence them before they can reveal any more. And we wouldn't be any closer to finding Pierce's murderer.'

'Right,' said Teddy. 'We need to build a dossier with thirteen names and supporting evidence, and hopefully while we're doing that, we'll discover which of them killed Pierce. Once that goes public the whole thing will start to tumble like a house of cards.'

'We should meet again when Jonny comes up with some names. You could come to our next meeting,' said Jasmine, smiling at DJ.

'You should be getting back to your rehearsal, or whatever atrocities you've planned for your banjo guy,' said Teddy. 'And I must get Jasmine home before her dad thinks I've abducted her.'

'So we'll see you at *Jasmine's* on Friday?'

DJ nodded. 'I'll try to get someone to cover at the shop, but that could be difficult. Can you meet in the evening?'

'Right,' said Teddy, downing the last of his pint. 'Which of us is going to break the news to Katya?'

29

J onny sat at his desk, with Harold snoring at his feet, and
booted up his computer. There was an email from Jasmine
with a short summary of the meeting she and Teddy had had
with DJ about the Followers of Herne. DJ had been right to
warn Jasmine not to have anything to do with them. If her account
was correct, they were a nasty lot. A dead end as far as Edwin
Eastman was concerned, on account of his alibi, although his involvement with Stella didn't let him off the hook entirely. Even if he wasn't
a member of the Followers, he could still be implicated in Pierce's
death.

His thoughts turned to the pendant in the tree. Ripped from
Pierce as part of his disgrace, perhaps, and left there as a reminder to
other members who might consider straying. Its location in the tree
suggested that Raymond was connected to them. If so, there would be
a case for investigating further and that was a job for the police. And
the police wouldn't be interested unless they could give them some
names. So it was time for him to get down to it and work on the list
that Lugs had sent Katya.

Half an hour later, Jonny hadn't made a lot of progress. He'd
expected it to be straightforward. His task was simply to find out

more about the owners of cars who had parked in the car park that night. It should be easy. Company directors appeared on websites, online lists, at Companies House and as members of golf clubs and charity organisations like the Lions Club. But he was not sure where that would get him. There was no way of linking the names he *did* find to any of the cars. It was all too anonymous. And even if his searches went well, he would only be halfway. There were only seven cars on the list, so they must have given each other lifts, which he found strange. Did it mean some of them lived near each other? Was membership of the Followers of Herne decided by area? Or it might be a way for members to keep an eye on each other. That was sinister. But the whole idea of meeting at night dressed in head-to-toe black was sinister. A lack of trust probably shouldn't surprise him.

After another half hour he still wasn't making much progress. He'd begun with the names on the list. He only had two actual names, the other five cars being registered to companies. The names meant nothing to him. They should. He was, or had been, a local businessman himself and had contacts with companies all over the country. He googled both names but found nothing helpful. They were not unusual names so there were thousands of results. He tried adding more search terms: CEO; company chairman; board of directors – nothing. He tried googling the registration numbers instead but that only told him what he already knew – the make of the cars, confirmation that they were insured and how old they were.

Perhaps he'd have more luck with the company cars. In his experience, company cars were usually driven by the sales teams or company directors. There were advantages to using a company car as a director, mostly tax ones, but that had never seemed quite honest. Jonny had always preferred to drive his own car and leave the contract cars to those of his employees who really needed them. No wonder, he thought, that he'd never been approached as a potential Follower of Herne. He wasn't ruthless enough. And his company was far too transparent. Not that he'd ever been interested in joining clandestine groups. He should warn Marcus, though. From what DJ had said, he could well be a target. If DJ was correct, FH members were involved in things like financial services, or import and export companies. Cardboard packaging had provided Jonny and his family with a comfortable lifestyle, but it was probably nothing compared to those of the people he was searching for. They'd have two or three houses, yachts and offshore bank accounts. But to get those, they'd have been ruthless and would have no scruples about squeezing the life out of smaller companies.

The first name to come up proved that. A company who operated worldwide in various commodity markets. Jonny wasn't sure what that implied, but it was probably way out of his league business-wise. The next four companies he searched were similar in the vagueness of their business. All were registered at Companies House, but that meant very little. People had been known to register companies with entirely fictitious names and stolen addresses. There was also a complete lack of information about the personal lives of those that ran them. No Facebook pages, nothing on Instagram, TikTok or any other social media site. He shouldn't be surprised by that. People operating at the darker ends of business wouldn't be posting pictures of their offspring, summer holidays and meals out.

It was disappointing not to find either Edwin Eastman or his waste management company on the list. Even if he wasn't a member of the followers, he might have been connected in some way and appeared on a list of directors or shareholders. That would have brought things together. A further connection between him and Pierce, as well as a link to Teddy Strang's research. Eastman was in hospital the night of Pierce's death, but that didn't let him off the hook completely.

Jonny had another idea and checked Eastman on the council website. He lived on the River at Bray, which made Jonny wonder what he was doing twenty miles away in Beaconsfield the night of the murder. They could rule out Eastman as a hands-on murderer on account of his alibi, and it was also looking increasingly unlikely that he had anything to do with the Followers of Herne. Jonny wondered if that let Stella off the hook as well. Probably not. It just meant she was not acting as Eastman's accomplice, or Eastman as hers. A pity.

Jonny had constructed a nice, tidy theory in which Stella returned from Spain for half a day, laced Raymond's drink with extra beta blockers and left Eastman to lure him to the Copper Horse, where he'd employed an assassin to finish him off. But the call to Raymond's phone had come from an advertising company, which was a long way from waste management and, as far as Jonny knew, Stella had nothing to do with either.

He returned to his search of cars. There were two more that he hadn't looked at in detail and both belonged to companies that were a long way from waste management. One was an upmarket property firm operating in west London, the other a vague-sounding organisation named only by the initials GH&L. He found some details of the CEO of the property company and decided he was pretty much what one would expect a director of a property company who also belonged to a covert group would look like – three grand suit, designer haircut and no doubt handmade shoes. He couldn't see the man's feet in the photo, but no one who wore a suit like that would wear shoes from a high street store. GH&L gave little away on their website. No photos or names of directors but they seemed to be something to do with international model agencies.

He'd failed, Jonny thought, shutting down his computer. Jasmine had Ivo and discovered amazing things. Teddy and Jasmine had found an important link through Darkjeweller. Katya had a way of eliciting useful information from her police friend as well as keeping them all on track. He almost expected her to appear with a huge crime board like the ones the police always used on TV. But Jonny had done nothing much. Except, he suddenly remembered, discovering that Stella had returned from Spain rather sooner than she had led them to believe. Katya had asked him to keep an eye on Stella, so that's what he should do. Right now. *No time like the present,* he thought with renewed enthusiasm. But he shouldn't confront Stella with the evidence he had, the copy of her boarding pass. Katya was right about that. It would scare her away and then they'd never know the truth or the extent of her involvement in her husband's death. It was possible she had a perfectly good reason for getting the dates wrong, or for returning for a day, but they needed to know what it was, if only to eliminate her as a suspect.

He could chat to Stella, see if he could elicit the truth without actually confronting her with the evidence. He wasn't sure how to do that, but perhaps he could lead her gently into the topic of her visits to her cousin in Spain and hope she'd inadvertently let something drop about her recent travel arrangements. He would pay her a visit on the pretext of offering to help with the funeral. No one would want to do that on their own and, as far as he knew, Stella had no one to help her. He knew the body had been released but had heard nothing from Stella about funeral arrangements. He would go right now. 'Come on, Harold,' he said, reaching for his lead. 'Let's go and see Stella. There could be a biscuit in it for you.' Harold wagged his tail. He had, Jonny discovered, learnt the word *biscuit*.

SOMETHING'S DIFFERENT, Jonny thought as he pulled up outside Stella's house. A sale board had appeared on the grass verge at the entrance to the drive. Stella clearly wasn't one for hanging around. Maybe she was making a quick getaway before anyone discovered her lie about when she'd returned from Spain. *But no, he thought, it can take months to sell a house, what with wrangling over offers, solicitors' searches and sorting out removals. Not to mention finding somewhere else to live.* Perhaps Stella had done that already. She'd mentioned moving abroad, but perhaps she'd changed her mind and was now reconsidering a development of luxury flats closer to the town centre. They were going to be popular with commuters using the nearby and recently opened Elizabeth line, which would whiz them from Slough to the centre of London at twice the speed they were used to. Stella might have snapped one of them up while there were still some to snap. But Jonny didn't think they were anywhere near ready to move into, so what would she do in the meantime? She'd need to delay completion if she sold her house quickly. Unless she planned to stay in a hotel for several months. Or go off to Spain again. People did that, he supposed. Having lived in the same house for nearly forty years, Jonny remembered very little about the hassle of selling up and moving.

He rang the doorbell and was greeted by Stella, who was clutching a cup of something and dressed in a rather fetching bright red trouser suit. She was really not the popular idea of a grieving widow. She should either be dressed in head-to-toe black, or look as if she didn't care one way or another about how she looked. Either way, red trouser suits just weren't appropriate. If he'd been remotely attracted to Stella, he'd probably prefer the slightly scruffy book-sorting outfit she'd worn when he last visited her. But he wasn't, so what she wore was none of his business. Except perhaps in his role of detective, which might lead him to speculate on what the average murder suspect wore.

As usual, she invited him inside. 'There's coffee on the go,' she said, waving her cup at him. Harold trotted into the house behind them, no doubt listening out for the rattle of the biscuit tin. He wasn't disappointed. Stella appeared in minutes with a second cup of coffee and a tin of biscuits.

'I was just wondering about funeral arrangements,' said Jonny, passing Harold a digestive biscuit while sitting in a comfortable chair by the French windows. The lounge looked considerably tidier than when he'd last been there. 'I heard they've released Raymond's body. Do you need any help?'

'All done,' she said, swallowing the last of her coffee and putting the cup down on a small table. 'Yesterday.'

He stared at her in surprise. Didn't funerals take a lot of planning? When his father died there'd been endless discussions about music, favourite hymns and who was going to speak or read something. And not least, who was going to pay for it all and where the wake would be held. He remembered discussions about the relative merits of sausage rolls and sandwiches over ham and salad. Stella must have put it all together in double-quick time. Was that suspicious? Did she need to dispose of Raymond as fast as possible in case someone suggested further investigations into the cause of his death? 'That was rather sudden, wasn't it?' he said, searching her expression for any sign of guilt.

'No point in waiting,' she said, her face a mask of blamelessness. 'The undertaker fitted us in at the last minute. Why? Did you want to come?'

How could he answer that? Saying no would sound rude, saying yes would be ghoulish. 'Many there?' he asked instead.

'No,' she said. 'Raymond wasn't a social type.'

'Not even his bridge pals, or people who belong to that group you told me about?'

'Catherine Wallace sent flowers, but I don't know who else was in this group so I couldn't let them know.'

'What about Edwin Eastman? I thought they were quite close. I know they played bridge together.'

'Edwin? He wasn't a close friend of Raymond's. And anyway, he couldn't have come. He's been in hospital.'

'Sorry to hear that,' said Jonny, wondering how she knew. 'Lives alone, I believe.'

'Yes,' she said, with a little smile. 'He's divorcing his wife. She moved out some time ago.'

'Ah,' said Jonny, not sure how to bring up the subject of Stella's visits to Spain.

'Look,' she said impatiently, piling his coffee cup onto her own and glancing towards the kitchen. 'It's lovely to see you and all that, but I need to get on. I have to leave soon.' She looked at him as if she hoped he was about to do the same.

Jonny nodded at a pile of suitcases near the door. 'Going away?'

'Yes, the taxi will be here any minute.'

'Back to Spain again?' he asked. 'You seem to go backwards and forwards to Madrid rather a lot.'

'So? I have a cousin there. Anyway, that's not where I'm going this time.'

'Right,' he said, zipping up his coat and picking up Harold's lead. 'I should be going too. But before I do, would you like to tell me why you didn't mention that you were not actually in Spain the night

Raymond died?' She was leaving anyway, and regardless of what Katya had said, this could be his only chance to uncover the truth.

'What? Why do you ask?'

'I saw your boarding card last time I was here. It fell out of one of your magazines. I just wondered why you didn't tell the police.'

She sat down suddenly, looking annoyed rather than scared. 'I suppose I'd better explain,' she said. 'Although it's really none of your business. Yes. I flew back that day.'

'Did you see Raymond?'

'No. I didn't come here at all. I was meeting someone, but he wasn't there, so I took a taxi back to Heathrow and flew to Madrid early the next morning.'

'Why didn't you tell the police?'

'Because they would have thought exactly what you are thinking right now. That I came back to kill my husband.'

'And you didn't?'

'No, of course I didn't. Raymond wasn't worth the effort. I was planning to divorce him and settle down with the man I'm in love with, but...'

'But?'

She sighed. 'I was very angry when he failed to turn up that night. I'd spent three hours waiting at the Bull in Gerrards Cross and was furious. The taxi cost me a fortune, a double fortune since I had to get another one and go straight back to Heathrow. I flew back to Madrid to think things over for a few days. I decided to come back here, put divorce proceedings in place, sell the house and my share of the company and start again somewhere sunny. On my own. But of course, when I got back...'

'Raymond was dead. Very convenient,' said Jonny.

'In some ways, yes.'

'And in other ways?'

'There's a lot to do when someone dies. It wasn't going to be the quick getaway I'd hoped for.'

So her plans had been disrupted; lover failed to turn up, husband dead. He had little sympathy for her.

There was a ring on the doorbell. 'That'll be my taxi,' said Stella, picking up her handbag and heading for the door. 'I'm sorry but I need you to leave.'

Not much to stay for, Jonny thought as he and Harold followed her into the entrance hall. 'Can I ask where you're going?'

'No,' she said abruptly. She opened the door and pointed the driver in the direction of her cases. 'Let me help,' said Jonny, picking up one of the larger ones and loading it into the boot of the waiting taxi.

'Thanks, mate,' said the driver.

'No problem,' said Jonny. 'Glad to help. Heading to the station?'

'Heathrow,' he said.

Stella climbed into the back seat of the taxi. 'Goodbye, Mr Cardew,' she said. 'Thank you for your company.' She slammed the door and didn't look back at him as the taxi turned into the road.

It was only when Jonny was turning into his own drive that something clicked in his memory. Gerrards Cross. Quite close to Beaconsfield, where Edwin Eastman had been involved in a road traffic accident the very night of Raymond's death. They already knew he couldn't have been at the Copper Horse when Raymond died. And if she was kicking her heels at the Bull, neither could Stella. But they could have been planning to be together. And now Stella was heading off to Heathrow. Was Edwin Eastman about to do the same?

30

'We don't have evening meetings.' Katya scowled. Pity they weren't on FaceTime, where Teddy would get the full benefit of her bad-tempered expression. 'We're the *breakfast* club detectives. There's a clue in the name.'

'Look,' said Teddy, his sigh audible over the phone. 'You asked me to follow up Darkjeweller, which I did yesterday evening. You didn't specify a time of day, so I didn't realise I was limited to breakfast hours. In any case, haven't you heard of all day breakfast? It's very popular at fashionable establishments.'

Katya hadn't, but it sounded like an idea she could go along with. All the same, a meeting in the evening? 'The café's closed in the evening. Are you expecting Jasmine to keep it open for us?'

'She doesn't need to serve food and it'll be easier for her if she hasn't got to keep one eye on the customers. We'll have her full attention. And DJ has to work during the day.'

'DJ's coming to the meeting?' Was Katya losing all control over *her* team? A team she'd put in place, encouraged, cajoled and organised.

'She's got some very useful stuff on the Followers of Herne, and an action plan. We don't want her going off on her own with that, do we? She'd be putting herself in danger, and if she's successful she'd get all the glory. Your detectives wouldn't even get a mention.'

Well, they could do with a bit of action. And yes, if there was a plan afoot, Katya wanted to be part of it. Dammit, she wanted to be in charge of it. She was the only one of them with any experience. A load of amateurs blundering around could make a complete dog's breakfast of the case. 'Okay,' she said. 'If you insist. And only if Jasmine doesn't mind.'

'She doesn't,' said Teddy.

'You already asked her?' Who the hell did he think he was, making plans?

'I'll explain when I see you,' said Teddy.

What did that mean? But she could see his point. So an evening meeting it would be. Katya had now been voted an honorary member of the breakfast club and she wanted to take full advantage of the free breakfasts. But if things were developing rapidly, an evening meeting when the café was closed probably wasn't such a bad idea. And DJ had something to share with them. Did that mean she was also now an unofficial member? Or even an official one because, Teddy having dropped a few hints about his meeting with her, she was the only one of them to have been personally involved with the Followers of Herne.

KATYA CALLED JONNY AND IVO, who were both happy about meeting in the evening. Ivo had a full day's work and told her an evening meeting was a good idea as it would mean not letting customers down. Jonny, always happy to go along with whatever was organised, told her he'd be on his own anyway. Belinda was attending a performance of *An Inspector Calls,* a collaborative production staged by Datchet Men in Sheds and the Eton Wick branch of the Women's Institute. 'Anything that gets me out of that can only be a good thing,' he told Katya. A call to Jasmine confirmed what Teddy had said, that she was quite happy for them to use the café in the evening.

'We'll have to call ourselves *all day breakfast detectives,*' said Katya with a laugh, but rather hoping the idea might catch on and that Jasmine would take the hint and serve them with a nice fry-up before they got started.

Jasmine had soup left over from her lunch customers, so it wasn't quite the meal Katya had hoped for. But beggars can't be choosers and you can't beat a nice bowl of home-made soup and some crusty rolls. By the time Katya arrived, Jasmine had moved two tables together and had six bowls ready on the counter. She looked up as Katya came through the door. 'The group's growing,' she said.

Katya agreed that it was indeed growing, but didn't feel too sure that she wanted it that way. She'd never have thought of partnering up with Teddy Strang, and if it hadn't been for that chance meeting at the coroner's office, it wouldn't have happened. Throughout her police career she'd gone along with the general mistrust of the press, who hounded them for information about cases and then reported it inaccurately. Her police colleagues would have thought she was crazy. It was akin to teaming up with the enemy. Well, not quite the enemy. That would be the criminals, although journalists came close and were definitely among those not to be trusted. But she had to admit now that Teddy had his uses. She wouldn't have known about Eastman if it hadn't been for him. Although, as things turned out, it was looking less and less likely that Eastman had anything to do with the murder.

She wasn't sure she trusted Darkjeweller either. How involved was she with the Followers of Herne? She made their pendants for them, but that didn't necessarily mean she was one of them, just someone who did business with them. It probably wasn't that easy to find makers of regalia for secret groups, and Darkjeweller advertised as catering for all pagan requirements. And she was local. They might not have had a lot of choice. But making pendants for them was fulfilling a commission. It didn't mean DJ was complicit in what- ever the group carried out. In fact, from what Katya had learnt about her involvement, DJ had more reason than any of them to uncover them for who they really were. Apart, of course, from Raymond Pierce, for whom it was too late to do anything.

But suppose DJ wasn't just a maker of pendants. Perhaps she was a spy planted by the Followers to find out how much Katya and her team knew about what they were up to. But DJ hadn't contacted *them*. Jasmine had contacted *her*, and Katya would be the first to admit that if Jasmine hadn't gone against orders and gone to find her, they'd not know as much as they did about the Followers of Herne.

Katya sighed. Leading a team of amateurs was far harder than being part of a police team who all knew their place, did what they were told and didn't tend to stray off and do things on their own. But Katya felt that, amateur though they were, they had made much more of the case than the police had. Apart from Lugs, none of the pros seemed remotely interested in the possibility that Pierce had been murdered. And being part of a police team wasn't always a walk in the park. She'd been taken off cases simply because pushy men wanted them, felt they were entitled to them. She had more than a suspicion that she'd been overlooked for promotion because she was a woman and she'd had to suffer a lot of behind the scenes banter.

Now all that had changed. Jasmine, Ivo and Jonny all looked up to her. Okay, sometimes she had to work hard to keep them on track. But their hearts were in the right place, bless them. Even Teddy had been a surprise. But she could hardly say he did what she told him. Perhaps he should be treated more as an adviser than a member of her team. She couldn't imagine him taking orders from her. She'd not tried giving him any, but he had come up with some very useful information and was probably about to do so again after his meeting with DJ.

Katya looked up from her notes as Ivo, Jonny and Harold arrived. An interesting friendship, Katya thought, Jonny and Ivo. Surprising what bonding over dog care could do. Absolutely nothing in common; different backgrounds, life experiences, ages. And yet they were the best of friends. She was even warming to Harold. Not really a dog person herself, Katya had never imagined owning one. And if for any reason she ever changed her mind, it would be something small and fluffy. And Harold was not, nor ever would be, small and fluffy. Pretty much the opposite. He looked like an ugly thug of a dog. But looks could be deceiving. She'd discovered that, battered though he was, Harold was sweet-natured and loyal. And you could do a lot worse than that in a dog.

Teddy and DJ arrived last. Another unusual partnership and one that Katya had instigated herself, mostly to protect Jasmine from any harm DJ might inflict on her. But it seemed to have turned out well. DJ had been a mine of information, Teddy told her. And it looked as if they got on well with each other, but that surprised her less. They were both more worldly than either Jonny or Ivo, and if Teddy's story came to anything it would probably do no harm to DJ's business. Unless, of course, DJ turned out to be a Follower of Herne spy, in which case Teddy's story, if successful, would probably destroy her and her business. And if not success- ful, it might well destroy Teddy. But she couldn't worry about that now.

THE SOUP WAS DELICIOUS, and Katya concentrated on enjoying it. The meeting could wait. Well-fed, they'd all pay more attention, and it didn't take long to polish off a bowl of soup. Katya wondered if there were any cakes left. She knew everything the café served was freshly baked each day and it wouldn't do for food to go to waste.

Once they'd all finished, Jasmine cleared away the bowls and made space on the table. She didn't mention cakes, but perhaps when the meeting finished...

They all remained seated around the table, apart from Harold who settled in his usual spot underneath it. 'I've asked Teddy and DJ to join us because they have important information to share,' said Katya, studying the notes she'd made on her clipboard. 'Let's get started.' She put her finger on the first item on her list. 'It looks as if we can now reject both Stella Pierce and Edwin Eastman as suspects. Jonny has talked to Stella, and she has explained her early return to the country. Everything she told Jonny can easily be verified. She's now leaving to start a new life abroad.'

'Do we know where?' Teddy asked.

'Again, if it matters it should be easy enough to find out. She was headed to Heathrow so it would just be a case of checking passenger lists.'

'And Eastman?' Ivo asked.

'Eastman's car accident gives him an alibi for the night of the murder. He is not connected to any of the parked cars whose numbers have all been checked, and in any case he was still in hospital until yesterday evening. It's very unlikely that he had anything to do with the Followers of Herne.' She tapped her pen on the table, feeling that their attention was wandering. 'What we do have is information from DJ that could take our enquiry in a new and interesting direction. DJ, would you like to explain?'

'Do you all know who Tommy Brooke is?' DJ asked.

'He's the one who used Pierce's bank card,' said Ivo.

'That's right. He plays the banjo in a band I sometimes sing with. And now it seems he's also involved with the Followers of Herne.'

'Really?' said Teddy. 'He doesn't sound like the type at all. From what you told me the other night I thought they were all rich businesspeople.'

'He's not a member. At least, I'm pretty sure he's not. I know him through the band and he's run some errands for us in the past. But now I've discovered that he also works for at least one of the members as a messenger. I realised after we talked that the night he failed to turn up to collect the amp was the night of Pierce's death. I hadn't made the connection before. I was too busy being angry about the gig it cost us. But we know he took the bank cards and he's already said he was in the park that night.'

'Parked in the road that crosses the Long Walk and within sight of the Copper Horse,' said Teddy. 'I admit I didn't make the connection either, but it puts him in the park at the time of Pierce's death, doesn't it?'

'So I was right,' said Ivo. 'He murdered Pierce for his wallet.'

'I don't think you're wrong,' said Teddy. 'But it's more complicated than that. Someone called Pierce while he was in the taxi. It was a premeditated killing, not just a robbery gone wrong.'

'Ah,' said Katya. 'It's beginning to make sense. Pierce upset one the Followers, or all of them, and one of them was elected to deal with him. Whoever that was enlisted Brooke to help them. They lured Pierce to the park and killed him. Perhaps it was Brooke's job to move the body to where it was found the following morning. And he got greedy, took the wallet and started using the cards.'

'What about the pendant?' asked Ivo. 'Pierce wasn't wearing it when he was found. Jonny and I spotted it in the tree a couple of days later.'

That, Katya admitted to herself, was a puzzle.

'I was just wondering,' said Jonny, 'what the weather was the morning the body was found.'

Jasmine started clicking on the keyboard of her laptop. 'Overcast,' she said, looking up a few moments later.

'And two days later, when Ivo and I found the pendant?'

'Sunny,' said Jasmine.

'So,' said Jonny. 'Perhaps the police missed it. There was no reason why they should look up into the tree while they were working on the scene. Ivo and I spotted it glinting in the sun.'

'It was actually Harold who saw it first,' said Ivo.

'That's right,' said Jonny. 'We only looked up into the tree because Harold was barking at something he saw in the branches. The police probably didn't have dogs with them, did they?'

'They wouldn't have,' said Katya. 'Not at a potential crime scene.'

'But why put the pendant there at all?' asked Jasmine.

Katya thought that through for a moment. 'Either,' she said slowly, 'so that it wouldn't be found on the body and mark him as a Follower, or for the exact opposite reason. To prove to the Followers that their orders had been carried out.'

'Or perhaps Brooke left it there intending to come back for it,' Teddy suggested. 'Are they worth anything?' he asked DJ.

'Not much,' said DJ. 'Not in materials, anyway. They're commissioned through a well-guarded website, so they do have a rarity value to anyone who knows what they are.'

'Does Brooke know you make them?'

'He might. He's collected packages from me for delivery to a PO box. I never thought of him as anything more than a delivery boy until yesterday evening.'

'What happened then?' Katya asked.

'I had a text message from an anonymous number.' She clicked on the message and handed it round:

> YOU'VE BEEN CALLED TO A MEETING [ANTLER EMOJI]
> TOMORROW NIGHT 11.30 IN THE DEER PARK
> [BANJO EMOJI] WILL ARRANGE TO PICK YOU UP
> AND ESCORT YOU TO THE MEETING
> COME ALONE

'Very cloak and dagger,' said Teddy, handing the phone back. 'If I didn't already know how dangerous this lot are, I'd think it was a teenage prank.'

'It could be just that,' said Katya. 'But we can't risk it.'

DJ nodded. 'I'd rather look stupid and get plastered all over TikTok by a load of teenagers than end up like Raymond Pierce.'

'Does Tommy Brooke go in for stupid pranks?' Jonny asked.

'He's never struck me as a prankster, and he's obviously not overly intelligent or he would never have risked using the bank cards. It's the first clue I've had that he's involved with the Followers, but alongside knowing he was in the park the night Pierce died, I think we need to assume he's taking orders from someone, not just tricking me for laughs.'

'We should definitely take it seriously,' said Katya. 'Do you know why they might have summoned you?'

'I think I must have been spotted in the park during their meeting the other night. And I'll be expected to account for myself.'

'Will you go?' Ivo asked. 'It sounds dangerous.'

'Of course I'll go,' said DJ. 'It's the only way I'm going to discover who they actually are. And if I don't go this time, they could try to get to me in some other way that I have no warning about. And that would definitely be dangerous.'

Katya made some notes on her clipboard and then tapped her pencil thoughtfully on what she'd written. 'We should go with you,' she said.

The others looked at her in surprise. 'How can we?' said Jonny. 'We can't all turn up at wherever Brooke arranges to meet DJ. Not if she's supposed to go on her own.'

He had a point, Katya thought. But she had the experience. She'd taken part in covert operations back in the day and there would be a way of doing it now. 'No,' said Katya. 'We need to follow her somehow, but without being noticed.' She just needed to work out how to do it.

'There won't be much time,' said Ivo. 'We don't know where Brooke is meeting DJ and if we follow her there, we'd be too easy to spot.'

'He might pick her up from where she lives,' said Katya. 'We could conceal ourselves outside her house and watch.'

'Where do you live?' asked Jasmine. 'Would it be possible to watch your house?'

'Block of flats in Datchet,' said DJ. 'There's not a lot of parking space. You'd have to kerb crawl.'

Not a good idea, Katya thought.

Teddy, who had been fiddling with his phone, looked up at them. 'We can track her,' he said. 'It's easy on a smartphone. We just need to set it up. There are several tracking apps, but actually as long as the person you want to track agrees, we won't need to do that. Just use *Find My Phone.* Would you be okay with that, DJ?'

'Yeah,' she said. 'I was hoping you might come up with something like that. I'd definitely feel safer if I thought you knew where I was.'

'What if DJ's made to leave her phone behind?' Jasmine asked. 'These Follower people are bound to know about phone tracking.'

'Easy,' said Teddy. 'We lend her one of ours. She can keep it in an inside pocket. I doubt they'll suspect her of having two phones. If she's told to leave her phone behind, we'll still have the second one to track her with.'

DJ was nodding. 'I'll make a fuss if Brooke tries to make me leave my phone. It will be more convincing. If I give in too easily it might make him suspicious.'

'So, Teddy, you can track one of the phones,' said Jonny. 'Who's going to track the other?'

'Me,' said Katya. *Damned if I'm going to be left out of any of this.* 'Teddy can track DJ's actual phone and I'll watch the other.'

'You don't drive, so you'll go with Teddy in his car?' said Jonny. 'How will he track DJ's phone if he's driving? Won't it be confusing?'

Katya was more indignant than confused. 'I can drive,' she said. 'I have special police training. I just don't own a car.'

Teddy was drawing a mind map on the back of an envelope. 'This is what we can do,' he said. 'Between us we have three cars.' He pointed to three circles that he'd drawn with the letters T, Jo and Ja inside them. 'I suggest we use two of them. Jasmine drove her dad's car the other night and there's a chance it could have been spotted, so we don't want to risk it being seen again.' He crossed out the 'Ja' circle. Then he drew lines from each of the other two and wrote names on them. One line said 'Teddy, Jasmine and Ivo'. On the other he wrote 'Katya and Jonny'. 'One driver and one tracker in each car, plus Ivo to keep contact between the two. Everyone agreed?'

'Fine with me,' said Jonny. 'You okay with me driving, Katya?'

Katya nodded. She'd prefer Jonny to Teddy any day.

'I'm hoping,' said Teddy, grinning at Jonny, 'that you don't drive some posh four-by-four in dazzling white, or with distinctive dayglo orange stripes.'

Jonny laughed. 'I wish,' he said. 'I'm not sure what Belinda's reaction would be to something flashy. It's just a boring, dark grey Honda.'

'Perfect,' said Teddy. 'That's settled then. We can follow at a discreet distance.' He rubbed his hands and grinned. 'All on for tomorrow night.'

He was enjoying this rather too much. All for the sake of a good story, Katya supposed. She tapped her pencil on the table again. It was time to reassert her control before Teddy took over the whole operation. 'Phones out, everyone,' she said. 'Check that we all have everyone's number. Who's going to lend DJ their phone? It can't be me or Teddy.'

'She can have mine,' said Jasmine. 'I'm in the café all day. If I need a phone, I can use Dad's.' She got out a phone in a bright pink case with a picture of kittens and handed it to DJ.

'Thanks,' said DJ, giving the kittens an unenthusiastic glance. 'I'll just take the phone. It'll be less bulky without the case.' She pulled the phone out of its case and slipped it into her pocket, handing the kittens back to Jasmine.

Not a cat person, Katya thought. *Not a pink person, either.* But DJ was right. Kittens aside, it would be a lot easier to conceal a phone without the case.

'Don't scratch it,' said Jasmine anxiously, putting the case in her pocket.

'Don't worry,' said DJ. 'I've got one of those long-sleeved thermal vests with an inside pocket. It will be quite safe. And I promise not to pretend to be you if anyone calls during the day.'

'You could redirect your calls to your dad's phone,' Teddy suggested. 'DJ can switch that to Ivo's in the evening if you give her your passcode.'

Jasmine wrote some numbers on a slip of paper and handed it to DJ.

'Good,' said Katya. 'That's all settled. We should meet here at ten tomorrow night. DJ, you must text us as soon as you hear from Brooke and we can track you from then on. Once you've made contact, we'll play it by ear. We might only need to keep an eye on where you are being taken, or we may need to intervene. We'll set off once we know you're headed for the park. It's only a few minutes' drive from here so you'll be easy to pick up. Ivo can make sure we all stay in contact. Jonny can have his phone on speaker when he's driving.'

'What about Harold?' Ivo asked.

'What about him?' said Katya, frowning. 'He can stay at Jonny's house for the evening, can't he?' They didn't need to take a dog with them.

'He could be useful,' said Ivo. 'He caught a burglar once.'

Katya sighed. Anyone would think he was a bloody police dog instead of an ugly mutt who spent his time snoring under tables.

'I don't mind if he comes in the car with us,' said Teddy.

'Yes,' said Jasmine. 'We can't leave him behind. He's one of the team.'

'And he was the one that found the pendant,' said Jonny. 'We'd never have come as far as this if he hadn't.'

'Oh, very well,' said Katya. *Pick your battles carefully. This one is not worth fighting.* 'As long as he stays in the car and keeps quiet.'

They spent the next half hour setting up their phones and checking that they worked. Jonny laughed when he saw the map with the six phones piled up on top of each other, each with a little cameo photo of the owner. 'Just remember that the photo of Jasmine will actually be DJ,' he said.

Katya gave him a withering look. 'And make sure they are all fully charged before we meet tomorrow,' she said. 'We can't risk losing touch with DJ because someone's phone is out of battery.'

'You'd better take this, then,' said Jasmine, unplugging her phone charger and handing it to DJ.

'Are you all clear about what you're doing?' asked Katya, looking around and noticing nods of agreement. 'If there are no more questions, we should go and get a good night's sleep and meet up here at ten tomorrow night.'

As they were standing up to leave, Katya pulled DJ into her arms. 'Just take care, love,' she said. 'Okay? And remember, we'll be watching you the whole way.'

DJ nodded. 'Thanks,' she said. 'Appreciate it.'

She's a lot more scared than she's letting on, Katya thought. They mustn't let her down.

Teddy took Jasmine's phone from her and fiddled with it for a few moments. Then he handed it back. 'I've put Jonny's number on emergency,' he said. 'Just press the side buttons if you get into any trouble.'

'Can you do the same for mine?' Jonny asked. 'Just in case I need to contact Ivo quickly.'

'Good thought,' said Teddy, tapping some keys on Jonny's phone and then handing it back to him.

They each hugged DJ in turn as she left.

Katya watched her with mixed feelings. Was this going to solve the case for them, as she hoped? Or would it all go horribly wrong?

Pull yourself together, she thought as she reached into her pocket for her hat and gloves and heaved herself out of her chair. *You've faced far worse than this. But not,* a small voice warned her, *with a bunch of amateurs.* People, she realised, that she'd grown very fond of.

KATYA DECIDED to call Lugs and give him the heads up about the plan. They might need backup if things didn't go well. There was no real evidence that any of it was dangerous, and she couldn't call the police out because of a few unsupported rumours that the Followers of Herne were anything more than a group of people who liked prancing around at night wearing cloaks. But if Lugs were to take her seriously, he would try to persuade her not to go. She decided instead to sound him out about whether or not he was on call.

'What are you up?' he asked in response to her question about his on-call nights that week.

'Just thinking you might like to go for a drink one evening when you're free,' she said.

'Pull the other one, Katya,' he said. 'If it was a drink you were after you'd have come straight out with it, not gone pussyfooting around with questions about my free time.'

Damn, she thought. *I've said too much.* She sighed. 'Look,' she said. 'It's probably nothing, but I've said I'll go with a young friend who's meeting someone in the park this evening. I'm just a bit concerned that this character she's meeting up with might be, well, you know, a bit dodgy.'

'Then tell her to meet them in a pub, somewhere there are plenty of people about.'

'It's not that kind of meeting and the pubs will be closed by then.'

'A night-time nature walk?' he asked. 'Look, I wasn't born yesterday. I know when you are planning something that's a bit, well, free range.'

She was going to have to be straight with him. She gave him a quick run-down on the Followers of Herne, but stressed Teddy's suspicions and possible story rather than Raymond Pierce's involvement. 'I'm just going with a group of friends to see what they are up to.'

'To spy on them, in other words.'

'I'm sure we won't be in any danger.'

'So why are you calling me?'

'Because I've not enough information to bring it to you officially but there's just a chance, a very small chance, that we might need help, and I want someone to know where we are.'

'In case you're abducted?'

'Don't be silly,' she growled. 'I'm just keeping you informed about my movements tonight.'

'Okay,' he laughed. 'Put my personal phone on speed dial. That way I can drum up help if you need it without going through official channels first. And you won't look stupid if it comes to nothing.'

'Perfect,' said Katya. 'You're a star. I'll owe you one.'

'Just take care. Any hint of trouble, you call me right away.'

'Will do,' she said. 'And trust me. I know not to put anyone in danger.'

AFTER SHE ENDED THE CALL, Katya thought about what to take with her. She'd caused some amusement shortly after she retired by buying an ex-army greatcoat from a second hand shop near the Victoria Barracks. A group of young squaddies had nudged each other and laughed at her. 'Planning to enlist, grandma?' one of them asked. She'd ignored them. They'd not be laughing now. For a few pounds, she'd kitted herself out with a coat that kept out the winter chill and which had enormous pockets. She wasn't a handbag person and those pockets had seen everything from her loose change to packs of sandwiches. She lifted the coat down from its place on a peg in the hall and emptied the pockets, examining each object in turn, deciding which she might or might not need. She rejected a pair of fingerless gloves, some sweet wrappers, a miniature Scots Guard in full uniform that she'd picked up from the gutter in St Leonards Road and a torn five-pound note. She kept a packet of Fisherman's Friends, a handy pack of Kleenex (almost full) and a ball of gardening string. Then she rummaged in her kitchen drawer and fished out a pair of handcuffs that she'd somehow forgotten to return when she retired. Pity she'd not been able to keep her taser, but that wasn't regular police issue. Tasers had to be signed out and accounted for, reports written when used and handed back for secure storage. She stuffed the handcuffs into her pocket, along with a length of washing line and a heavy torch. Then she set out for *Jasmine's,* calling DJ as soon as she arrived.

'Nothing yet,' said DJ. 'If he's taking me to the Deer Park, I'd expect him at around eleven, so you may have a bit of a wait. He might have been lying about the meeting place, I suppose, but I can't see why. As far as he knows, there's no one else involved. But the Deer Park could be a decoy to stop me letting anyone know where I'm going.'

'No worries,' said Katya, looking up as Teddy arrived with a rolled-up map under his arm. 'We'll be tracking you as soon as you give us the heads up that you're on your way. Wherever he takes you, we will know where you are.' Or at least where her phone was.

Teddy spread the map out on one of the tables and by the time Ivo and Jonny arrived, he'd marked some possible meeting places, approach roads to the Deer Park and a couple of likely parking spots.

'What's the plan?' Jonny asked.

'As soon as we know where they're headed, we'll set out and follow them,' said Katya. 'We'll stay close, even if it means giving ourselves away. We're not taking any risks with DJ's safety. Hopefully we can stay out of sight and listen to what they are saying, but if I think it's necessary, we'll intervene.'

They sat and waited for what seemed to all of them like a very long half hour. Then, at last, two phones pinged with a message. Katya clicked hers and read it. *He's here,* was all it said. 'We thought he was going to arrange a meeting place,' said Katya. 'Looks like he's picking her up at home.'

'Datchet to the Deer Park is only ten or fifteen minutes,' said Jonny, checking his own phone. 'They'll be there well before eleven-thirty.'

'We don't know exactly where they're meeting. It might not be the Deer Park at all,' said Teddy. 'And if it is the park, it could be quite a long way from the road.'

Katya's eyes were fixed on her phone screen. 'They've left,' she said, suddenly. 'Turned right into Victoria Road. They'll be headed to Albert Bridge, so it looks like the park after all.'

'Yup,' said Teddy. 'And she's got both phones with her.'

'We should go,' said Katya. 'We don't want them arriving too soon before us. It might be difficult to track them accurately once they're off the main road.'

Teddy handed his phone to Jasmine, who would be tracking DJ while he drove. 'I've disabled the login code,' he said. 'You don't need to worry if it turns off.' He picked up his keys and headed for the door, with Jasmine and Ivo close behind.

'Wait a minute,' said Jasmine, staring at the phone screen. 'They've turned left. That's away from Windsor. And now they've stopped.'

'They're at Boris the Bear,' said Katya, who'd also been checking.

'Boris the who?' asked Ivo.

'It's a big statue of a bear,' said Katya. 'On a patch of grass near some houses.'

'That can't be the meeting place, can it?' said Jonny. 'It's in the middle of the village and only about half a mile from DJ's flat.'

'No,' said Katya. 'They're moving again. They've turned round and headed back towards the bridge.'

'Why would they have gone there?' Ivo asked. 'Doesn't Brooke know where he's going?'

'They left DJ's phone there,' said Jasmine. 'So now we're relying on my phone to follow her.'

'Keep watching her phone,' said Katya. 'It could be a trap.'

'Okay,' said Jasmine.

'They've just crossed the bridge,' said Katya. 'So it looks like they are going to the park. Time to leave if we're not going to let them get too far ahead. I'm assuming they are going to stop as close as they can to the Deer Park, park somewhere along Albert Road and walk from there. Teddy, you follow us.'

THEY PILED into two cars and set off, Katya holding a phone in each hand, with Jonny's on speaker in case Ivo called them. Jonny's phone was connected to Ivo's and Katya was able to give a commentary about where DJ and Brooke were heading. They'd just left the round-about at the end of King's Road and Jonny had swung round onto the A308 and into the park when Katya looked up from her phone. 'They're about half a mile away,' she said. 'They're going quite slowly and are off the road, so they must have left the car and headed into the park on foot. I think they are probably going towards where the meeting was the other night.'

'That makes sense,' said Jonny. 'There's good tree cover there.' A few hundred yards further on, he pulled off the road onto a track, where their way was blocked by a gate and a sign that said *Entry to Crown Estates only.* Teddy followed them and pulled up alongside Jonny's car.

'They've gone that way,' said Katya, waving her arms towards a group of trees a hundred yards down the track.

'Look,' said Jasmine, staring in the same direction and pointing towards a glimmer of light in the distance.

'Right,' said Katya. 'This is what we'll do. Jonny and I will head straight for the trees. The rest of you go that way and approach from the other side.' She waved an arm in an arc to the left. 'It's in the open and there's some moonlight so you should be able to see your way. Don't use your torches unless you absolutely have to. And for God's sake, keep that dog quiet.' She frowned at Harold, who had jumped out of the car and was sniffing some grass on the verge. Hadn't she told them to leave him in the car? Not worth arguing about now, she supposed. 'When you can see them, send Jonny a text. We'll do the same if we get there first.'

Katya and Jonny watched as Jasmine, Teddy and Ivo took a path through the grass, Harold trotting obediently on his lead at Ivo's side. They waited until they were out of sight and then headed towards the clump of trees. As they grew nearer, it turned out to be a larger area than Katya had expected, although they could still see a beam of light ahead of them. 'Don't turn your torch on, or they will be able to see us,' she hissed. It was slow going, with dead leaves underfoot hiding tree roots that might trip them up. They were still picking their way through the undergrowth towards the light when Jonny's phone buzzed with a text from Ivo.

> We can see them. Looks like DJ's tied up and someone in a black cloak is threatening her. Can't see much but be careful. He may have spotted you.

They stopped walking and Jonny passed the phone to Katya. 'Ask how many of them,' she said.

Jonny tapped a message.

> Just two. Don't think the one in the cloak is Brooke.

Jonny turned on his own tracker and could see that Ivo's phone was about a quarter of a mile away to their left. They were going in the wrong direction. 'We need to go more that way,' said Jonny, pointing.

Katya took the phone from him and studied it. Jonny was right. She swung round and started to head towards the left-hand edge of the trees. But where was Brooke? There was no other car on the track where they had parked. He could either have driven away or hidden somewhere nearby. 'Send Ivo a text and tell them to stay where they are unless they think DJ's in danger,' she said. 'We'll head in that direction and then close in on the two of them when we know the others are close enough to back us up.' She set off, glancing over her shoulder to see if Jonny was following. He was standing still to send the text. Katya was ahead of him now, but Jonny was not out of sight. He'd soon catch her up. She was several yards further ahead when she realised how quiet it was. She turned to see if Jonny was following her but could see nothing. She peered into the darkness, straining to listen. Nothing. She reached into her pocket for her torch. She'd hoped not to attract attention by using it, but a sudden yelp made her forget that. This was an emergency. She swung the torch in the direction of the voice and could see two figures. One prone on the ground and the other sitting on top of him, pushing his face into the leaves, presumably in an effort to silence him. Katya charged towards them, still unheard by the attacker – Brooke, she assumed – who was shouting something into Jonny's ear. She lunged forward and grabbed Brooke by his jacket, pulling him off Jonny and flinging him heavily onto the ground at her feet. She reached into her pocket for the handcuffs and, pulling Brooke's arms behind his back, she snapped them on. *Still got it,* she thought. Should she tie his feet as well? She had a length of washing line in her pocket, but they might need that for whoever it was that had tied DJ to a tree. Brooke wouldn't be going far with his hands fastened behind his back. Even if he did escape, they knew who he was.

Jonny turned over and groaned.

'You okay, Jonny?' she asked.

'Think so,' said Jonny, spitting out some dead leaves and staggering to his feet, clutching his arm. 'Didn't see that coming.'

'Me neither,' said Katya. 'I ought to have been on the lookout. We should have stayed together.'

'Sorry,' said Jonny. 'I just stopped to send Ivo the message.'

'Not your fault,' said Katya, patting him on the shoulder and noticing that he winced with pain. 'But look at it this way. One's out of action. That means it's four of us against the other one.'

'Are we just going to leave him here?'

'Unless you want to stay and watch him. I don't think he's going anywhere with his hands out of action. We'll come back and deal with him later. I'll take these, though.' She reached into Brooke's pocket and pulled out a phone and some car keys.

'You can't do that,' Brooke objected.

'Can't quite see how you can stop us,' said Katya. Delving again into her own pocket, she pulled out a large, red and white spotted handkerchief and twisted it into a gag, which she fastened with a stout knot at the back of his head. 'Sorry about that,' she said. 'But we don't want you shouting and giving us away, do we?' She tapped a message into her own phone and grinned at Jonny. 'Calling in the cavalry,' she said. 'Right, let's go.'

JONNY, still clutching the arm he'd fallen heavily onto, blundered after Katya as she headed towards the trees. He'd always thought of Katya as someone who was built for comfort rather than speed, but he'd just been proved wrong. He was having trouble keeping up with her. *Is this wise?* he wondered. His arm was throbbing, and he felt a wave of nausea. They had no idea what they were going to find in the clearing. It might be better to go a bit slower and more quietly. But he could hardly call out to Katya. For one thing, she wouldn't be the only one who heard him, and for another, he was out of breath. And suddenly it was no longer an issue. Well, not that issue. They had stumbled straight into another one that looked way more dangerous.

Katya stopped abruptly, Jonny almost running into the back of her. They were no longer concealed by trees but were standing in a clearing, with someone shining a strong light at them. Jonny held up his pain-free arm to shield his eyes and stared ahead.

'Stop pointing that bloody light at me,' said Katya, and rather to Jonny's surprise the beam was swung away from them and towards the figure of DJ, who was fastened with rope, noose-like around her wrists, to a high branch of a tree, her feet just about making contact with the ground. A figure in a black cloak, their face concealed by a hood, stood in front of her, holding a knife at her throat.

'Come a step closer and she's dead.'

It was a woman's voice. One that Jonny thought he recognised but couldn't place where he'd heard it before. It definitely wasn't Stella Pierce's.

'You'd never get away with it,' said Katya.

'You think not? You don't think I'm capable of outrunning a fat old woman and a weedy man still in the throes of covid?'

How the hell did she know that? Jonny was still wondering where they'd met. She obviously knew him.

'I'd be out of here before you could draw breath. You two would be prime suspects if you're found here with a body. I'll leave my knife behind to make sure of that. And you've no way of identifying me.'

Don't be so sure. We've met and sooner or later I'm going to remember how and where. That is, if I don't pass out first. Jonny was beginning to feel weak in the legs as well as nauseous.

'We know who your accomplice is,' said Katya.

'That little wimp,' the woman scoffed. 'He can't help you. I covered my tracks. He's no idea who I am.'

Katya looked as if she was quite happy to just stand there and see how things panned out. Should Jonny leap forward and wrestle the knife from this woman's grasp? It would be the brave and gentlemanly thing to do. It would also probably get them both killed. Where the hell were the others? Were they close by and able to hear every word that was being said? Or were they waiting out there somewhere with no clue about what was going on? It was then that he remembered the emergency key Teddy had set up on his phone. The phone was in his jacket pocket. Unfortunately, it was in the pocket on the side of his injured arm. He tried moving the arm, an action that resulted in a stab of pain running from the tips of his fingers to the base of his neck. He could probably stretch his other arm across. It would just about reach his pocket but would involve him twisting, and that would attract the woman's attention. He needed to cause a diversion. Hell, a lifetime in packaging hadn't prepared him for this. His one foray into crime detection had involved collating paperwork and spying covertly for evidence. He'd never had to rescue anyone held at knifepoint before. He looked across the clearing at DJ. If she could just do something to distract the woman for a second or two.

Jonny caught DJ's eye and she must have been able to read his mind. She started to twist and moan. 'My arms are going numb,' she complained.

The cloaked woman turned towards her and scowled. 'That's the least of your problems,' she hissed, pushing the knife tighter against her throat.

For a few seconds she looked away from Katya and Jonny. It was just enough time for him to reach over and press the side button on his phone. He prayed that Ivo would feel his own phone buzz and that they weren't too far away. He sensed that they didn't have very long. How long did it take to slit someone's throat? Seconds, he supposed, and then a mad woman would be on the loose somewhere. She was right. They'd never be able to catch her. And unless he could get his brain working again, they wouldn't even be able to say who she was.

There was a sudden commotion from the other side of the clearing as Harold charged toward them, closely followed by Ivo and a few seconds later by Teddy and Jasmine.

'Turning out to be quite a party,' said the woman in the cloak. 'Anyone else coming along? No?'

Teddy stepped forward, holding up his arms in a conciliatory gesture. 'Come on,' he said. 'You don't want to do that. Just drop the knife and we can talk about it.'

'Nothing to talk about,' she said, digging the point of the knife into DJ's throat and drawing a drop of blood. 'This woman betrayed me. She deserves what's about to happen to her.'

'You'll never get away with it,' said Teddy. 'The police are on their way.'

'Really? I can't hear them, can you? Anyway, I can disappear like a ghost. It's one of my skills. Never liked dogs,' she said, looking down at Harold. 'I might just finish him off first. He's the only one capable of catching me.'

'No,' gasped Ivo, trying to rush towards her, but Jasmine was holding him back.

Harold sank to the ground and growled. Before they realised what was happening, he lurched forward, grabbed the hem of the woman's cloak and tugged at it. Ivo struggled free and lurched towards them. He grabbed Harold, holding him tightly in his arms, and dragged him back towards the trees. Harold was nothing if not determined. He hung on to the cloak which, in spite of the woman's efforts, started to unravel, after a few seconds revealing a slim figure in tight jeans and skinny jumper. And shining in the light of several torches, her bright red hair. 'Hermia Rutherford,' Jonny gasped, before he sank unconscious onto the ground, dimly aware of the sound of police sirens.

Not bad for a dog, Katya thought. Harold was still growling and tugging at the cloak, and in her efforts to free herself from it, Hermia dropped the knife. Katya rushed forward and grabbed it at the same time as Teddy ran out from the trees and threw Hermia to the ground. 'Here,' said Katya, tossing him a length of rope that she had pulled out of one of the pockets in her overcoat. Lucky she had come prepared to tie people up. None of the others had thought of that. But then, why should they? She was the professional here.

Teddy caught the rope, but she could see that he was struggling. Journalists, she supposed, didn't often have to deal with murderers hell bent on escaping. Hermia was face down on the ground, writhing and kicking. Teddy was sitting astride her, warding off kicks from her feet. He grabbed the rope but didn't look too sure about what to do with it. 'Tie her wrists,' Katya shouted. But at that moment Hermia shook Teddy off her back, scrambled to her feet and ran into the trees. Harold looked set to follow her, but Ivo held him back. *A wise move,* Katya thought. If Harold caught her, goodness only knew what he'd do to her. She could sue him under the Dangerous Dogs Act, claim that she'd been taking an innocent walk in the woods when she was set upon by a mad dog. She knew Lugs and his methods. He'd have pinpointed where they were and surrounded the area. This Hermia Rutherford woman didn't stand a chance. She could be the world's fastest, most scheming criminal but she'd not escape Lugs and his team. Katya knew them. She'd worked with them, and they'd not lost a suspect yet. All Katya and *her* team had to do now was wait. *That's all good,* she thought. *I provided the brains. Lugs just needs to appear with the brawn.* They still worked well together.

'I don't want to seem impatient,' said DJ, pulling Katya back to reality. 'But since you now have the knife, do you suppose you could cut me down from this tree?'

'Sorry, love,' said Katya. She started hacking through the rope, eventually freeing DJ, who sank to the ground, rubbing her wrists.

'You okay?' Katya asked.

'Well, you took your time and I'm a bit stiff in the shoulders. But I guess I'll live. Shouldn't you do something about him?' She nodded towards Jonny, who was still lying on the damp grass.

'You're right,' said Katya. 'Look after DJ, Teddy, while I see if Jonny's okay.'

'Be happy to,' said Teddy, removing his coat and wrapping it around DJ. He reached into one of the pockets and found a hip flask, which he handed to her. 'It's just sweet coffee laced with a little brandy,' he said. 'Good for shock.'

DJ took a sip and pulled a face. 'It's disgusting,' she said. 'But thanks for the thought.'

Katya knelt beside Jonny and, noticing the awkward angle of his left arm, decided it was best not to move him. Jonny opened his eyes and managed to smile weakly at her. 'Don't try to move,' she said, taking his uninjured hand and rubbing it to keep him warm.

Ivo was trying to control Harold, who still had Hermia's cloak in his mouth. He looked as if he was trying to kill it. Stupid dog. Didn't he realise there was no one inside it now? All the same, if he hadn't lunged forward and grabbed it when he did, Katya wasn't sure how things would have worked out.

Jasmine was standing on her own at the edge of the clearing, looking pale and shaken. She needed something to do. And Jonny was now shivering. *He must be in shock, or he would be howling in pain from that arm.* Katya hadn't realised that Brooke had used so much force. She pulled off her coat and tossed it to Jasmine. 'Look after Jonny,' she said. 'Cover him with this, but be careful not to move him. I think his arm's broken.'

'What are we going to do?' Jasmine asked, tearfully. 'I really want us all to go home, but how will we get Jonny to the car?'

'The police should be here any minute,' said Katya, looking at her watch. It must have been fifteen minutes since she'd called Lugs. She was just thinking that they were taking their time, when a couple of paramedics appeared through the trees.

Jasmine looked relieved, the colour returning to her face. Harold had now let go of Hermia's cloak and was lying down next to Jonny, licking his face. 'Good dog,' Jonny muttered. 'Yeah,' said the paramedic. 'You chat to the dog while I give you a shot of something to ease the pain a bit. They're bringing an ambulance across from the road. We'll soon have you tucked up in hospital.'

They were joined by the second paramedic. 'The lady's fine,' he said. 'That gentleman will see her home.' He nodded in Teddy's direction.

The ambulance arrived and Jonny was loaded in and driven off. Teddy would drive Ivo, Jasmine and DJ back to the café, where Jasmine promised them a hot meal. Katya would drive Jonny's car and join them as soon as she'd handed over to Lugs, who was currently apprehending Hermia. He'd called Katya, saying they'd caught her heading for the Copper Horse, where apparently she'd expected to meet up with Brooke again. Brooke himself had been found by two of Lugs' team where Katya and Jonny had left him. He'd been arrested and driven off to Slough nick. Lugs said he didn't expect to be long and had volunteered Katya to secure the scene, hoping that they hadn't destroyed too much evidence. Pity Katya hadn't thought of bringing some evidence bags with her. She still had some tucked away in one of her kitchen cupboards. She delved into the pocket of her trousers and found an empty paper bag that had once contained a kilo of bruised apples she had bought for a knock-down price in the market. Not ideal, but it would have to do. She wrapped the knife in it and pushed it into the back pocket of her trousers. Then at last she saw the flash of blue lights. Two police cars had pulled up at the gate. Katya picked up her torch and flashed at them through the trees, wondering if they would breach the Crown Estates privacy sign and drive across the park. The ambulance had done that but there were exceptions for injuries. She had reported a crime and there was no sign of the palace security patrol. *For once,* she thought, *the local police should take precedence.* Someone would smooth things over with the castle authorities if necessary. That had always been way above her pay grade. Then she was pleased to see that the police cars were on the move again, bouncing across the grass towards her.

'No stopping you, is there?' said Lugs, as he and two sergeants climbed out of the cars and began cordoning off the area with crime scene tape.

Katya handed over the knife, still wrapped in the paper bag. One of the sergeants transferred it to an evidence bag and wrote a label for it.

'There'll be prints,' said Katya. 'But some will be mine. I had to cut DJ down and that was all we had.'

'Not to worry,' said Lugs kindly. 'Technology has moved on since your day. There'll be plenty left for us to work with.'

'Huh,' said Katya. 'I do keep up with developments. And it's not that many years since I retired.'

'Only joking,' said Lugs. 'You did a grand job here today.' He patted her on the back and she headed back to where they'd left Jonny's car.

31

Jonny woke up, yawned and stretched out his legs. He was warm and comfortable and in his own bed. What had happened? And how had he got there? The last thing he remembered was being in the park on a dark night. Then, as his head began to clear, he recalled being pushed to the ground, landing painfully on his arm and being pinned face down and with a mouthful of dead leaves. He'd been following Katya into the woods and he needed his phone to send Ivo a text. He'd pushed it back into his pocket just before he was attacked. And then he'd needed it again, he remembered hazily, and it was agony reaching into his pocket for it. And there was a woman with a knife. He knew her but her name had deserted him until he saw her red hair and recognised Hermia Rutherford. After that he must have blacked out because the next thing he knew he was in an ambulance being wrapped in tin foil. That was a brief memory, because someone gave him a shot of something and after that he woke up in a hospital bed, his arm in plaster and Belinda trying to coax him into some clean clothes, reassuring him that DJ was safe and that arrests had been made. He must have still been drugged up on painkillers because he remembered very little about the drive home.

But there he was, awake in his own bedroom, the sun streaming in through the windows. He glanced at the clock by the bed. It was eleven o'clock. In the morning, presumably, or it would have been dark. And now he felt safe, free of pain and with details of the evening beginning to seep back into his brain. He climbed out of bed, feeling encouragingly steady on his feet, and pulled on some clothes. He wasn't sure about showering with an arm in a cast, so he didn't bother. He cleaned his teeth and splashed his face with cold water. A scent of coffee and bacon was wafting up the stairs, and Jonny realised it must have been hours since his last meal.

He made his way downstairs, hanging onto the stair rail with his good arm just in case of a sudden dizzy spell. He was probably still stuffed full of anaesthetic, and he must be on painkillers or he wouldn't have slept so well. What time had they arrived home? How long had he been asleep?

In the kitchen he found Belinda dishing up plates of scrambled egg and bacon to Katya and Lugs. Belinda poured him a coffee and he sat down opposite Katya.

'You look surprisingly well,' said Katya. 'You had us worried, passing out like that.'

'He's fine,' said Belinda. 'They reset his arm and sent him home. He was a bit groggy when we got back, but nothing a good night's sleep couldn't fix. Eggs?' she asked, waving a spatula at him.

'You bet,' he said. 'I'm starving.'

Belinda passed him a plate of food and he tucked in. He hadn't tasted anything so good for a long time. Jasmine served up superb breakfasts, but they didn't usually follow a night of chasing criminals. That definitely gave the meal an edge.

'This came for you,' said Belinda, handing him a brown A4 envelope.

Jonny took it from her and reached out to put it on the sideboard, to leave room for his breakfast. Nothing interesting; it felt like a catalogue. At this time of year, he got plenty of those from travel companies who wanted him to go on a cruise or a skiing holiday. What was going on here was much more interesting than that. 'Glad you're here,' he said to Katya. 'I want to hear everything that happened last night after I blacked out.'

'Well,' said Katya, helping herself to a piece of toast and spreading it liberally with butter. 'Lugs here arrived with his squad. Two of his team found Brooke pretty much where we'd left him, and he's now been charged with assaulting you. They arrived in the clearing after Hermia Rutherford made off through the trees, but in spite of her boast that she was a record runner, Lugs and his officers caught her before she got too far. She was detained and later arrested for the attempted murder of DJ.'

'Plenty of witnesses,' said Lugs, scraping his plate clean. 'Thanks to you lot.'

'Happy to help,' said Katya.

'I've always wanted to solve crimes,' said Jonny. 'And catch criminals.'

Lugs stared at Jonny, half a sausage poised on his fork. 'Of course,' he said. 'We've met before. You solved that case of people trafficking. Bloke in your factory, wasn't it?'

Jonny looked modestly down at his food and nodded. 'A while ago,' he said. 'No crime solving since then.'

'I don't remember that,' said Katya.

'It was just before you joined my team,' said Lugs. 'Bloody good breakfast.' He smiled at Belinda. 'Pardon my language.'

Belinda shrugged. 'I've heard worse,' she said. 'And after last night, a good breakfast is no more than you deserve.'

'Where's Harold?' Jonny asked, looking at the empty rug near the radiator.

'Jasmine said he and Ivo should stay with her last night. They're probably both asleep on her sofa.'

'Looks like the dog saved the day,' said Lugs. 'He'll be nominated for a Thin Blue Paw Award if he carries on like that.'

'Do you know why Hermia wanted to kill DJ?' Jonny asked, finishing his eggs and reaching for the toast.

'Not entirely clear yet,' said Lugs. 'She wasn't making a lot of sense last night. We're holding her for forty-eight hours pending a psychiatric report.'

'And how was Brooke involved?' Hadn't the police cleared him of any involvement? Although, as Jonny remembered, it was following the most cursory of interviews.

'She'd promised him membership of the Followers of Herne if he did as she told him. But once he cottoned on that she was stringing him along, and when he realised we were about to charge him with Pierce's murder, he became very cooperative.'

'Was he the murderer?'

'Doubt it,' said Lugs. 'But we didn't tell him that. What we did say was that the charge might be reduced to assault if he told us all he knew about Hermia Rutherford. Couldn't stop him talking after that.'

'So do you know what actually happened the night Pierce died?'

'According to Brooke, Hermia bribed him to frighten Pierce.'

'Why?' asked Jonny. Murder by scaring someone wasn't usual.

'She said it was revenge for his betrayal of the Followers. But although they do some pretty horrible stuff, they haven't, as far as we know, murdered anyone. After Pierce died, his wife discovered a folder of evidence that he'd been collecting. It turns out he wasn't a loyal follower at all. He was more interested in selling the informa-tion to the highest bidder. He'd discovered things that incriminated a lot of the members, Hermia in particular. Stella Pierce was black-mailing her.'

Jonny had never expected that. He'd clearly underestimated Stella. Hermia had too, apparently. 'But Stella Pierce is a rich woman. Why would she need to blackmail anyone?'

'Seems she was not quite as well off as she made out. The house was heavily mortgaged, and the company was doing very badly; no one buying carpets, I suppose. She wanted to leave Pierce and needed escape money.'

'Which Hermia paid her?'

'We're still looking into that. All the relevant bank accounts will be forensically scrutinised.'

'So where is Stella now?'

'No idea. She was last seen boarding a flight to Madrid a couple of days ago.'

'She seems to do that a lot,' said Katya.

'Yes, but she's not there now. Her cousin hasn't seen her since she left shortly after Pierce died.'

'And did Hermia actually kill Pierce or was it a heart attack brought on by fear?'

'Well,' said Lugs. 'According to Brooke, he and Hermia were waiting for him at the Copper Horse. Brooke hid in the trees while Hermia pretended to seduce Pierce, first with a drink of something from a hip flask and then by leading him into the trees where Brooke was waiting, pretending to be the ghost of Herne the Hunter, and instructed to frighten the shit out of him. At that point Pierce did indeed take fright and legged it, but he'd been drugged and probably didn't know where he was going. Brooke told us that he and Hermia followed him until he was almost back on the Long Walk. Then she threw her cloak over him, and he fell to the ground. We're not sure what happened next, because Brooke decided he'd had enough and escaped. He made a run for his car, which was parked in the road that crosses the Long Walk and he says he just drove home.'

'When did he take the wallet?' Jonny asked.

'He told us Pierce dropped it while he was fumbling with his phone trying to turn the flashlight on. Brooke picked it up and slipped it into his own pocket.'

'And he left Hermia behind?'

'So he says. We don't know how she got home. But a few days ago, she called him and threatened to tell us he was the killer unless he did what she told him.'

'Which was to drive DJ to meet her last night,' said Jonny.

'We assume Hermia suspected that DJ knew about the murder and planned to silence her,' said Lugs.

'What did DJ have to say about that?'

'She told us all she wanted was the downfall of the Followers. With the evidence she has about what they did to her friend, we believed her.'

'Where is she now?'

'DJ?' said Katya. 'She's with Teddy, helping him with his story. He's probably got enough evidence now for an exciting bit of investigative journalism. He was hoping to bring Edwin Eastman down, but what he has on the Followers could be a lot more explosive.'

'Where is Eastman now?'

'Another mystery,' said Lugs. 'He was last seen leaving his home with a suitcase and getting into a taxi. We traced the driver who took him to Heathrow. Interestingly, on the same day that Stella flew to Madrid.'

'Were they together?'

'Not unless he was flying under an assumed name. But there's not a lot we can do. Eastman is an unlikeable type, but he hasn't actually been accused of anything. Anyway,' he said, draining his coffee, 'I'd better get going. Just dropped in to check you were okay after last night. I'll send one of my team to take your statement if that's okay.'

'He'll be here,' said Belinda. 'He won't be going anywhere for a day or two.'

'Excellent,' said Lugs. 'Want a lift, Katya?'

'Wouldn't mind,' she said, patting Jonny on the back. 'See you in a day or two.'

BELINDA SHOWED them to the door and then returned to the kitchen. 'Jonny,' she said, sitting down and pouring herself a coffee. 'That package. The one that arrived this morning. That was from Spain, wasn't it?'

Jonny reached for it. Belinda was right. It had been posted in Madrid two days previously. He tore it open and stared open-mouthed at its contents. A cardboard folder of notes; lists of names and addresses; photographs; cuttings from newspapers; printouts from websites and some blurred photographs obviously taken at night. Stapled to the front of the folder was a handwritten note:

Jonny

Just a small thank you for your help.

Do what you think best with the attached. You are better placed to decide what Raymond would have wanted.

I wasn't a good wife - Raymond probably deserved better but it's all water under the bridge now. I won't be returning.

Stella

JONNY EMPTIED the folder and flicked through some of the pages. 'It's Raymond's evidence,' said Jonny. 'Everything he'd collected about the Followers of Herne.'

'Evidence that Stella used to blackmail Hermia Rutherford?' Belinda asked.

'Looks like it. I suppose that means Hermia didn't pay Stella anything or she wouldn't have kept the folder.'

'What are you going to do with it?'

'I'm going to pass it on to Teddy,' said Jonny, reaching for his phone.

32

I t was seven in the morning when Jasmine pulled back the shutters and flipped the sign on the door to *Open*. She peered out into the street, which looked damp and dreary. She'd preferred it last week, when there had been a heavy frost every night, even a light dusting of snow. But now the air was mild again. If anyone had put their money on a white Christmas this year, their hopes would be dashed. She returned inside, turned on the Christmas tree lights and checked that the heating was on. She wanted the café warm and welcoming this morning, not that it wasn't always, but this was the first time they'd opened on Christmas Day. 'No one will come, love,' her dad had said, when she first broached her plan with him. But she'd insisted. Since the breakfast club had opened, she'd promised herself they would always be there for their members. She wasn't going to assume every member had somewhere else to be at Christmas. The food bank was hosting a Christmas dinner later in the day with entertainers, and a team of chiropodists, dentists and hairdressers. But that still meant people were wandering the streets in the early morning, having been thrown out of hostels or maybe after spending a night out of doors. They needed to start the day with something warm inside them.

She couldn't expect any of the regular staff to come in, although a couple had volunteered. Offers Jasmine accepted, because perhaps they had no one to spend Christmas with. Ivo, Jonny and even Katya were all coming in to help. Teddy, too, had said he might pop in, although she imagined he could be the worse for wear after a boozy Christmas Eve with colleagues. Teddy was still celebrating the success of his story; the uncovering and subsequent disbanding of the Followers of Herne. Names had been revealed and arrests made for intimidation and financial misdemeanours. Not as many as Teddy had first hoped for, but more information was emerging every day as more and more people came forward with complaints. Police enquiries were still ongoing. Teddy had written a touching tribute to Raymond Pierce – the victim who had given his life in his attempt to collect evidence against the Followers. Evidence without which Teddy could never have written his article.

No one admitted to nailing the pendant to the tree. Jonny and Ivo went to take it down and it was decided that they would auction it and give the proceeds to charity.

And that wasn't Teddy's only story. The local paper had carried the story of the brave band of amateur sleuths who had solved a murder case. They had been thanked by the police for their work and had attended a reception given by the mayor in their honour. Breakfast club membership had soared, and they now had a waiting list. Jonny was beginning to think of raising the funds to expand. There was an empty shop close by, but Jasmine suggested it might be better to start up a similar enterprise somewhere else. Other towns, she told him, were more needy. They'd not made any decisions yet. Research needed to be done. The balance between paid and free membership was crucial to the way the club operated and Jonny was going to be kept busy in the new year working out the best way to operate.

THE FIRST PUNTERS started drifting into the café and the kitchen was busy, with Katya making toast and Ivo frying eggs. Jonny and Jasmine were serving plates of food to a dozen or so customers. *Just the right number,* Jasmine thought. They could stay there and keep warm for as long as they wanted to. Many more and she'd have had to operate a shift system, and turning people out onto the street just because they had finished eating wasn't something she wanted to do.

'Belinda at home preparing the turkey?' she asked Jonny when the initial rush was over.

'No, we're going to my family for the day when I've finished here. But...'

'Everything okay?' Jasmine asked, wondering if they'd had a row.

'Absolutely,' said Jonny with a wink. 'She'll be here soon and... well, you'll just have to wait and see.'

He was bursting to tell her something, Jasmine could see that, but she wasn't going to dig any deeper and spoil his surprise, whatever it was. And she didn't have to wait long. As they were clearing the tables, Belinda arrived with Harold on a lead, Teddy and DJ following in her wake. Jasmine cleared a table for them, Jonny poured them coffee and Katya appeared from the kitchen with a plate of toast.

'Is it going to work out?' Jonny whispered to Belinda.

She nodded. 'All sorted,' she said.

'Teddy and I went round there first thing this morning,' said DJ.

'Where is Ivo?' Belinda asked, just as Ivo himself appeared, still wearing a striped apron. Harold jumped up and down, wagging his tail.

'I think he already knows,' said Jonny, patting him on the head.

'What does he know?' Ivo asked.

'Sit down, Ivo,' said Belinda. 'The three of us,' she indicated Teddy and DJ, 'have been making a few enquiries and have a proposition for you. No pressure to accept if you don't want to. Harold's a very welcome guest in our house for as long as he wants. But take a look in here and tell us what you think.'

She handed Ivo a padded envelope. 'Open it,' she said, as Ivo stared at it suspiciously, turning it over in his hands.

Ivo slipped open the envelope and pulled out a sheet of paper and a set of keys. 'I don't understand,' he said.

'Teddy has been working on a piece on local housing,' said Belinda. 'He came to me for some inside information and you and Harold came up in the conversation. He's also become very friendly with DJ over the last few weeks.'

'I've got this friend,' said DJ. 'He inherited a piece of land and he's putting up twenty pre-built cabin style houses, which he'll rent out. Small but affordable homes.'

'He can rent one to me?' Ivo asked.

'No,' said DJ. 'Not exactly. He needs someone onsite who can keep an eye on the cabins, keep them maintained and do small repairs. He wants to offer you the job. It doesn't pay very well, but you'd have time for other jobs, and you'd get a cabin rent-free.'

'But he doesn't know me,' said Ivo, who looked as if he was having trouble grasping what was happening.

'He knows all about you after Teddy's piece in the paper, and Belinda and Jonny are happy to give you a reference.'

'Me too,' said Jasmine. 'And Dad.'

'And Harold can live there too?'

'Of course,' said Belinda.

'We can take you to see it before you decide,' said Teddy, picking up the bunch of keys and waving them at him. 'It's a bit of a walk out of town, but you'll notice that one of these keys is for a small van that goes with the job.'

'What do you think?' asked DJ. 'We can go and look at it now if you like, and then you can join me and Teddy for Christmas dinner. I bet Harold wouldn't say no to some turkey.'

He looked shell-shocked, Jasmine thought. 'Give him a bit of space to think,' she said. 'Let's open our presents and have a glass of Buck's Fizz to celebrate.'

'When can we move in?' asked Ivo.

AROUND THE SAME time the breakfast club detectives were opening presents and celebrating their success, a middle-aged couple were sunning themselves on the balcony of a hotel in the Cayman Islands. The woman took a sip of champagne and opened the professionally wrapped present the man had just given her. She knew perfectly well that he'd phoned down to the hotel reception for it when he woke up that morning with the mother and father of all hangovers and realised it was Christmas day. She also knew that whatever it was would be flashy, expensive and in bad taste, and that she would hate it.

FOR THE BREAKFAST DETECTIVES' next case read **Death in the River.**

Click here to get your copy

ACKNOWLEDGMENTS

I would also like to thank my editor, Sally Silvester-Wood at *Black Sheep Books*, my cover designer, Anthony O'Brien and all my fellow writers at *Quite Write* who have patiently listened to extracts and offered suggestions.

Discover more about Hilary Pugh and download the Breakfast Club Detectives prequel novella **Crime about Town** FREE at www.hilary-pugh.com

COMING SOON

I would like to thank you so much for reading **Death in the Long Walk** I do hope you enjoyed it.

Book 2 **Death in the River** will be available in September 2023
Pre-order here:
https://books2read.com/u/4D8Pee

<u>Available in 2024</u>
Book 3 Death on the Carousel
Book 4 Death at the Festival

ALSO BY HILARY PUGH

<u>The Ian Skair: Private Investigator series</u>

Finding Lottie – series prequel

<u>Free</u> **when you join my mailing list:**

https://storyoriginapp.com/giveaways/61799962-7dc3-11eb-b5c8-7b3702734d0c

The Laird of Drumlychtoun

https://books2read.com/u/bwrEky

Postcards from Jamie

https://books2read.com/u/4X28Ae

Mystery at Murriemuir

https://books2read.com/u/mgj8Bx

The Diva of Dundas Farm

https://books2read.com/u/bMYMJA

The Man in the Red Overcoat

https://books2read.com/u/4DJRge

Printed in Great Britain
by Amazon